Thieves, harlots, godlings, hired swords and sorcerous beings beyond imagining lurk in the shadows of Sanctuary—the seediest town in the Rankan Empire—and each of them has a tale to tell. . . .

Seven top fantasy authors, including C. J. Cherryh, Vonda McIntyre, and Andrew Offutt, tell the stories of those who live and die in the infamous town of Sanctuary in the latest volume of the unique anthology series that has captured the imaginations of fans, critics, and authors from coast to coast.

Join us—but be warned: keep one hand on your money and the other on your sword; in Sanctuary they play for keeps.

*   *   *

"Delightful . . . easily one of the best ideas in years."

—Andre Norton

edited by **ROBERT LYNN ASPRIN**

SHADOWS OF SANCTUARY

ACE FANTASY BOOKS
NEW YORK

SHADOWS OF SANCTUARY

An Ace Fantasy Book / published by arrangement with
the editor

PRINTING HISTORY
Ace Original / October 1981
Second printing / October 1982
Third printing / April 1983
Fourth printing / October 1983

ISBN: 0-441-76029-5

Ace Fantasy Books are published by The Berkley Publishing Group,
200 Madison Avenue, New York, New York 10016.
PRINTED IN THE UNITED STATES OF AMERICA

SHADOWS OF SANCTUARY

Introduction, Robert Asprin   1

Looking for Satan, Vonda N. McIntyre ...   7

Ischade, C. J. Cherryh 77

A Gift in Parting, Robert Asprin 133

The Vivisectionist, Andrew Offutt 163

The Rhinoceros and the Unicorn,
    Diana L. Paxson 209

Then Azyuna Danced, Lynn Abbey 245

A Man and His God, Janet Morris 279

Essay: Things the Editor Never Told Me,
    Lynn Abbey 333

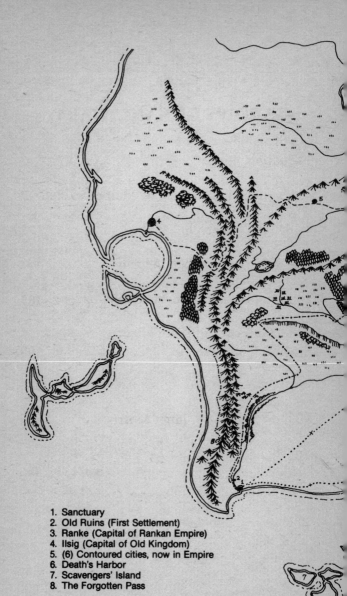

1. Sanctuary
2. Old Ruins (First Settlement)
3. Ranke (Capital of Rankan Empire)
4. Ilsig (Capital of Old Kingdom)
5. (6) Contoured cities, now in Empire
6. Death's Harbor
7. Scavengers' Island
8. The Forgotten Pass

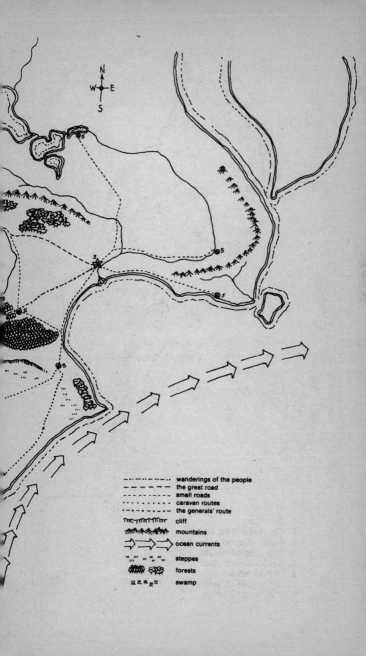

wandering of the people
the great road
small roads
caravan routes
the generals' route
cliff
mountains
ocean currents
steppes
forests
swamp

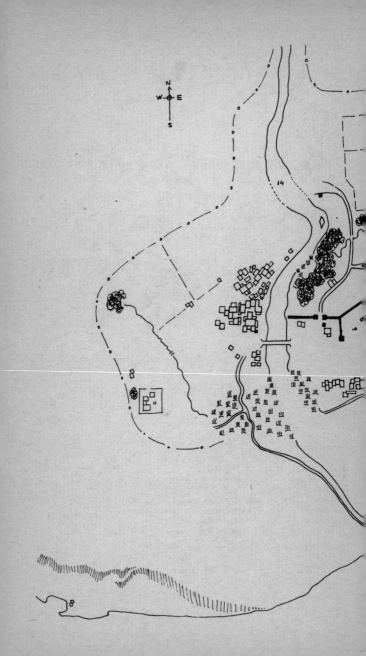

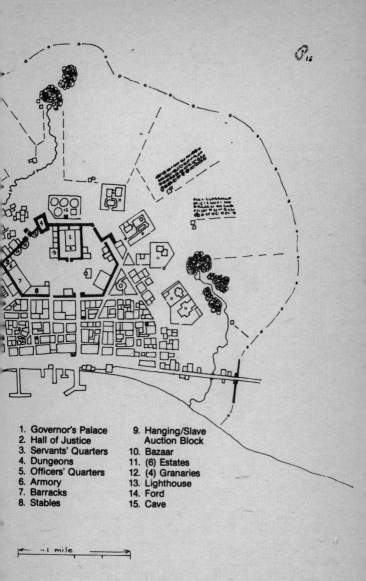

1. Governor's Palace
2. Hall of Justice
3. Servants' Quarters
4. Dungeons
5. Officers' Quarters
6. Armory
7. Barracks
8. Stables
9. Hanging/Slave
   Auction Block
10. Bazaar
11. (6) Estates
12. (4) Granaries
13. Lighthouse
14. Ford
15. Cave

|← -1 mile →|

INTRODUCTION

Robert Asprin

It was a slow night at the Vulgar Unicorn. Not slow in the sense that there had been no fights (there hadn't) or that there weren't many customers (there weren't) but rather a different kind of slow; the slow measured pace of a man on his way to the gallows, for the Unicorn was dying, as was the entire town of Sanctuary. More people were leaving every day and those left were becoming increasingly desperate and vicious as the economy dipped to new lows.

Desperate people were dangerous; they were quick to turn predator at the smallest imagined opportunity, which in turn made them vulnerable to the *real* predators drawn to the town like

wolves to a sick animal. Anyone with an ounce
of sense and a good leg to hobble on would have
deserted Sanctuary long ago.

Such were the thoughts of Hakiem, the
Storyteller, as he sat brooding over a cup of
cheap wine. Tonight he did not even bother
adopting his usual guise of dozing drunkenly
while eavesdropping on conversations at the
neighboring tables. He knew all the patrons
present and not one of them was worth spying
on—hence no need to fake disinterest.

He would leave Sanctuary tomorrow. He
would go somewhere, anywhere, where people
were freer with their money and a master
storyteller would be appreciated. Hakiem smiled
bitterly at himself even as he made the
resolution—for he knew it to be a lie.

He loved this bedraggled town as he loved the
tough breed of people it spawned. There was a
raw, stubborn vitality that surged and ebbed just
below the surface. Sanctuary was a storyteller's
paradise. When he left, if he ever did, he would
have stories enough for a lifetime . . . no, two
lifetimes. Big stories and little ones, tailored to
the buyer's purse. Stories of violent battle between warriors and between sorcerors. Tiny
stories of people so common they would move
the hearts of any who listened. From the princely
military-governor with his Hell-Hound elite
guard to the humblest thief, they were all grist
for Hakiem's mill. If he had personally commanded their performances they could not have
performed their roles better.

The storyteller's smile was more sincere as he
raised his cup for another sip. Then his eye was

caught by a figure lurching through the door and he froze in mid-movement.

One-Thumb!

The Vulgar Unicorn's owner had been absent for some time, causing no small question among the patrons about his fate. Now, here he was, large as life . . . well, not quite as large as life.

Hakiem watched with narrowed eyes as One-Thumb slumped against the bar, seizing a crock of wine while his normally practiced fingers fumbled with the stopper like a youth with his first woman. Unable to contain his curiosity longer, the old storyteller untangled himself from his chair and skuttled forward with a speed that belied his age.

"One-Thumb," he cackled with calculated joviality, "welcome back!"

The massive figure straightened and turned, focusing vacant eyes on the intruder. "Hakiem!" The fleshy face suddenly wrinkled with a wide smile. "By the gods—the world is normal."

To the storyteller's amazement, One-Thumb seemed on the verge of tears as he stepped forward, arms extended to embrace the old man like a long lost son. Recoiling, Hakiem hastily interposed his wine cup between them.

"You've been gone a long time," he said, abandoning all semblance of subtlety. "Where have you been?"

"Gone?" The eyes were vacant again. "Yes, I've been gone. How long has it been?"

"Over a year." The storyteller was puzzled, and insatiable.

"A year," One-Thumb murmured. "It seems like . . . the tunnels! I've been in the tunnels. It was . . ." He paused to take a long swallow of wine, then absently filled Hakiem's cup as he launched into his story.

Accustomed to piecing together tales from half-heard words and phrases, the storyteller rapidly grasped the essence of One-Thumb's ordeal.

He had been trapped by a magician's spell in the tangle of tunnels below Sanctuary's streets. Confronted by an image of himself, he had killed it and been slain in turn—over and over until this night when he miraculously found himself alone and unscathed.

As One-Thumb redoubled his lurid description, describing the feel of cold metal as it found its home in one's innards—again and again, Hakiem pondered the facts of the story. It fit.

Lately someone had been stalking wizards, slaying them in their own beds. Apparently the hunter's knife had struck down the spell-weaver who was holding One-Thumb in painful thrall, freeing him suddenly to his normal life. An interesting story, but totally useless to Hakiem.

First: One-Thumb was obviously willing to spill the tale to anyone who would stand still long enough to listen, ruining the market for second-hand renditions. Second, and more important: it was a bad story. Its motive was unclear; the ending hazy and inactive; there was no real interplay between the characters. The only real meat was the uniqueness of One-Thumb's ability to tell the tale in the first-person and even that weakened through repetition. In short, it was boring.

It didn't take a master storyteller to reach this

conclusion. It was obvious. In fact, Hakiem was already growing weary listening to the whine and prattle.

"You must be tired," he interrupted. "It's wrong of me to keep you. Maybe we can talk again after you've rested." He turned to leave the Unicorn.

"What about the wine?" One-Thumb called angrily. "You haven't paid yet."

Hakiem's response was habitual: "Pay? I didn't order it. It was you who filled the cup. Pay for it yourself." He regretted the words immediately. One-Thumb's treatment of drinkers who refused to pay was legendary throughout the Maze. To his surprise, then, it was One-Thumb who gave ground.

"Well, all right," the big man grumbled. "Just don't make a habit of it."

The old storyteller felt a rare twinge of remorse as he left the Unicorn. While he had no love for One-Thumb, neither had he any reason to wish him ill.

The big man hadn't just lost a year of his life—he'd lost his fire—that core of ferocity which had earned him the respect of the town's underworld. Though One-Thumb was unmarked physically, he was only the empty shell of his former self. This town was no place for a man without the strength to back his bluster.

The end of One-Thumb's story was in sight—and it wouldn't be pleasant. Maybe with a few revisions the story—if not the man—had a future.

Lost in his thoughts, Hakiem faded once more into the shadows of Sanctuary.

LOOKING FOR SATAN

Vonda N. McIntyre

The four travellers left the mountains at the end of the day, tired, cold, and hungry, and they entered Sanctuary.

The inhabitants of the city observed them and laughed, but they laughed behind their sleeves or after the small group passed. All its members walked armed. Yet there was no belligerence in them. They looked around amazed, nudged each other, and pointed at things, for all the world as if none had ever seen a city before. As, indeed, they had not.

Unaware of the amusement of the townspeople, they passed through the marketplace toward the city proper. The light was fading. The farmers culled their produce and took down their awnings. Limp cabbage leaves and rotten fruit littered the roughly cobbled street, and bits of unrecognizable stuff floated down the open central sewer.

Beside Wess, Chan shifted his heavy pack.

"Let's stop and buy something to eat," he said, "before everybody goes home."

Wess hitched her own pack higher on her shoulders and did not stop. "Not here," she said. "I'm tired of stale flatbread and raw vegetables. I want a hot meal tonight."

She tramped on. She knew how Chan felt. She glanced back at Aerie, who walked wrapped in her long dark cloak. Her pack weighed her down. She was taller than Wess, as tall as Chan, but very thin. Worry and their journey had deepened her eyes. Wess was not used to seeing her like this. She was used to seeing her freer.

"Our tireless Wess," Chan said.

"I'm tired, too!" Wess said. "Do you want to try camping in the street again?"

"No," he said. Behind him, Quartz chuckled.

In the first village they had ever seen—it seemed years ago now, but was only two months—they tried to set up camp in what they thought was a vacant field. It was the village common. Had the village possessed a prison, they would have been thrown into it. As it was they were escorted to the edge of town and invited never to return. Another traveller explained inns to them—and prisons—and now they all could laugh, with some embarrassment, at the episode.

But the smaller towns they had passed through did not even approach Sanctuary in size

and noise and crowds. Wess had never imagined
so many people or such high buildings or any
odor so awful. She hoped it would be better
beyond the marketplace. Passing a fish stall, she
held her breath and hurried. It was the end of the
day, true, but the end of a cool late fall's day.
Wess tried not to wonder what it would smell
like at the end of a long summer's day.

"We should stop at the first inn we find,"
Quartz said.

"All right," Wess said.

By the time they reached the street's end,
darkness was complete and the market was deserted. Wess thought it odd that everyone should
disappear so quickly, but no doubt they were
tired too and wanted to get home to a hot fire and
dinner. She felt a sudden stab of homesickness
and hopelessness: their search had gone on so
long, with so little chance of success.

The buildings closed in around them as the
street narrowed suddenly. Wess stopped: three
paths faced them, and another branched off only
twenty paces farther on.

"Where now, my friends?"

"We must ask someone," Aerie said, her voice
soft with fatigue.

"If we can find anyone," Chan said doubtfully.

Aerie stepped toward a shadow-filled corner.

"Citizen," she said, "would you direct us to
the nearest inn?"

The others peered more closely at the dim
niche. Indeed, a muffled figure crouched there. It
stood up. Wess could see the manic glitter of its
eyes, but nothing more.

"An inn?"

"The closest, if you please. We've travelled a long way."

The figure chuckled. "You'll find no inns in this part of town, foreigner. But the tavern around the corner—it has rooms upstairs. Perhaps it will suit you."

"Thank you." Aerie turned back, a faint breeze ruffling her short black hair. She pulled her cloak closer.

They went the way the figure gestured, and did not see it convulse with silent laughter behind them.

In front of the tavern, Wess puzzled out the unfamiliar script: The Vulgar Unicorn. An odd combination, even in the south where odd combinations were the style of naming taverns. She pushed open the door. It was nearly as dark inside as out, and smoky. The noise died as Wess and Chan entered—then rose again in a surprised buzz when Aerie and Quartz followed.

Wess and Chan were not startlingly different from the general run of southern mountain folk: he fairer, she darker. Wess could pass unnoticed as an ordinary citizen anywhere; Chan's beauty often attracted attention. But Aerie's tall white-skinned black-haired elegance everywhere aroused comment. Wess smiled, imagining what would happen if Aerie flung away her cloak and showed herself as she really was.

And Quartz: she had to stoop to come inside. She straightened up. She was taller than anyone else in the room. The smoke near the ceiling swirled a wreath around her hair. She had cut it short for the journey, and it curled around her

face, red, gold, and sand-pale. Her gray eyes reflected the firelight like mirrors. Ignoring the
stares, she pushed her blue wool cloak from her
broad shoulders and shrugged her pack to the
floor.

The strong heavy scent of beer and sizzling
meat made Wess' mouth water. She sought out
the man behind the bar.

"Citizen," she said, carefully pronouncing the
Sanctuary language, the trade-tongue of all the
continent, "are you the proprietor? My friends
and I, we need a room for the night, and dinner."

Her request seemed ordinary enough to her,
but the innkeeper looked sidelong at one of his
patrons. Both laughed.

"A room, young gentleman?" He came out
from behind the bar. Instead of replying to Wess,
he spoke to Chan. Wess smiled to herself. Like all
Chan's friends, she was used to seeing people
fall in love with him on sight. She would have
done so herself, she thought, had she first met
him when they were grown. But they had known
each other all their lives and their friendship was
far closer and deeper than instant lust.

"A room?" the innkeeper said again. "A meal
for you and your ladies? Is that all we can do for
you here in our humble establishment? Do you
require dancing? A juggler? Harpists and haut-
bois? Ask and it shall be given!" Far from being
seductive, or even friendly, the innkeeper's tone
was derisive.

Chan glanced at Wess, frowning slightly, as
everyone within earshot burst into laughter.
Wess was glad her complexion was dark enough

to hide her blush of anger. Chan was bright pink from the collar of his homespun shirt to the roots of his blond hair. Wess knew they had been insulted but she did not understand how or why, so she replied with courtesy.

"No, citizen, thank you for your hospitality. We need a room, if you have one, and food."

"We would not refuse a bath," Quartz said.

The innkeeper glanced at them, an irritated expression on his face, and spoke once more to Chan.

"The young gentleman lets his ladies speak for him? Is this some foreign custom, that you are too high-bred to speak to a mere tavern-keeper?"

"I don't understand you," Chan said. "Wess spoke for us all. Must we speak in chorus?"

Taken aback, the man hid his reaction by showing them, with an exaggerated bow, to a table.

Wess dumped her pack on the floor next to the wall behind her and sat down with a sigh of relief. The others followed. Aerie looked as if she could not have kept on her feet a moment longer.

"This is a simple place," the tavern-keeper said. "Beer or ale, wine. Meat and bread. Can you pay?"

He was speaking to Chan again. He took no direct note of Wess or Aerie or Quartz.

"What is the price?"

"Four dinners, bed—you break your fast somewhere else, I don't open early. A piece of silver. In advance."

"The bath included?" Quartz said.

"Yes, yes, all right."

"We can pay," said Quartz, whose turn it was

to keep track of what they spent. She offered him a piece of silver.

He continued to look at Chan, but after an awkward pause he shrugged, snatched the coin from Quartz, and turned away. Quartz drew back her hand, then, under the table, surreptitiously wiped it on the leg of her heavy cotton trousers.

Chan glanced over at Wess. "Do you understand anything that has happened since we entered the city's gates?"

"It is curious," she said. "They have strange customs."

"We can puzzle them out tomorrow," Aerie said.

A young woman carrying a tray stopped at their table. She wore odd clothes, summer clothes by the look of them, for they uncovered her arms and shoulders and almost completely bared her breasts. It is hot in here, Wess thought. That's quite intelligent of her. Then she need only put on a cloak to go home, and she will not get chilled or overheated.

"Ale for you, sir?" the young woman said to Chan. "Or wine? And wine for your wives?"

"Beer, please," Chan said. "What are 'wives'? I have studied your language, but this is not a word I know."

"The ladies are not your wives?"

Wess took a tankard of ale off the tray, too tired and thirsty to try to figure out what the woman was talking about. She took a deep swallow of the cool bitter brew. Quartz reached for a flask of wine and two cups, and poured for herself and Aerie.

"My companions are Westerly, Aerie, and

Quartz," Chan said, nodding to each in turn. "I am Chandler. And you are—?"

"I'm just the serving girl," she said, sounding frightened. "You could not wish to be troubled with my name." She grabbed a mug of beer and put it on the table, spilling some, and fled.

They all looked at each other, but then the tavern-keeper came with platters of meat. They were too hungry to wonder what they had done to frighten the barmaid.

Wess tore off a mouthful of bread. It was fairly fresh, and a welcome change from trail rations—dry meat, flatbread mixed hurriedly and baked on stones in the coals of a campfire, fruit when they could find or buy it. Still, Wess was used to better.

"I miss your bread," she said to Quartz in their own language. Quartz smiled.

The meat was hot and untainted by decay. Even Aerie ate with some appetite, though she preferred meat raw.

Halfway through her meal, Wess slowed down and took a moment to observe the tavern more carefully.

At the bar, a group suddenly burst into raucous laughter.

"You say the same damned thing every damned time you turn up in Sanctuary, Bauchle," one of them said, his loud voice full of mockery. "You have a secret or a scheme or a marvel that will make your fortune. Why don't you get an honest job—like the rest of us?"

That brought on more laughter, even from the large, heavyset young man who was being made fun of.

"You'll see, this time," he said. "This time I've got something that will take me all the way to the court of the Emperor. When you hear the criers tomorrow, you'll know." He called for more wine. His friends drank and made more jokes, both at his expense.

The Unicorn was much more crowded now, smokier, louder. Occasionally someone glanced toward Wess and her friends, but otherwise they were let alone.

A cold breeze thinned the odor of beer and sizzling meat and unwashed bodies. Silence fell suddenly, and Wess looked quickly around to see if she had breached some other unknown custom. But all the attention focused on the tavern's entrance. The cloaked figure stood there casually, but nothing was casual about the aura of power and self-possession.

In the whole of the tavern, not another table held an empty place.

"Sit with us, sister!" Wess called on impulse.

Two long steps and a shove: Wess' chair scraped roughly along the floor and Wess was rammed back against the wall, a dagger at her throat.

"Who calls me 'sister'?" The dark hood fell back from long, gray-streaked hair. A blue star blazed on the woman's forehead. Her elegant features grew terrible and dangerous in its light.

Wess stared up into the tall, lithe woman's furious eyes. Her jugular vein pulsed against the point of the blade. If she made a move toward her knife, or if any of her friends moved at all, she was dead.

"I meant no disrespect—" She almost said

"sister" again. But it was not the familiarity that had caused offense: it was the word itself. The woman was travelling incognito, and Wess had breached her disguise. No mere apology would repair the damage she had done.

A drop of sweat trickled down the side of her face. Chan and Aerie and Quartz were all poised on the edge of defense. If Wess erred again, more than one person would die before the fighting stopped.

"My unfamiliarity with your language has offended you, young gentleman," Wess said, hoping the tavern-keeper had used a civil form of address, if not a civil tone. It was often safe to insult someone by the tone, but seldom by the words themselves. "Young gentleman," she said again when the woman did not kill her, "someone has made sport of me by translating 'frejôjan,' 'sister.' "

"Perhaps," the disguised woman said. "What does frejôjan mean?"

"It is a term of pace, an offer of friendship, a word to welcome a guest, another child of one's own parents."

"Ah. 'Brother' is the word you want, the word to speak to men. To call a man 'sister,' the word for women, is an insult."

"An insult!" Wess said, honestly surprised.

But the knife drew back from her throat.

"You are a barbarian," the disguised woman said, in a friendly tone. "I cannot be insulted by a barbarian."

"There is the problem, you see," Chan said. "Translation. In our language, the word for outsider, for foreigner, also translates as 'barbarian.' " He smiled, his beautiful smile.

Wess pulled her chair forward again. She reached for Chan's hand under the table. He squeezed her fingers gently.

"I meant only to offer you a place to sit, where there is no other."

The stranger sheathed her dagger and stared down into Wess' eyes. Wess shivered slightly and imagined spending the night with Chad on one side, the stranger on the other.

Or you could have the center, if you liked, she thought, holding the gaze.

The stranger laughed. Wess could not tell if the mocking tone were directed outward or inward.

"Then I will sit here, as there is no other place." She did so. "My name is Lythande."

They introduced themselves, and offered her—Wess made herself think of Lythande as "him" so she would not damage the disguise again—offered him wine.

"I cannot accept your wine," Lythande said. "But to show I mean no offense, I will smoke with you." He rolled shredded herbs in a dry leaf, lit the construction, inhaled from it, and held it out. "Westerly, *frejôjan*."

Out of politeness Wess tried it. By the time she stopped coughing her throat was sore, and the sweet scent made her feel lightheaded.

"It takes practice," Lythande said smiling.

Chan and Quartz did no better, but Aerie inhaled deeply, her eyes closed, then held her breath. Thereafter she and Lythande shared it while the others ordered more ale and another flask of wine.

"Why did you ask me, of all this crowd, to sit here?" Lythande asked.

"Because . . ." Wess paused to try to think of a way to make her intuition sound sensible. "You look like someone who knows what's going on. You look like someone who might help us."

"If information is all you need, you can get it less expensively than by hiring a sorcerer."

"Are you a sorcerer?" Wess asked.

Lythande looked at her with pity and contempt. "You child! What do your people mean, sending innocents and children out of the north!" He touched the star on his forehead. "What did you think this means?"

"I'll have to guess, but I guess it means you are a mage."

"Excellent. A few years of lessons like that and you might survive, a while, in Sanctuary—in the Maze—in the Unicorn!"

"We haven't got years," Aerie whispered. "We have, perhaps, overspent the time we *do* have."

Quartz put her arm around Aerie's shoulders, for comfort, and hugged her gently.

"You interest me," Lythande said. "Tell me what information you seek. Perhaps I will know whether you can obtain it less expensively—not cheaply, but less expensively—from Jubal the Slavemonger, or from a seer—" At their expressions, he stopped.

"Slavemonger!"

"He collects information as well. You needn't worry that he'll abduct you from his sitting-room."

They all started speaking at once, then fell silent, realizing the futility.

"Start at the beginning."

"We're looking for someone," Wess said.

"This is a poor place to search. No one will tell you anything about any patron of this establishment."

"But he's a friend."

"There's only your word for that."

"Satan wouldn't be here anyway," Wess said. "If he were free to come here he'd be free to go home. We'd have heard something of him, or he would have found us, or—"

"You fear he was taken prisoner. Enslaved, perhaps."

"He must have been. He was hunting, alone. He liked to do that, his people often do."

"We need solitude sometimes," Aerie said.

Wess nodded. "We didn't worry about him till he didn't come home for Equinox. Then we searched. We found his camp, and a cold trail . . ."

"We tried to hope for kidnapping," Chan said. "But there was no ransom demand. The trail was so old—they took him away."

"We followed, and we heard some rumors of him," Aerie said. "But the road branched, and we had to choose which way to go." She shrugged, but could not maintain the careless pose; she turned away in despair. "I could find no trace . . ."

Aerie, with her longer range, had met them after searching all day at each evening's new camp, ever more exhausted and more driven.

"Apparently we chose wrong," Quartz said.

"Children," Lythande said, "children, frejôjans—"

"Frejôjani," Chan said automatically, then shook his head and spread his hands in apology.

"Your friend is one slave out of many. You could not trace him by his papers, unless you discovered what name they were forged under. For someone to recognize him by a description would be the greatest luck, even if you had an homuncule to show. Sisters, brother, you might not recognize him yourselves, by now."

"I would recognize him," Aerie said.

"We'd all recognize him, even in a crowd of his own people. But that makes no difference. Anyone would know him who had seen him. But no one *has* seen him, or if they have they will not say so to us." Wess glanced at Aerie.

"You see," Aerie said, "he is winged."

"Winged!" Lythande said.

"Winged folk are rare, I believe, in the south."

"Winged folk are myths, in the south. Winged? Surely you mean . . ."

Aerie started to shrug back her cape, but Quartz put her arm around her shoulders again. Wess broke into the conversation quickly.

"The bones are longer," she said, touching the three outer fingers of her left hand with the forefinger of her right. "And stronger. The webs between fold out."

"And these people fly?"

"Of course. Why else have wings?"

Wess glanced at Chan, who nodded and reached for his pack.

"We have no homuncule," Wess said. "But we

have a picture. It isn't Satan, but it's very like him."

Chan pulled out the wooden tube he had carried all the way from Kaimas. From inside it, he drew the rolled kidskin, which he opened out onto the table. The hide was carefully tanned and very thin; it had writing on one side and a painting, with one word underneath it, on the other.

"It's from the library at Kaimas," Chan said. "No one knows where it came from. I believe it is quite old, and I think it is from a book, but this is all that's left." He showed Lythande the written side. "I can decipher the script but not the language. Can you read it?"

Lythande shook his head. "It is unknown to me."

Disappointed, Chan turned the illustrated side of the manuscript page toward Lythande. Wess leaned toward it too, picking out the details in the dim candlelight. It was beautiful, almost as beautiful as Satan himself. It was surprising how like Satan it was, for it had been in the library since long before he was born. The slender and powerful winged man had red-gold hair and flame-colored wings. His expression seemed composed half of wisdom and half of deep despair.

Most flying people were black or deep iridescent green or pure dark blue. But Satan, like the painting, was the color of fire. Wess explained that to Lythande.

"We suppose this word to be this person's name," Chan said. "We cannot be sure we have the pronunciation right, but Satan's mother liked the sound as we say it, so she gave it to him as his name, too."

Lythande stared at the gold and scarlet painting in silence for a long time, then shook his head and leaned back in his chair. He blew smoke toward the ceiling. The ring spun, and sparked, and finally dissipated into the haze.

"Frejôjani," Lythande said, "Jubal—and the other slavemongers—parade their merchandise through the town before every auction. If your friend were in the coffle, everyone in Sanctuary would know. Everyone in the Empire would know."

Beneath the edges of her cape, Aerie clenched her hands into fists.

Chan slowly, carefully, blankly, rolled up the painting and stored it away.

This was, Wess feared, the end of their journey.

"But it might be . . ."

Aerie looked up sharply, narrowing her deep-set eyes.

"Such an unusual being would not be sold at public auction. He would be offered in private sale, or exhibited, or perhaps even offered to the emperor for his menagerie."

Aerie flinched, and Quartz traced the texture of her short-sword's bone haft.

"It's better, children, don't you see? He'll be treated decently. He's valuable. Ordinary slaves are whipped and cut and broken to obedience."

Chan's transparent complexion paled to white. Wess shuddered. Even contemplating slavery they had none of them understood what it meant.

"But how will we find him? Where will we look?"

"Jubal will know," Lythande said, "if anyone does. I like you, children. Sleep tonight. Perhaps tomorrow Jubal will speak with you." He got up, passed smoothly through the crowd, and vanished into the darkness outside.

In silence with her friends, Wess sat thinking about what Lythande had told them.

A well-set-up young fellow crossed the room and leaned over their table toward Chan. Wess recognized him as the man who had earlier been made sport of by his friends.

"Good evening, traveller," he said to Chan. "I have been told these ladies are not your wives."

"It seems everyone in this room has asked if my companions are my wives, and I still do not understand what you are asking," Chan said pleasantly.

"What's so hard to understand?"

"What does 'wives' mean?"

The man arched one eyebrow, but replied. "Women bonded to you by law. To give their favors to no one but you. To bear and raise your sons."

" 'Favors'?"

"Sex, you clapperdudgeon! Fucking! Do you understand me?"

"Not entirely. It sounds like a very odd system to me."

Wess thought it odd, too. It seemed absurd to decide to bear children of only one gender; and bonded by law sounded suspiciously like slavery. But—three women pledged solely to one man? She glanced across at Aerie and Quartz and saw they were thinking the same thing. They burst out laughing.

"Chan, Chad-love, think how exhausted you'd be!" Wess said.

Chan grinned. They often slept and made love all together, but he was not expected to satisfy all his friends. Wess enjoyed making love with Chad, but she was equally excited by Aerie's delicate ferocity, and by Quartz' inexhaustible gentleness and power.

"They're not your wives, then," the man said. "So how much for that one?" He pointed at Quartz.

They all waited curiously for him to explain.

"Come on, man! Don't be coy! You're obvious to everyone—why else bring women to the Unicorn? With that one, you'll get away with it till the madams find out. So make your fortune while you can. What's her price? I can pay, I assure you."

Chan started to speak, but Quartz gestured sharply and he fell silent.

"Tell me if I interpret you correctly," she said. "You think coupling with me would be enjoyable. You would like to share my bed tonight."

"That's right, lovey." He reached for her breast but abruptly thought better of it.

"Yet you speak, not to me, but to my friend. This seems very awkward, and very rude."

"You'd better get used to it, woman. It's the way we do things here."

"You offer Chan money, to persuade me to couple with you."

The man looked at Chan. "You'd best train your whores to manners yourself, boy, or your customers will help you and damage your merchandise."

Chan blushed scarlet, embarrassed, flustered, and confused. Wess began to think she knew what was going on, but she did not want to believe it.

"You are speaking to me, *man*," Quartz said, using the word with as much contempt as he had put into "woman." "I have but one more question for you. You are not ill-favored, yet you cannot get someone to bed you for the joy of it. Does this mean you are diseased?"

With an incoherent sound of rage, he reached for his knife. Before he touched it, Quartz' short-sword rasped out of its scabbard. She held its tip just above his belt-buckle. The death she offered him was slow and painful.

Everyone in the tavern watched intently as the man slowly spread his hands.

"Go away," Quartz said. "Do not speak to me again. You are not unattractive, but if you are not diseased you *are* a fool, and I do not sleep with fools."

She moved her sword a handsbreadth. He backed up three fast steps and spun around, glancing spasmodically from one face to another, to another. He found only amusement. He bolted, through a roar of laughter, fighting his way to the door.

The tavern-keeper sauntered over. "Foreigners," he said, "I don't know whether you've made your place or dug your graves tonight, but that was the best laugh I've had since the new moon. Bauchle Meyne will never live it down."

"I did not think it funny in the least," Quartz said. She sheathed her short-sword. She had not even touched her broadsword. Wess had never seen her draw it. "And I am tired. Where is our room?"

He led them up the stairs. The room was small and low-ceilinged. After the tavern-keeper left, Wess poked the straw mattress of one of the beds, and wrinkled her nose.

"I've got this far from home without getting lice, I'm not going to sleep in a nest of bed-bugs." She threw her bedroll to the floor. Chan shrugged and dropped his gear.

Quartz flung her pack into the corner. "I'll have something to say to Satan when we find him," she said angrily. "Stupid fool, to let himself be captured by these creatures."

Aerie stood hunched in her cloak. "This is a wretched place," she said. "You can flee, but he cannot."

"Aerie, love, I know, I'm sorry." Quartz hugged her, stroking her hair. "I didn't mean it, about Satan. I was angry."

Aerie nodded.

Wess rubbed Aerie's shoulders, unfastened the clasp of her long hooded cloak, and drew it from Aerie's body. Candlelight rippled across the black fur that covered her, as sleek and glossy as sealskin. She wore nothing but a short thin blue silk tunic and her walking boots. She kicked off the boots, dug her clawed toes into the splintery floor, and stretched.

Her outer fingers lay close against the backs of her arms. She opened them, and her wings unfolded.

Only half-spread, her wings spanned the room. She let them droop, and pulled aside the leather curtain over the tall narrow window. The next building was very close.

"I'm going out. I need to fly."

"Aerie, we've come so far today—"

"Wess, I am tired. I won't go far. But I can't fly in the daytime, not here, and the moon is waxing. If I don't go now I may not be able to fly for days."

"It's true," Wess said. "Be careful."

"I won't be gone long." She slid sideways out the window and climbed up the rough side of the building. Her claws scraped into the adobe. Three soft footsteps overhead, the shushh of her wings: she was gone.

The others pushed the beds against the wall and spread their blankets, overlapping, on the floor. Quartz looped the leather flap over a hook in the wall and put the candle on the window-ledge.

Chan hugged Wess. "I never saw anyone move as fast as Lythande. Wess, love, I feared he'd killed you before I even noticed him."

"It was stupid, to speak so familiarly to a stranger."

"But he offered us the nearest thing to news of Satan we've heard in weeks."

"True. Maybe the fright was worth it." Wess

looked out the window, but saw nothing of
Aerie.

"What made you think Lythande was a woman?"

Wess glanced at Chan sharply. He gazed back
at her with a mildly curious expression.

He doesn't know, Wess thought, astonished.
He didn't realize—

"I . . . I don't know," she said. "A silly mistake. I made a lot of them today."

It was the first time in her life she had deliberately lied to a friend. She felt slightly ill, and
when she heard the scrape of claws on the roof
above, she was glad for more reasons than simply that Aerie had returned. Just then the
tavern-keeper banged on their door announcing
their bath. In the confusion of getting Aerie inside and hidden under her cloak before they
could open the door, Chan forgot the subject of
Lythande's gender.

Beneath them, the noise of revelry in the Unicorn gradually faded to silence. Wess forced
herself to lie still. She was so tired that she felt as
if she were trapped in a river, with the current
swirling her around and around so she could
never get her bearings. Yet she could not sleep.
Even the bath, the first warm bath any of them
had had since leaving Kaimas, had not relaxed
her. Quartz lay solid and warm beside her, and
Aerie lay between Quartz and Chan. Wess did
not begrudge Aerie or Quartz their places, but
she did like to sleep in the middle. She wished
one of her friends were awake, to make love with,

but she could tell from their breathing that they were all deeply asleep. She cuddled up against Quartz, who reached out, in a dream, and embraced her.

The darkness continued, without end, without any sign of dawn, and finally Wess slid out from beneath Quartz' arm and the blankets, silently put on her pants and shirt, and, barefoot, crept down the stairs, past the silent tavern, and outside. On the doorstep, she sat and pulled on her boots.

The moon gave a faint light, enough for Wess. The street was deserted. Her heels thudded on the cobblestones, echoing hollowly against the close adobe walls. Such a short stay in the town should not make her uneasy, but it did. She envied Aerie her power to escape, however briefly, however dangerous the escape might be. Wess walked down the street, keeping careful track of her path. It would be very easy to get lost in this warren of streets and alleys, niches and blank canyons.

The scrape of a boot, instantly stilled, brought her out of her mental wanderings. They wished to try to follow her? Good luck to them.

Wess was a hunter. She tracked her prey so silently that she killed with a knife; in the dense rain forest where she lived, arrows were too uncertain. She had crept up on a panther and stroked its smooth pelt—then vanished so swiftly that she left the creature yowling in fury and frustration, while she laughed with delight. She grinned, and quickened her step, and her footfalls turned silent on the stone.

Her unfamiliarity with the streets hampered her slightly. A dead-end could trap her. But she found, to her pleasure, that her instinct for seeking out good trails translated into the city. Once she thought she would have to turn back, but the high wall barring her way had a deep diagonal fissure from the ground to its top. She found just enough purchase to clamber over it. She jumped into the garden the wall enclosed, scampered across it and up a grape arbor, and swung down into the next alley.

She ran smoothly, gladly, as her exhaustion lifted. She felt good, despite the looming buildings and twisted dirty streets and vile odors.

She faded into a shadowed recess where two houses abutted but did not line up. Listening, she waited.

The soft and nearly silent footsteps halted. Her pursuer hesitated. Grit scraped between stone and leather as the person turned one way, then the other, and, finally, chose the wrong turning and hurried off. Wess grinned, but she felt respect for any hunter who could follow her this far.

Moving silently through shadows, she started back toward the tavern. When she came to a tumbledown building she remembered, she found finger- and toe-holds and climbed to the roof of the next house. Flying was not the only talent Aerie had that Wess envied. Being able to climb straight up an undamaged adobe wall would be useful sometimes, too.

The rooftop was deserted. Too cold to sleep outside, no doubt; the inhabitants of the city went to ground at night, in warmer, unseen warrens.

The air smelled cleaner here, so she travelled by rooftop as far as she could. But the main passage through the Maze was too wide to leap across. From the building that faced the Unicorn, Wess observed the tavern. She doubted that her pursuer could have reached it first, but the possibility existed, in this strange place. She saw no one. It was near dawn. She no longer felt exhausted, just deliciously sleepy. She climbed down the face of the building and started across the street.

Someone flung open the door behind her, leaped out as she turned, and punched her in the side of the head.

Wess crashed to the cobblestones. The shadow stepped closer and kicked her in the ribs. A line of pain wrapped around her chest and tightened when she tried to breathe.

"Don't kill her. Not yet."

"No. I have plans for her."

Wess recognized the voice of Bauchle Meyne, who had insulted Quartz in the tavern. He toed her in the side.

"When I'm done with you, bitch, you can take me to your friends." He started to unbuckle his belt.

Wess tried to get up. Bauchle Meyne's companion stepped toward her, to kick her again.

His foot swung toward her. She grabbed it and twisted. As he went down, Wess struggled up. Bauchle Meyne, surprised, lurched toward her and grabbed her in a bear hug, pinioning her

arms so she could not reach her knife. He pressed
his face down close to hers. She felt his whisker
stubble and smelled his yeasty breath. He could
not hold her and force his mouth to hers at the
same time, but he slobbered on her cheek. His
pants slipped down and his penis thrust against
her thigh.

Wess kneed him in the balls as hard as she
could.

He screamed and let her go and staggered
away, holding himself, doubled up and moaning, stumbling over his fallen breeches. Wess
drew her knife and backed against a wall, ready
for another attack.

Bauchle Meyne's accomplice rushed her. Her
knife sliced quickly toward him, slashing his
arm. He flung himself backwards and swore violently. Blood spurted between his fingers.

Wess heard the approaching footsteps a moment before he did. She pressed her free hand
hard against the wall behind her. She was afraid
to shout for help. In this place whoever answered
might as easily join in attacking her.

But the man swore again, grabbed Bauchle
Meyne by the arm, and dragged him away as fast
as the latter, in his present distressed state, could
go.

Wess sagged, sliding down the wall to the
ground. She knew she was still in danger, but her
legs would not hold her up anymore.

The footsteps ceased. Wess looked up, clench-
ing her fingers around the handle of her knife.

"Frejôjan," Lythande said softly, from ten
paces away, "sister, you led me quite a chase."

She glanced after the two men. "And not only me, it seems."

"I never fought a person before," Wess said shakily. "Not a real fight. Only practice. No one ever got hurt." She touched the side of her head. The shallow scrape bled freely. She thought about its stopping, and the flow gradually ceased.

Lythande sat on his heels beside her. "Let me see." He probed the cut gently. "I thought it was bleeding, but it's stopped. What happened?"

"I don't know. Did you follow me? Did they? I thought I was eluding one person."

"I was the only one following you," Lythande said. "They must have come back to bother Quartz again."

"You know about that?"

"The whole city knows, child. Or anyway, the whole Maze. Bauchle will not soon live it down. The worst of it is he will never understand what it is that happened, or why."

"No more will I," Wess said. She looked up at Lythande. "How can you live here?" she cried.

Lythande drew back, frowning. "I do not live here. But that is not really what you are asking. We cannot speak so freely on the public street." He glanced away, hesitated, and turned back. "Will you come with me? I haven't much time, but I can fix your cut, and we can talk safely."

"All right," Wess said. She sheathed her knife and pushed herself to her feet, wincing at the sharp pain in her side. Lythande grasped her elbow, steadying her.

"Perhaps you've cracked a rib," he said. They

started slowly down the street.

"No," Wess said. "It's bruised. It will hurt for a while, but it isn't broken."

"How do you know?"

Wess glanced at him quizzically. "I may not be from a city, but my people aren't completely wild. I paid attention to my lessons when I was little."

"Lessons? Lessons in what?"

"In knowing whether I am hurt, and what I must do if I am, in controlling the processes of my body—surely your people teach their children these things?"

"My people don't know these things," Lythande said. "I think we have more to talk about than I believed, frejôjan."

The Maze confused even Wess, by the time they reached the small building where Lythande stopped. Wess was feeling dizzy from the blow to her head, but she was confident that she was not dangerously hurt. Lythande opened a low door and ducked inside. Wess followed.

Lythande picked up a candle. The wick sparked. In the center of the dark room, a shiny spot reflected the glow. The wick burst into flame and the spot of reflection grew. Wess blinked. The reflection spread into a sphere, taller than Lythande, the color and texture of deep water, blue-gray, shimmering. It balanced on its lower curve, bulging slightly so it was not quite perfectly round.

"Follow me, Westerly."

Lythande walked toward the sphere. Its surface rippled at her approach. She stepped into it.

It closed around her, and all Wess could see was a wavering figure, beyond the surface, and the spot of light from the candle flame.

She touched the sphere gingerly with her fingertip. It was wet. Taking a deep breath, she put her hand through the surface.

It froze her fast; she could not proceed, she could not escape, she could not move. Even her voice was captured.

After a moment Lythande surfaced. Her hair sparkled with drops of water, but her clothes were dry. She stood frowning at Wess, lines of thought bracketing the star on her forehead. Then her brow cleared and she grasped Wess' wrist.

"Don't fight it, little sister," she said. "Don't fight me."

The blue star glittered in the darkness, its points sparking with new light. Against great resistance, Lythande drew Wess' hand from the sphere. The cuff of Wess' shirt was cold and sodden. In only a few seconds the water had wrinkled her fingers. The sphere freed her suddenly and she nearly fell, but Lythande caught and supported her.

"What happened?"

Still holding her up, Lythande reached into the water and drew it aside like a curtain. She urged Wess toward the division. Unwillingly, Wess took a shaky step forward, and Lythande helped her inside. The surface closed behind them. Lythande eased Wess down on the platform that flowed out smoothly from the inside curve. Wess expected it to be wet, but it was resilient and smooth and slightly warm.

"What happened?" she asked again.

"The sphere is a protection against other sorcerers."

"I'm not a sorcerer."

"I believe you believe that. If I thought you were deceiving me, I would kill you. But if you are not a sorcerer, it is only because you are not trained."

Wess started to protest, but Lythande waved her to silence.

"Now I understand how you eluded me in the streets."

"I'm a hunter," Wess said irritably. "What good would a hunter be, who couldn't move silently and fast?"

"No, it was more than that. I put a mark on you, and you threw it off. No one has ever done that before."

"I didn't do it, either."

"Let us not argue, frejôjan. There isn't time."

She inspected the cut, then dipped her hand into the side of the sphere, brought out a handful of water, and washed away the sticky drying blood. Her touch was warm and soothing, as expert as Quartz'.

"Why did you bring me here?"

"So we could talk unobserved."

"What about?"

"I want to ask you something first. Why did you think I was a woman?"

Wess frowned and gazed into the depths of the floor. Her boot dimpled the surface, like the foot of a water-strider.

"Because you *are* a woman," she said. "Why you pretend you are not, I don't know."

"That is not the question," Lythande said. "The question is why you called me 'sister' the moment you saw me. No one, sorcerer, or otherwise, has ever glanced at me once and known me for what I am. You could place me, and yourself, in great danger. How did you know?"

"I just knew," Wess said. "It was obvious. I didn't look at you and wonder if you were a man or a woman. I saw you, and I thought, how beautiful, how elegant she is. She looks wise. She looks like she could help us. So I called to you."

"And what did your friends think?"

"They . . . I don't know what Quartz and Aerie thought. Chan asked whatever was I thinking of."

"What did you say to him?"

"I . . ." She hesitated, feeling ashamed. "I lied to him," she said miserably. "I said I was tired and it was dark and smoky, and I made a foolish mistake."

"Why didn't you try to persuade him you were right?"

"Because it isn't my business to deny what you wish known about yourself. Even to my oldest friend, my first lover."

Lythande stared up at the curved surface of the inside of the sphere. The tension eased in the set of her shoulders, the expression on her face.

"Thank you, little sister," she said, her voice full of relief. "I did not know if my identity were safe with you. But I think it is."

Wess looked up suddenly, chilled by insight. "You brought me here—you would have killed me!"

"If I had to," Lythande said easily. "I am glad it

was not necessary. But I could not trust a promise made under threat. You do not fear me; you made your decision of your own free will."

"That may be true," Wess said. "But it isn't true that I don't fear you."

Lythande gazed at her. "Perhaps I deserve your fear, Westerly. You could destroy me with a thoughtless word. But the knowledge you have could destroy you. Some people would go to great lengths to discover what you know."

"I'm not going to tell them."

"If they suspected—they might force you."

"I can take care of myself," Wess said.

Lythande rubbed the bridge of her nose with thumb and forefinger. "Ah, sister, I hope so. I can give you very little protection." She—*he*, Wess reminded herself—stood up. "It's time to go. It's nearly dawn."

"You asked questions of me—may I ask one of you?"

"I'll answer if I can."

"Bauchle Meyne—if he hadn't behaved so stupidly, he could have killed me. But he taunted me till I recovered myself. He made himself vulnerable to me. His friend knew I had a knife, but he attacked me unarmed. I've been trying to understand what happened, but it makes no sense."

Lythande drew a deep breath. "Westerly," she said, "I wish you had never come to Sanctuary. You escaped for the same reason that I first chose to appear as I now must remain."

"I still don't understand."

"They never expected you to fight. To struggle a little, perhaps, just enough to excite them.

They expected you to acquiesce to their wishes whether it was to beat you, to rape you, or to kill you. Women in Sanctuary are not trained to fight. They are taught that their only power lies in their ability to please, in bed and in flattery. Some few excel. Most survive.''

"And the rest?"

"The rest are killed for their insolence. Or—'' She smiled bitterly and gestured to herself. "Some few . . . find their talents are stronger in other areas."

"But why do you put up with it?"

"That is the way it is, Westerly. Some would say that is the way it must be—that it is ordained."

"It isn't that way in Kaimas." Just speaking the name of her home made her want to return. "Who ordains it?"

"Why, my dear," Lythande said sardonically, "the gods."

"Then you should rid yourselves of gods."

Lythande arched one eyebrow. "You should, perhaps, keep such ideas to yourself in Sanctuary. The gods' priests are powerful." She drew her hand up the side of the sphere so it parted as if she had slit it with a knife, and held the skin apart so Wess could leave.

Wess thought the shaky uncertain feeling that gripped her would disappear when she had solid ground beneath her feet again.

But it did not.

Wess and Lythande returned to the Unicorn in silence. As the Maze woke, the street began to fill with laden carts drawn by scrawny ponies, with beggars and hawkers and pickpockets. Wess bought fruit and meat rolls to take to her friends.

The Unicorn was closed and dark. As the tavern-keeper had said, he did not open early. Wess went around to the back, but at the steps of the lodging door, Lythande stopped.

"I must leave you, frejôjan."

Wess turned back in surprise. "But I thought you were coming upstairs with me—for breakfast, to talk . . ."

Lythande shook his head. His smile was odd, not, as Wess had come to expect, sardonic, but sad. "I wish I could, little sister. For once, I wish I could. I have business to the north that cannot wait."

"To the north! Why did you come this way with me?" She had got her bearings on the way back, and while the twisted streets would not permit a straight path, they had proceeded generally southward.

"I wanted to walk with you," Lythande said.

Wess scowled at him. "You thought I hadn't enough sense to get back by myself."

"This is a strange place for you. It isn't safe even for people who have always lived here."

"You—" Wess stopped. Because she had promised to safeguard his true identity, she could not say what she wished: that Lythande was treating her as Lythande himself did not wish to be treated. Wess shook her head, flinging aside her anger. Stronger than her anger in Lythande's lack of confidence in her, stronger than her disappointment that Lythande was going away, was her surprise that Lythande had pretended to hint at finding Satan. She did not wish to think too deeply on the sorcerer's motives.

"You have my promise," she said bitterly. "You may be sure that my word is important to me. May your business be profitable." She turned away and fumbled for the latch, her vision blurry.

"Westerly," Lythande said gently, "do you think I came back last night only to coerce an oath from you?"

"It doesn't matter."

"Well, perhaps not, since I have so little to give in return."

Wess turned around. "And do you think I made that promise only because I hoped you could help us?"

"No," Lythande said. "Frejôjan, I wish I had more time—but what I came to tell you is this. I spoke with Jubal last night."

"Why didn't you tell me? What did he say? Does he know where Satan is?" But she knew she would have no pleasure from the answer. Lythande would not have put off good news. "Will he see us?"

"He has not seen your friend, little sister. He said he had no time to see you."

"Oh."

"I did press him. He owes me, but he has been acting peculiar lately. He's more afraid of something else than he is of me, and that is very strange." Lythande looked away.

"Didn't he say *anything*?"

"He said . . . this evening, you should go to the grounds of the governor's palace."

"Why?"

"Westerly . . . this may have nothing to do with Satan. But the auction block is there."

Wess shook her head, confused.

"Where slaves are offered for sale."

Fury and humiliation and hope: Wess' reaction was so strong that she could not answer. Lythande came up the steps in one stride and put his arms around her. Wess held him, trembling, and Lythande stroked her hair.

"If he's there—is there no law, Lythande? Can a free person be stolen from their home, and . . . and . . ."

Lythande looked at the sky. The sun's light showed over the roof of the easternmost building.

"Frejôjan, I must go. If your friend is to be sold, you can try to buy him. The merchants here are not so rich as the merchants in the capital, but they are rich enough. You'd need a great deal of money. I think you should, instead, apply to the governor. He is a young man, and a fool—but he is not evil." Lythande hugged Wess one last time and stepped away. "Good-bye, little sister. Please believe I'd stay if I could."

"I know," she whispered.

Lythande strode away without looking back, leaving Wess alone among the early-morning shadows.

Wess returned to the room at the top of the stairs. When she entered, Chan propped himself up on one elbow.

"I was getting worried," he said.

"I can take care of myself!" Wess snapped.

"Wess, love, what's the matter?"

She tried to tell him, but she could not. Wess stood, silent, staring at the floor, with her back turned on her best friend.

She glanced over her shoulder when Chan stood up. The ripped curtain let in shards of light that cascaded over his body. He had changed, like all of them, on the long journey. He was still beautiful, but he was thinner and harder.

He touched her shoulder gently. She shrank away.

He saw the bloodstains on her collar. "You're hurt!" he said, startled. "Quartz!"

Quartz muttered sleepily from the bed. Chan tried to lead Wess over to the window, where there was more light.

"Just don't touch me!"

"Wess—"

"What's wrong?" Quartz said.

"Wess is injured."

Quartz padded barefoot toward them and Wess burst into tears and flung herself into her arms.

Quartz held Wess, as Wess had held her a few nights before, when Quartz had cried silently in bed, homesick, missing her children. "Tell me what happened," she said softly.

What Wess managed to say was less about the attack than about Lythande's explanations of it, and of Sanctuary.

"I understand," Quartz said after Wess had told her only a little. She stroked Wess' hair and brushed the tears from her cheeks.

"I don't," Wess said. "I must be going crazy, to act like this!" She started to cry again. Quartz led her to the blankets, where Aerie sat up, blinking and confused. Chan followed, equally bewildered. Quartz made Wess sit down, sat beside her and hugged her. Aerie rubbed her back and neck and let her wings unfold around them.

"You aren't going crazy," Quartz said. "It's that you aren't used to the way things are here."

"I don't want to get used to things here, I hate this place, I want to find Satan, I want to go home."

"I know," Quartz whispered. "I know."

"But I don't," Chan said.

Wess huddled against Quartz, unable to say anything that would ease the hurt she had given Chad.

"Just leave her alone for a little while, Chad," Quartz said to him. "Let her rest. Everything will be all right."

Quartz eased Wess down and lay beside her. Cuddled between Quartz and Aerie, with Aerie's wing spread over them all, Wess fell asleep.

At midmorning, Wess awoke. Her head ached fiercely and the black bruise across her side hurt every time she took a breath. She looked around the room. Sitting beside her, mending a strap on her pack, Quartz smiled down at her. Aerie was brushing her short smooth fur, and Chan stared out the window, his arm on the sill and his chin resting on his arm, his other shirt abandoned unpatched on his knee.

Wess got up and crossed the room. She sat on her heels near Chan. He glanced at her, and out the window, and at her again.

"Quartz explained, a little . . ."

"I was angry," Wess said.

"Just because barbarians act like . . . like barbarians, isn't a good reason to be angry with me."

He was right. Wess knew it. But the fury and bewilderment mixed up in her were still too strong to shrug off with easy words.

"You know—" he said, "you *do* know I couldn't act like that . . ."

Just for an instant Wess actually tried to imagine Chad acting like the innkeeper, or Bauchle Meyne, arrogantly, blindly, with his self-interest and his pleasure considered above everything and everyone else. The idea was so ludicrous that she burst out in sudden laughter.

"I know you wouldn't," she said. She had been angry at the person he *might* have been, had all the circumstances of his life been different. She had been angry at the person *she* might have been, even more. She hugged Chan quickly. "Chad, I've got to get free of this place." She took his hand and stood up. "Come, I saw Lythande last night, I have to tell you what he said."

They did not wait till evening to go to the governor's palace, but set out earlier, hoping to gain an audience with the prince and persuade him not to let Satan be sold.

But no one else was waiting till evening to go to the palace, either. They joined a crowd of people streaming toward the gate. Wess' attempt to slip through the throng earned her an elbow in her sore ribs.

"Don't push, girl," said the ragged creature she had jostled. He shook his staff at her. "Would you knock over an old cripple? I'd never get up again, after I'd been trompled."

"Your pardon, citizen," she said. Ahead she could see that the people had to crowd into a narrower space. They were, more or less, in a line. "Are you going to the slave auction?"

"Slave auction? Slave auction! No slave auction today, foreigner. The carnival come to town!"

"What's the carnival?"

"A carnival! You've never heard of a carnival? Well, ne'mind, nor has half the people in Sanctuary, nor seen one neither. Two twelve-years since one came. Now the prince is governor, we'll see more, I don't doubt. They'll come wanting an admission to his brother the emperor—out of the hinterlands and into the capital, if you know."

"But I still don't know what a carnival is."

The old man pointed.

Over the high wall of the palace grounds, the great drape of cloth that hung limply around a tall pole slowly began to spread, and open—like a huge mushroom, Wess thought. The guy ropes tightened, forming the canvas into an enormous tent.

"Under there—magic, foreign child. Strange animals. Prancing horses with pretty girls in feathers dancing on their backs. Jugglers, clowns, acrobats on high wires—and the freaks!" He chuckled. "I like the freaks best, the last time I saw a carnival they had a sheep with two heads and a man with two—but that's not a story to tell a young girl unless you're fucking her." He reached out to pinch her. Wess jerked back, drawing her knife. Startled, the old man said, "There, girl, no offense." She let the blade slide back into its sheath. The old man laughed again. "And a special exhibition, this carnival—special, for the prince. They won't say what 'tis. But it'll be a sight, you can be sure."

"Thank you, citizen," Wess said coldly, and stepped back among her friends. The ragged man was swept forward with the crowd.

Wess caught Aerie's gaze. "Did you hear?"

Aerie nodded. "They have him. What else could their great secret be?"

"In this skyforsaken place, they might have overpowered some poor troll, or a salamander." She spoke sarcastically, for trolls were the gentlest of creatures, and Wess herself had often stretched up to scratch the chin of a salamander who lived on a hill where she hunted. It was entirely tame, for Wess never hunted salamanders. Their hide was too thin to be useful and no one in the family liked lizard meat. Besides, one could not pack out even a single haunch of fullgrown salamander, and she would not waste her kill. "In this place, they might have a winged snake in a box, and call it a great secret."

"Wess, their secret is Satan and we all know it," Quartz said. "Now we have to figure out how to free him."

"You're right, of course," Wess said.

At the gate, two huge guards glowered at the rabble they had been ordered to admit to the parade-ground. Wess stopped before one of them.

"I want to see the prince," she said.

"Audience next week," he replied, hardly glancing at her.

"I need to see him before the carnival begins."

This time he did look at her, amused. "You do, do you? Then you've no luck. He's gone, won't be back till the parade."

"Where is he?" Chan asked.

She heard grumbling from the crowd piling up behind them.

"State secret," the guard said. "Now go in, or clear the way."

They went in.

The crowd thinned abruptly, for the parade-ground was enormous. Even the tent seemed small; the palace loomed above it like a cliff. If the whole population of Sanctuary had not come here, then a large proportion of every section had, for several merchants were setting up stalls: beads here, fruit there, pastries farther on; a beggar crawled slowly past; and a few paces away a large group of noblefolk in satins and fur and gold walked languidly beneath parasols held by naked slaves. The thin autumn sunlight was hardly enough to mar the complexion of the most delicate noble, or to warm the back of the most vigorous slave.

Quartz looked around, then pointed over the heads of the crowd. "They're making a pathway, with ropes and braces. The parade will come through that gate, and into the tent from this side." She swept her hand from right to left, east to west, in a long curve from the Processional gate. The carnival tent was set up between the auction block and the guards' barracks.

They tried to circle the tent, but the area beyond it all the way to the wall was blocked by rope barriers. In the front, a line of spectators already snaked back far beyond any possible capacity.

"We'll never get in," Aerie said.

"Maybe it's for the best," Chan said. "We don't need to be inside with Satan—we need to get him out."

The shadows lengthened across the palace grounds. Wess sat motionless and silent, waiting. Chan bit his fingernails and fidgeted. Aerie hunched under her cloak, her hood pulled low to shadow her face. Quartz watched her anxiously, and fingered the grip of her sword.

After again being refused an audience with the prince, this time at the palace doors, they had secured a place next to the roped-off path. Across the way, a work crew put the finishing touches on a platform. When it was completed, servants hurried from the palace with rugs, a silk-fringed awning, several chairs, and a brazier of coals. Wess would not have minded a brazier of coals herself; as the sun fell, the air was growing chill.

The crowd continued to gather, becoming denser, louder, more and more drunk. Fights broke out in the line at the tent, as people began to realize they would never get inside. Soon the mood grew so ugly that criers spread among the people, ringing bells and announcing that the carnival would present one more performance, several more performances, until all the citizens of Sanctuary had the opportunity to glimpse the carnival's wonders. And the secret. Of course, the secret. Still, no one even hinted at the secret's nature.

Wess pulled her cloak closer. She knew the nature of the secret; she only hoped the secret would see his friends and be ready for whatever they could do.

The sun touched the high wall around the palace grounds. Soon it would be dark.

Trumpets and cymbals: Wess looked toward the Processional gate, but a moment later realized that all the citizens around her were straining for a view of the palace entrance. The enormous doors swung open and a phalanx of guards marched out, followed by a group of nobles wearing jewels and cloth of gold. They strode across the hard-packed ground. The young man at the head of the group, who wore a gold coronet, acknowledged his people's shouts and cries as if they all were accolades—which, Wess thought, they were not. But above the mutters and complaints, the loudest cry was, "The prince! Long live the prince!"

The phalanx marched straight from the palace to the new-built platform. Anyone shortsighted enough to sit in that path had to snatch up their things and hurry out of the way. The route cleared as swiftly as water parting around a stone.

Wess stood impulsively, about to sprint across the parade route to try once more to speak to the prince.

"Sit down!"

"Out of the way!"

Someone threw an apple core at her. She knocked it away and crouched down again, though not because of the threats or the flying garbage. Aerie, too, with the same thought, started to her feet. Wess touched her elbow.

"Look," she said.

Everyone within reach or hearing of the procession seemed to have the same idea. The crowd surged in, every member clamoring for attention. The prince flung out a handful of coins, which drew the beggars scuffling away from him. Others, more intent on their claims, continued to press him. The guards fell back, surrounding him, nearly cutting off the sight of him, and pushed at the citizens with spears held broadside.

The tight cordon parted and the prince mounted the platform. Standing alone, he turned all the way around, raising his hands to the crowd.

"My friends," he cried, "I know you have claims upon me. The least wrong to one of my people is important to me."

Wess snorted.

"But tonight we are all privileged to witness a wonder never seen in the Empire. Forget your troubles tonight, my friends, and enjoy the spectacle with me." He held out his hand, and brought a member of his party up beside him on the stage.

Bauchle Meyne.

"In a few days, Bauchle Meyne and his troupe will journey to Ranke, there to entertain the Emperor my brother."

Wess and Quartz glanced at each other, startled. Chan muttered a curse. Aerie tensed, and Wess held her arm. They all drew up their hoods.

"Bauchle goes with my friendship, and my seal." The prince held up a rolled parchment secured with scarlet ribbons and ebony wax.

The prince sat down, with Bauchle Meyne in the place of honor by his side. The rest of the royal party arrayed themselves around, and the parade began.

Wess and her friends moved closer together, in silence.

They would have no help from the prince.

The Processional gates swung open to the sound of flutes and drums. The music continued for some while before anything else happened. Bauchle Meyne began to look uncomfortable. Then abruptly a figure staggered out onto the path, as if he had been shoved. The skeletally thin, red-haired man regained his balance, straightened up, and gazed from side to side. The jeers confounded him. He pushed his long cape off his shoulders to reveal his star-patterned black robe, and took a few hesitant steps.

At the rope barrier's first wooden supporting post, he stopped again. He gestured toward it tentatively and spoke a gutteral word.

The post sputtered into flame.

The people nearby drew back shouting, and the wizard lurched along the path, first to one side, then the other, waving his hands at each wooden post in turn.

The foggy white circles melded together to light the way. Wess saw that the posts were not, after all, burning. When the one in front of her began to shine, she brought her hand toward it, palm forward and fingers outspread. When she felt no heat she touched the post gingerly, then gripped it. It held no warmth, and it retained its ordinary texture, splintery rough-hewn wood.

She remembered what Lythande said, about her having a strong talent. She wondered if she could do the same thing. It would be a useful trick, though not very important. She had no piece of wood to try it on, nor any idea how to start to try in the first place. She shrugged and let go of the post. Her handprint—she blinked. No, it was her imagination, not a brighter spot that she had touched.

At the prince's platform, the wizard stood staring vacantly around. Bauchle Meyne leaned forward intently, glaring, his worry clear and his anger barely held in check. The wizard gazed at him. Wess could see Bauchle Meyne's fingers tense around a circle of ruby chain. He twisted it. Wess gasped. The wizard shrieked and flung up his hands. Bauchle Meyne slowly relaxed his hold on the talisman. The wizard spread his arms. He was trembling. Wess, too, was shaking. She felt as if the chain had whipped around her body like a lash.

The wizard's trembling hands moved: the prince's platform, the wooden parts of the chairs, the poles supporting the fringed awning, all burst suddenly into a fierce white fire. The guards leaped forward in fury and confusion, but stopped at a word from their prince. He sat calm and smiling, his hands resting easily on the bright arms of his throne. Shadowy flames played across his fingers, and the light spun up between his feet. Bauchle Meyne leaned back in satisfaction, and nodded to the wizard. The other nobles on the platform stood disconcerted, awash in the light from the boards between the patterned rugs. Nervously, but following the example of their ruler, they sat down again.

The wizard stumbled onward, lighting up the rest of the posts. He disappeared into the darkness of the tent. Its supports began to shine with the eerie luminescence. Gradually, the barrier-ropes and the carpets on the platform and the awning over the prince and the canvas of the tent became covered with a soft gentle glow.

The prince applauded, nodding and smiling toward Bauchle Meyne, and his people followed his lead.

With a sharp cry, a jester tumbled through the Processional gates and somersaulted along the path. After him came the flutists and drummers, and then three ponies with bedraggled feathers attached to their bridles. Three children in spangled shorts and halters rode them. The one in front jumped up and stood balanced on her pony's rump, while the two following did shoulder-stands, braced against the ponies' withers. Wess, who had never been on a horse in her life and found the idea quite terrifying, applauded. Others in the audience applauded, too, here and there, and the prince himself idly clapped his hands. But nearby a large grizzled man laughed sarcastically and yelled, "Show us more!" That was the way most of the audience reacted, with hoots of derision and laughter. The child standing up stared straight ahead. Wess clenched her teeth, angry for the child but impressed by her dignity. Quartz' oldest child was about the same age. Wess took her hand, and Quartz squeezed her fingers gratefully.

A cage, pulled by a yoke of oxen, passed through the dark gate. Wess caught her breath. The oxen pulled the cage into the light. It carried an elderly troll, hunched in the corner on dirty straw. A boy poked the troll with a stick as the oxen drew abreast of the prince. The troll leaped up and cursed in a high-pitched angry voice.

"You uncivilized barbarians! You, prince— prince of worms, I say, of maggots! May your penis grow till no one will have you! May your best friend's vagina knot itself with you inside! May you contract water on the brain and sand in the bladder!"

Wess felt herself blushing: she had never heard a troll speak so. Ordinarily they were the most cultured of forest people, and the only danger in them was that one might find oneself listening for a whole afternoon to a discourse on the shapes of clouds or the effects of certain shelf-fungi. Wess looked around, frightened that someone would take offense at what the troll was saying to their ruler. Then she remembered that he was speaking the Language, the real tongue of intelligent creatures, and in this place no one but she and her friends understood.

"Frejôjan!" she cried on impulse. "To- night—be ready—if I can—!"

He hesitated in the midst of a caper, stumbled, but caught himself and gamboled around, mak- ing nonsense noises till he faced her. She pulled her hood back so he could recognize her later. She let it fall again as the cart passed, so Bauchle Meyne would not see her from the other side of the path.

The gray-gold furry little being gripped the

bars of his cage and looked out, making horrible faces at the crowd, horrible noises in reaction to their jeers. But between the shrieks and the gibberish, he said, "I wait—"

After he passed them, he began to wail.

"Wess—" Chan said.

"How could I let him go by without speaking to him?"

"He isn't a friend, after all," Aerie said.

"He's enslaved, just like Satan!" Wess looked from Aerie's face to Chan's, and saw that neither understood. "Quartz—?"

Quartz nodded. "Yes. You're right. A civilized person has no business being in this place."

"How are you going to find him? How are you going to free him? We don't even know how we're going to free Satan! Suppose he needs help?" Aerie's voice rose in anger.

"Suppose we need help?"

Aerie turned her back on Wess and stared blankly out into the parade. She even shrugged off Quartz' comforting hug.

Then there was no more time for arguing. Six archers tramped through the gate. A cart followed. It was a flatbed, curtained all around, and pulled by two large skewbald horses, one with a wild blue eye. Six more archers followed. A mutter of confusion rippled over the crowd, and then cries of "The secret! Show us the secret!"

The postillion jerked the draft horses to a standstill before the prince. Bauchle Meyne climbed stiffly off the platform and onto the cart.

"My lord!" he cried. "I present you—a myth of our world!" He yanked on a string and the curtains fell away.

On the platform, Satan stood rigid and withdrawn, staring forward, his head high. Aerie moaned and Wess tensed, wanting to leap over the glowing ropes and lay about with her knife, in full view of the crowd, whatever the consequences. She cursed herself for being so weak and stupid this morning. If she had had the will to attack, she could have ripped out Bauchle Meyne's guts.

They had not broken Satan. They would kill him before they could strip him of his pride. But they had stripped him naked, and shackled him. And they had hurt him. Streaks of silver-gray cut across the red-gold fur on his shoulders. They had beaten him. Wess clenched her fingers around the handle of her knife.

Bauchle Meyne picked up a long pole. He was not fool enough to get within reach of Satan's talons.

"Show yourself!" he cried.

Satan did not speak the trade-language, but Bauchle Meyne made himself well enough understood with the end of the pole. Satan stared at him without moving until the young man stopped poking at him, and, with some vague awareness of his captive's dignity, backed up a step. Satan looked around him, his large eyes reflecting the light like a cat's. He faced the prince. The heavy chains clanked and rattled as he moved.

He raised his arms. He opened his hands, and his fingers unfolded.

He spread his great red wings. Wizard-light glowed through the translucent webs. It was as if he had burst into flame.

The prince gazed upon him with silent satisfaction as the crowd roared with surprise and
astonishment.

"Inside," Bauchle Meyne said, "when I release
him, he will fly."

One of the horses, brushed by Satan's wingtip,
snorted and reared. The cart lurched forward.
The postillion yanked the horse's mouth to a
bloody froth and Bauchle Meyne lost his balance
and stumbled to the ground. His face showed
pain and Wess was glad. Satan barely shifted.
The muscles tensed and slid in his back as he
balanced himself with his wings.

Aerie made a high, keening sound, almost
beyond the limits of human hearing. But Satan
heard. He did not flinch; unlike the troll he did
not turn. But he heard. In the bright white
wizard-light, the short fur on the back of his
shoulders rose. He made an answering cry, a
sighing: a call to a lover. He folded his wing-
fingers back along his arms. The webbing trembled and gleamed.

The postillion kicked his horse and the cart
lumbered forward. For the crowd outside, the
show was over.

The prince stepped down from the platform,
and, walking side by side with Bauchle Meyne
and followed by his retinue, proceeded into the
carnival tent.

The four friends stood close together as the
crowd moved past them. Wess was thinking,
They're going to let him fly, inside. He'll be free
. . . She looked at Aerie. "Can you land on top of
the tent? And take off again?"

Aerie looked at the steep canvas slope. "Easily," she said.

The area behind the tent was lit by torches, not wizard-light. Wess stood leaning against the grounds' wall, watching the bustle and chaos of the troupe, listening to the applause and laughter of the crowd. The show had been going on a long time now; most of the people who had not got inside had left. A couple of carnival workers kept a bored watch on the perimeter of the barrier, but Wess knew she could slip past any time she pleased.

It was Aerie she worried about. Once the plan started, she would be very vulnerable. The night was clear and the waxing moon bright and high. When she landed on top of the tent she would be well within range of arrows. Satan would be in even more danger. It was up to Wess and Quartz and Chan to create enough chaos so the archers would be too distracted to shoot either of the flyers.

Wess was rather looking forward to it.

She slipped under the rope when no one was looking and strolled through the shadows as if she belonged with the troupe. Satan's cart stood at the performers' entrance, but Wess did not go near her friend now. Taking no notice of her, the children on their ponies trotted by. In the torchlight the children looked thin and tired and very young, the ponies thin and tired and old. Wess slid behind the rank of animal cages. The carnival did, after all, have a salamander, but a piteous poor and hungry-looking one, barely the size of a

large dog. Wess broke the lock on its cage. She
had only her knife to pry with; she did the blade
no good. She broke the locks on the cages of the
other animals, the half-grown wolf, the pygmy
elephant, but did not yet free them. Finally she
reached the troll.

"Frejôjan," she whispered. "I'm behind you."

"I hear you, frejôjan." The troll came to the
back of his cage. He bowed to her. "I regret my
unkempt condition, frejôjan; when they captured me I had nothing, not even a brush." His
golden gray-flecked hair was badly matted. He
put his hand through the bars and Wess shook it.

"I'm Wess," she said.

"Aristarchus," he said. "You speak with the
same accent as Satan—you've come for him?"

She nodded. "I'm going to break the lock on
your cage," she said. "I have to be closer to the
tent when they take him in to make him fly. It
would be better if at first they didn't notice anything was going wrong . . ."

Aristarchus nodded. "I won't escape till
you've begun. Can I be of help?"

Wess glanced along the row of cages. "Could
you—would it put you in danger to free the animals?" He was old; she did not know if he could
move quickly enough.

He chuckled. "All of us animals have become
rather good friends," he said. "Though the salamander is rather snappish."

Wess wedged her knife into the padlock and
wrenched it open. Aristarchus snatched it off the
door and flung it into the straw. He smiled,
abashed, at Wess.

"I find my own temper rather short in these poor days."

Wess reached through the bars and gripped his hand again. Near the tent, the skewbald horses wheeled Satan's cart around. Bauchle Meyne yelled nervous orders. Aristarchus glanced toward Satan.

"It's good you've come," he said. "I persuaded him to cooperate, at least for a while, but he does not find it easy. Once he made them angry enough to forget his value."

Wess nodded, remembering the whip scars.

The cart rolled forward; the archers followed.

"I have to hurry," Wess said.

"Good fortune go with you."

She moved as close to the tent as she could. But she could not see inside; she had to imagine what was happening, by the tone of the crowd. The postillion drove the horses around the ring. They stopped. Someone crawled under the cart and unfastened the shackles from below, out of reach of Satan's claws. And then—

She heard the sigh, the involuntary gasp of wonder as Satan spread his wings, and flew.

Above her, Aerie's shadow cut the air. Wess pulled off her cloak and waved it, signalling. Aerie dived for the tent, swooped, and landed.

Wess drew her knife and started sawing at a guy-rope. She had been careful enough of the edge so it sliced through fairly quickly. As she hurried to the next line, she heard the tone of the crowd gradually changing, as people began to notice something amiss. Quartz and Chan were doing their work, too. Wess chopped at the second rope. As the tent began to collapse, she heard tearing canvas above where Aerie ripped through the roof with her talons. Wess sliced through a third rope, a fourth. The breeze flapped the sagging fabric against itself. The canvas cracked and howled like a sail. Wess heard Bauchle Meyne screaming, "The ropes! Get the ropes, the ropes are breaking!"

The tent fell from three directions. Inside, people began to shout, then to scream, and they tried to flee. A few spilled out into the parade-ground, then a mob fought through the narrow opening. The shriek of frightened horses pierced the crowd-noise, and the scramble turned to panic. The skewbald horses burst through the crush, scattering people right and left, Satan's empty cart lurching and bumping along behind. More terrified people streamed out after them. All the guards from the palace fought against them, struggling to get inside to their prince.

Wess turned to rejoin Quartz and Chan, and froze in horror. In the shadows behind the tent, Bauchle Meyne snatched up an abandoned bow, ignored the chaos, and aimed a steel-tipped arrow into the sky. Wess sprinted toward him, crashed into him, and shouldered him off-balance. The bowstring twanged and the arrow fishtailed up, falling back spent to bury itself in the limp canvas.

Bauchle Meyne sprang up, his high complexion scarlet with fury.

"You, you little bitch!" He lunged for her, grabbed her, and backhanded her across the face. "You've ruined me for spite!"

The blow knocked her to the ground. This time

Bauchle Meyne did not laugh at her. Half-blinded Wess scrambled away from him. She heard his boots pound closer and he kicked her in the same place in the ribs. She heard the bone crack. She dragged at her knife but its edge, roughened by the abuse she had given it, hung up on the rim of the scabbard. She could barely see and barely breathe. She struggled with the knife and Bauchle Meyne kicked her again.

"You can't get away this time, bitch!" He let Wess get to her hands and knees. "Just try to run!" He stepped toward her.

Wess flung herself at his legs, moved beyond pain by fury. He cried out as he fell. The one thing he could never expect from her was attack. Wess lurched to her feet. She ripped her knife from its scabbard as Bauchle Meyne lunged at her. She plunged it into him, into his belly, up, into his heart.

She knew how to kill, but she had never killed a human being. She had been drenched by her prey's blood, but never the blood of her own species. She had watched creatures die by her hand, but never a creature who knew what death meant.

His heart still pumping blood around the blade, his hands fumbling at her hands, trying to push them away from his chest, he fell to his knees, shuddered, toppled over, convulsed, and died.

Wess jerked her knife from his body. Once more she heard the shrieks of frightened horses and the curses of furious men, and the howl of a half-starved wolf cub.

The tent shimmered with wizard-light.

I wish it were torches, Wess screamed in her mind. Torches would burn you, and burning is what you deserve.

But there was no fire, and nothing burned. Even the wizard-light was fading.

Wess looked into the sky. She raked her sleeve across her eyes to wipe away her tears.

The two flyers soared toward the moon, free.

And now—

Quartz and Chan were nowhere in sight. She could find only terrified strangers: performers in spangles, Sanctuary people fighting each other, and more guards coming to the rescue of their lord. The salamander lumbered by, hissing in fear.

Horses clattered toward her and she spun, afraid of being run down. Aristarchus brought them to a halt and flung her the second horse's reins. It was the skewbald stallion from Satan's cart, the one with the wild blue eye. It smelled the blood on her and snorted and reared. Somehow she kept hold of the reins. The horse reared again and jerked her off her feet. Bones ground together in her side and she gasped.

"Mount!" Aristarchus cried. "You can't control him from the ground!"

"I don't know how—" She stopped. It hurt too much to talk.

"Grab his mane! Jump! Hold on with your knees."

She did as he said, found herself on the horse's back, and nearly fell off his other side. She clamped her legs around him and he sprang forward. Both the reins were on one side of his neck—Wess knew that was not right. She pulled on them and he twisted in a circle and almost threw her again. Aristarchus urged his horse forward and grabbed the stallion's bridle. The animal stood spraddle-legged, ears flat back, nostrils flaring, trembling between Wess' legs. She hung onto his mane, terrified. Her broken ribs hurt so badly she felt faint.

Aristarchus leaned forward, blew gently into the stallion's nostrils, and spoke to him so quietly Wess could not hear the words. Slowly, easily, the troll straightened out the reins. The animal gradually relaxed, and his ears pricked forward again.

"Be easy on his mouth, frejôjan," the troll said to Wess. "He's a good creature, just frightened."

"I have to find my friends," Wess said.

"Where are you to meet them?"

Aristarchus' calm voice helped her regain her composure.

"Over there." She pointed to a shadowed recess beyond the tent. Aristarchus started for it, still holding her horse's bridle. The animals stepped delicately over broken equipment and abandoned clothing.

Quartz and Chan ran from the shadowed side of the tent. Quartz was laughing. Through the chaos she saw Wess, tagged Chan on the shoulder to get his attention, and changed direction to hurry toward Wess.

"Did you see them fly?" Quartz cried. "They outflew eagles!"

"As long as they outflew arrows," Aristarchus said dryly. "Hurry, you, the big one, up behind me, and you," he said to Chan, "behind Wess."

They did as he ordered. Quartz kicked the

horse and he sprang forward, but Aristarchus reined him in.

"Slowly, children," the troll said. "Slowly through the dark, and no one will notice."

To Wess' surprise, he was quite correct.

In the city they kept the horses at the walk, and Quartz concealed Aristarchus beneath her cloak. The uproar fell behind them, and no one chased them. Wess clutched the stallion's mane, still feeling very insecure so high above the ground.

A direct escape from Sanctuary did not lead them past the Unicorn, or indeed into the Maze at all, but they decided to chance going back; the risk of travelling unequipped through the mountains this late in the fall was too great. They approached the Unicorn through back alleys, and saw almost no one. Apparently the denizens of the Maze were as fond of entertainments as anyone else in Sanctuary. No doubt the opportunity to watch their prince extricate himself from a collapsed tent was almost the best entertainment of the evening. Wess would not have minded watching that herself.

Leaving the horses hidden in shadow with Aristarchus, they crept quietly up the stairs to their room, stuffed belongings in their packs, and started out again.

"Young gentleman and his ladies, good evening."

Wess spun around, Quartz right beside her gripping her sword. The tavern-keeper flinched back from them, but quickly recovered himself.

"Well," he said to Chan, sneering. "I thought they were one thing, but I see they are your bodyguards."

Quartz grabbed him by the shirt front and lifted him off the floor. Her broadsword scraped from its scabbard. Wess had never seen Quartz draw it, in defense or anger; she had never seen the blade. But Quartz had not neglected it. The edge gleamed with transparent sharpness.

"I foreswore the frenzy when I abandoned war," Quartz said very quietly. "But you are very nearly enough to make me break my oath." She opened her hand and he fell to his knees before the point of the sword.

"I meant no harm, my lady—"

"Do not call me 'lady'! I am not of noble birth! I was a soldier and I am a woman. If that cannot deserve your courtesy, then you cannot command my mercy!"

"I meant no harm, I meant no offense. I beg your pardon . . ." He looked up into her unreadable silver eyes. "I beg your pardon, northern woman."

There was no contempt in his voice now, only terror, and to Wess that was just as bad. She and Quartz could expect nothing here, except to be despised or feared. They had no other choices.

Quartz sheathed her sword. "Your silver is on the table," she said coldly. "We had no mind to cheat you."

He scrabbled up and away from them, into the room. Quartz grabbed the key from the inside, slammed the door, and locked it.

"Let's get out of here."

They clattered down the stairs. In the street, they tied the packs together and to the horses' harnesses as best they could. Above, they heard the innkeeper banging at the door, and when he failed to break it down, he came to the window.

"Help!" he cried. "Help, kidnappers! Brigands!" Quartz vaulted up behind Aristarchus and Chan clambered up behind Wess. "Help!" the innkeeper cried. "Help, fire! Floods!"

Aristarchus gave his horse its head and it sprang forward. Wess' stallion tossed his mane, blew his breath out hard and loud, and leaped from a standstill into a gallop. All Wess could do was hold on, clutching the mane and the harness, hunching over the horse's withers, as he careered down the street.

They galloped through the outskirts of Sanctuary, splashed across the river at the ford, and headed north along the river trail. The horses sweated into a lather and Aristarchus insisted on slowing down and breathing them. Wess saw the sense of that, and, too, she could detect no pursuit from the city. She scanned the sky, but darkness hid any sign of the flyers.

Abandoning the headlong pace, they walked the horses or let them jog. Each step jarred Wess' ribs. She tried to concentrate on pushing out the pain, but to do it well she needed to stop, dismount, and relax. That was impossible right now. The road and the night led on forever.

At dawn, they reached the faint abandoned trail Wess had brought them in on. It led away from the road, directly up into the mountains.

The trees, black beneath the slate-blue sky, closed in overhead. Wess felt as if she had fought her way out of a nightmare world into a world she knew and loved. She did not yet feel free, but she could consider the possibility of feeling free again.

"Chad?"

"I'm here, love."

She took his hand, where he held her gingerly around the waist, and kissed his palm. She leaned back against him, and he held her.

A stream gushed between the gnarled roots of trees, beside the nearly invisible trail.

"We should stop and let the horses rest," Aristarchus said. "And rest, ourselves."

"There's a clearing a little way ahead," Wess said. "It has grass. They eat grass, don't they?"

Aristarchus chuckled. "They do, indeed."

When they reached the clearing, Quartz jumped down, stumbled, groaned, and laughed. "It's a long time since I rode horseback," she said. She helped Aristarchus off. Chan dismounted and stood testing his legs after the long ride. Wess sat where she was. She felt as if she were looking at the world through Lythande's secret sphere.

The sound of great wings filled the cold dawn. Satan and Aerie landed in the center of the clearing and hurried toward them.

Wess twined her fingers in the skewbald's striped mane and slid off his back. She leaned against his shoulder, exhausted, taking short shallow breaths. She could hear Chan and Quartz greeting the flyers. But Wess could not move.

"Wess?"

She turned slowly, still holding the horse's

mane. Satan smiled down at her. She was used to flyers' being lean, but they were sleek: Satan was gaunt, his ribs and hips sharp beneath his skin. His short fur was dull and dry, and besides the scars on his back he had marks on his ankles, and around his throat, where he had been bound.

"Oh, Satan—" She embraced him, and he enfolded her in his wings.

"It's done," he said. "It's over." He kissed her gently. Everyone gathered around him. He brushed the back of his hand softly down the side of Quartz' face, and bent down to kiss Chad.

"Frejôjani . . ." He looked at them all, then, as a tear spilled down his cheek, he wrapped himself in his wings and cried.

They held him and caressed him until the racking sobs ceased. Ashamed, he scrubbed away the tears with the palm of his hand. Aristarchus stood nearby, blinking his large green eyes.

"You must think me an awful fool, Aristarchus, a fool, and weak."

The troll shook his head. "I think, when I can finally believe I'm free . . ." He looked at Wess. "Thank you."

They sat beside the stream to rest and talk.

"It's possible that we aren't even being followed," Quartz said.

"We watched the city, till you entered the forest," Aerie said. "We saw no one else on the river road."

"Then they might not have realized anyone but another flyer helped Satan escape. If no one saw us fell the tent—"

Wess reached into the stream and splashed her
face, cupped her hand in the water, and lifted it
to her lips. The first rays of direct sunlight
pierced the branches and entered the clearing.

Her hand was still bloody. The blood was mix-
ing with the water. She choked and spat, lurched
to her feet, and bolted. A few paces away she fell
to her knees and retched violently.

There was nothing in her stomach but bile.
She crawled to the stream and scrubbed her
hands, then her face, with sand and water. She
stood up again. Her friends were staring at her,
shocked.

"There was someone," she said. "Bauchle
Meyne. But I killed him."

"Ah," Quartz said.

"You've given me another gift," Satan said.
"Now I don't have to go back and kill him myself."

"Shut up, Satan, she's never killed anyone
before."

"Nor have I. But I would have ripped out his
throat if just once he'd left the chains slack
enough for me to reach him!"

Wess wrapped her arms around herself, trying
to ease the ache in her ribs. Suddenly Quartz was
beside her.

"You're hurt—why didn't you tell me?"

Wess shook her head, unable to answer. And
then she fainted.

She woke up at midafternoon, lying in the
shade of a tall tree in a circle of her friends. The
horses grazed nearby, and Aristarchus sat on a

stone beside the stream, combing the tangles from his fur. Wess got up and went to sit beside him.

"Did you call my name?"

"No," he said.

"I thought I heard—" She shrugged. "Never mind."

"How are you feeling?"

"Better." Her ribs were bandaged tight. "Quartz is a good healer."

"No one is following. Aerie looked, a little while ago."

"That's good. May I comb your back for you?"

"That would be a great kindness."

In silence, she combed him, but she was paying very little attention. The third time the comb caught on a knot, Aristarchus protested quietly.

"Sister, please, that fur you're plucking is attached to my skin."

"Oh, Aristarchus, I'm sorry . . ."

"What's wrong?"

"I don't know," she said. "I feel—I want—I . . ." She handed him the comb and stood. "I'm going to walk up the trail a little way. I won't be gone long."

In the silence of the forest she felt easier, but there was something pulling her, something calling to her that she could not hear.

And then she did hear something, a rustling of leaves. She faded back off the trail, hiding herself, and waited.

Lythande walked slowly, tiredly, along the trail. Wess was so surprised that she did not speak as the wizard passed her, but a few paces on, Lythande stopped and looked around, frowning.

"Westerly?"

Wess stepped into sight. "How did you know I was there?"

"I felt you near . . . How did you find me?"

"I thought I heard someone call me. Was that a spell?"

"No. Just a hope."

"You look so tired, Lythande."

Lythande nodded. "I received a challenge. I answered it."

"And you won—"

"Yes." Lythande smiled bitterly. "I still walk the earth and wait for the days of Chaos. If that is winning, then I won."

"Come back to camp and rest and eat with us."

"Thank you, little sister. I will rest with you. But your friend—you found him?"

"Yes. He's free."

"You all escaped unhurt?"

Wess shrugged, and was immediately sorry for it. "I did crack my ribs this time." She did not want to talk about the deeper hurts.

"And now—are you going home?"

"Yes."

Lythande smiled. "I might have known you would find the Forgotten Pass."

They walked together back toward camp. A little scared by her own presumption, Wess reached out and took the wizard's hand in hers. Lythande did not draw away, but squeezed her fingers gently.

"Westerly—" Lythande looked at her straight

on, and Wess stopped. "Westerly, would you go back to Sanctuary?"

Stunned and horrified, Wess said, "Why?"

"It isn't as bad as it seems at first. You could learn many things . . ."

"About being a wizard?"

Lythande hesitated. "It would be difficult, but—it might be possible. It is true that your talents should not be wasted."

"You don't understand," Wess said. "I don't want to be a wizard. I wouldn't go back to Sanctuary if that were the reason."

Lythande said, finally, "That isn't the only reason."

Wess took Lythande's hand between her own, drew it to her lips, and kissed the palm. Lythande reached up and caressed Wess' cheek. Wess shivered at the touch.

"Lythande, I can't go back to Sanctuary. You would be the only reason I was there—and it would change me. It *did* change me. I don't know if I can go back to being the person I was before I came here, but I'm going to try. Most of what I did learn there I would rather never have known. You must understand me!"

"Yes," Lythande said. "It was not fair of me to ask."

"It isn't that I wouldn't love you," Wess said, and Lythande looked at her sharply. Wess took as deep a breath as she could, and continued. "But what I feel for you would change, too, as I changed. It wouldn't be love anymore. It would be . . . need, and demand, and envy."

Lythande sat on a tree root, shoulders

slumped, and stared at the ground. Wess knelt beside her and smoothed her hair back from her forehead.

"Lythande . . ."

"Yes, little sister," the magician whispered, as if she were too tired to speak aloud.

"You must have important work here." How could she bear it otherwise? Wess thought. *She is going to laugh at you for what you ask her, and explain how foolish it is, and how impossible.* "And Kaimas, my home . . . you would find it dull—" She stopped, surprised at herself for her hesitation and her fear. "You come with me, Lythande," she said abruptly. "You come home with me."

Lythande stared at her, her expression unreadable. "Did you mean what you said—"

"It's so beautiful, Lythande. And peaceful. You've met half my family already. You'd like the rest of them, too! You said you had things to learn from us."

"—about loving me?"

Wess caught her breath. She leaned forward and kissed Lythande quickly, then, a second time, slowly, as she had wanted to since the moment she saw her.

She drew back a little.

"Yes," she said. "Sanctuary made me lie, but I'm not in Sanctuary now. With any luck I'll never see it again, and never have to lie any-more."

"If I had to go—"

Wess grinned. "I might try to persuade you to stay." She touched Lythande's hair. "But I

wouldn't try to hold you. As long as you wanted
to stay, and whenever you wanted to come back,
you'd have a place in Kaimas."

"It isn't your resolve I doubt, little sister, it's
my own. And my own strength. I think I would
not want to leave your home, once I'd been there
for a while."

"I can't see the future," Wess said. Then she
laughed at herself, for what she was saying to a
wizard. "Perhaps you can."

Lythande made no reply.

"All I know," Wess said, "is that anything
anyone does might cause pain. To oneself, to a
friend. But you cannot do nothing." She stood
up. "Come. Come sleep, with me and my friends.
And then we'll go home."

Lythande stood up too. "There's so much you
don't know about me, little sister. So much of it
could hurt you."

Wess closed her eyes, wishing, like a child at
twilight seeking out a star. She opened her eyes
again.

Lythande smiled. "I will come with you. If
only for a while."

They walked together, hand in hand, to join
the others.

ISCHADE

C.J. Cherryh

1

Shadows slipped along the cobbles in this deepest sink of the Maze, in that small light of the moon which wended its way among the overhangs and glistened wetly off noisome moistures. A well-dressed woman had no place here, even shadow-clad in black, robed and hooded—but she went deliberately, weaving only from the course of the foulest and widest streams, stepping over most.

And a ruffler, a bravo, a sometime thief— Sjekso by name—he took to the alleys as a matter of course.

Sjekso belonged here, had been whelped here, wove in his steps too, but not from fastidiousness, as he came from the opposite direction down the web of dark ways. A handsome fellow, was Sjekso Kinzan, a blond youth with curling locks, a short and carefully kept beard, his shirt and jerkin open from the recent heat of the common room of the *Vulgar Unicorn*—from the heat, and, truth be told, from a certain vanity. He radiated sex, wine vapors, and a certain peevishness: was out of pocket from the dice, had lost even Minsy's purchasable favors to a bad throw . . . his absolute nadir of discomfort. Minsy was off with that whoreson Hanse, while he—

He staggered his hazed way back toward his lodgings and his own doorway off the Serpentine. He snuffed and faltered and lamented his misfortune with himself. He hated Hanse, at least for the evening, and plotted elaborate and public revenge . . . .

And blinking in the vapors up from the harbor and in the uncertain focus of his eyes, he found his way intersected with a woman's in the alleyway. No ordinary doxy, this: a courtesan of quality strayed from some rendezvous, an opportunity some fickle god had tossed into his path or him into hers.

"Well," he said, and flung wide his arms, leaned from one side of the way to the other to block her attempt to walk around him . . . a little fun, he reckoned. And again, owlishly: "*Well*,"—but she made a quick move to go past him and he seized her in that swift pass, grabbed and grasped and felt female roundnesses in delightful proportions. His prey writhed and pushed and kneed at him, and he gripped her hair through the hood, drew her head back and kissed her with fair aim and rising passion.

She struggled, which motion only felt the better in his hands, and she gave out muffled cries, which were far from loud, his mouth covering hers the while. He held her tight and sought with his eyes for some more convenient alcove among the broken amphorae and barrels, a place where they might not be disturbed.

All at once another sound penetrated the fog of sense and sound, the scuff of another foot near him. Sjekso started to spin himself and his victim about, went the least bit over to that foot and had a hand clamped onto his own chin, his head jerked back, and a deadly keen blade at his throat in the same instant.

"Let the lady go," a male whisper suggested, and he carefully, trading in all his remaining advantage, relaxed his hands and let them fall, wondering wildly all the while whether his only chance might be in some wild try at escape. The woman in the edge of his vision stepped back, brushed at her robes, adjusted her hood. The knife rode razor-edged at his throat and the hand which held his chin gave him nothing.

Mradhon Vis kept his grip and held the ruffian just off his balance, looked in a moment's distraction at the lady in question . . . at a severe and dusky face in the faint light of the alleyway. She was beautiful. His romantical soul was touched—that seldom-afforded self which launched itself mostly in the wake of more prof-

itable motives. "Be off," he told Sjekso, and
flung the villain a good several body lengths
down the alley; and Sjekso scrambled up and set
to his heels without stopping to see anything.

"*Wait!*" the woman called after Sjekso. The
would-be rapist spun about with his back to a
wall, ducking an imagined blow from behind.
Mradhon Vis, dagger still in hand, stood facing
him, utterly confounded.

"The boy and I are old friends," she said—and
to Sjekso: "Isn't it so?"

Sjekso straightened with his back against the
wall and managed a bow, if a wobbling one . . .
managed a sneer, his braggadocio recovered in
the face of a man he, after all, knew from the dice
table that night—and Mradhon Vis took a tighter
and furious grip on his dagger, knowing this
vermin at least from the tables at the *Unicorn*.

But feminine fingers touched very lightly on
his bare arm. "A misunderstanding," the woman
said, very soft and low. "But thank you for stepping in, all the same. You have some skill, don't
you? Out of the army, maybe—I ask you, sir . . . I
I have need to find someone . . . with that skill.
To guard me. I have to come and go hereabouts. I
could pay, if you could find me someone like
yourself,   a   friend   maybe—who   might
serve. . . ."

"At your service," Sjekso said, with a second
grander flourish. "I know my way around."

But the woman never turned to see. Her eyes
were all for Mradhon, dark and glittering in the
night. "He's one, in fact, I might sometimes want
protection *from.*—Do you know someone who
might be interested?"

Mradhon straightened his back and took a superior stance. "I've served as bodyguard now and again. And as it happens, I'm at liberty."

"Ah," she said, a hand to her robed breast, which outlined female curves in the shadow. And she turned at once to the confused villain, who had taken advantage of the moment to slip toward the shadows and the corner. "No, no, wait. I did promise you this evening. I had no right to put you off; and I want to talk with you. Be patient."—A glance then back, her hand bringing a purse from beneath her robes. She loosed the strings and took out a gold coin that caught Mradhon's whole attention, the more so when she dropped the heavy purse into his hand. Only the one coin she held, it winking colorless bright in the moonlight, and she held that up like an icon for Sjekso's eyes—another look at Mradhon: "I lodge seventh down from this corner, the first steps you'll come to that have a newel on the rail: on your right as you go. Go there. Learn the place so you can find it to-morrow morning, and be waiting there for me at midmorning. I'll be there. And the purse is yours."

He considered the weight in his palm, heavy as with gold. "I'll find it," he said, and, less than confident of the situation at hand: "Are you sure you don't want me to stay about?"

Black brows drew together, a frown uncommonly grim. "I have no doubts to my safety.— Ah, your name, sir. When I pay, I like to know that."

"Vis. Mradhon Vis."

"From—"

"Northward. A lot of places."

"We'll talk. Tomorrow morning. Go on, now. Believe me, that the quarrel wasn't what it seemed."

"Lady," he murmured—he had known polite company once. He clenched the purse in his fist and turned off in the direction she had named—not without a backward look. Sjekso still waited where he had fixed himself against the wall; but the lady seemed to know he would look back, and turned a shadowy look on him.

Mradhon moved on quickly and further along the winding way, stopped and anxiously shook out the purse into his hand, a spill of five heavy pieces in gold and half a dozen of silver. Hot and cold went through him, like the shock of a blow, a tremor through things that were . . . A second glance back, but buildings had come between him and the woman and her bought-boy Sjekso. Well, he had hired to stranger folk and no few worse to look on. He gave a twitch of his shoulders at that proceedings back there and shrugged it off. There was gold in his possession, a flood of gold. His gallantry had come from his own poverty, from one look at the woman's fine clothing and a sure knowledge that Sjekso Kinzan was all hollow when pushed. And for that gold in his hand he would have waited in the alley all night, or beaten Sjekso to fine rags, no questions asked.

It occurred to him while he went that it might involve more than that, but he went, all the same.

The woman looked back at Sjekso and smiled, a fervid smile which made wider and wider chaos of Sjekso's grasp of the situation. He stood away from his wall and—sobered as he had been in the encounter, deprived of the vaporous warmth of the wine in his blood—still he recovered something of anticipation, reestimated his own considerable animal charm in the light of the lady's sultry dark eyes, in the moonlike gleam of the gold coin she held up before him. He grinned, his confidence restored, stood easier still as she came to him—it might have been the wine after all, this new blush of heat; it might have been her slim fingers which touched at his collar and drew a line with the edge of the coin down amongst the fine hairs of his chest, disturbing there the chain of the luckpiece he wore.

His luck had improved, he reckoned, laying it all to his way with women. She had liked it after all . . . they all did; and she might be parted from more than a golden coin, and if she thought of using him and that bastard northerner one against the other, good: there was a chance of paying off Mradhon Vis. He had skills the northerner did not; and he knew how to get the most out of them. He took most of his living from women, in one way or the other.

"What's your name?" she asked him.

"Sjekso Kinzan."

"Sjekso. I have a place . . . not the lodgings where I sent that fellow; that's business. But my real house . . . near the river. A little wine, a soft bed . . . I'll bet you're good."

He laughed. "I make it a rule never to go out of my own territory till I know the terms. Here's good enough. Right over here. And I'll bet you don't care."

"Mine's Ischade," she murmured distractedly,

as he put his hands up under the robes. She
swayed against him, her own hands on him, and
he found the coin and took it from her unresist-
ing fingers. She brushed his lips with her own
and urged him on. "My name's Ischade."

2

A corpse was no uncommon sight in the Maze.
But one sprawled in the middle of the Serpentine, in the first light of the sun—the potboy of
the *Unicorn* found the blond male corpse when
he came out to heave the slops, a corpse on the
inn's very doorstep, a body quite stiff and cold,
and he knew Sjekso Kinzan. He spun on his heel
and started to run back in—thought again and
darted back to search for valuables . . . after all,
some less acquainted and deserving person
might come along. He found the brass luckpiece,
found the purse . . . empty, except for an old
nail and a bit of lint—dropped the luckpiece
down his own collar, jumped up and ran inside
in breathless haste, to spill his news to the morning's first stirrers-forth in the tavern; and the fact
of one of the *Unicorn's* regular patrons lying stiff
at the door brought a stamping up and down the
stair and a general outpouring of curious and
half-awake overnighters.

That was how it came to Hanse, a disturbance
under Minsy Zithyk's rented window next door.

The gathering around the body in the street
was solemn . . . partly a kind of respect and

partly morning headaches, more and more onlookers arriving as the commotion became its
own reason for being. Hanse was one of the first,
stood with his arms clenched into a tight fold—
he had his daggers: had them about his person
natural as breathing. His scowl and awakened-
owl stare at the corpse of Sjekso Kinzan, his arms
about his ribs holding his spine stiff—warned
Minsy Zithyk off. She stood snuffling and holding her own ribs, doubtless with the other half of
a throbbing headache. Hanse wanted no
hanging-on, now, of Sjekso's longtime woman.
The dice game and the wager stuck in his mind
and he felt eyes on him, himself part of the morning's gossip, with a man he had diced with lying
cold in the soiled stream of a drain.

"Who got him?" Hanse asked finally, and
there was a general shrugging of shoulders.
"Who?" Hanse snapped, looking round at the
onlookers. A corpse was indeed no novelty in the
Maze, but an otherwise young and healthy one,
with no mark of violence on it . . . but a man on
the doorstep of the tavern he frequented, a turn
or two of the alleys to his own lodgings . . . .

There were amenities like territory. A man was
never assured . . . but there were places and
places, and when he was in his own place, he
was least likely to end up among the morning's
debris. There were stirrings among the crowd,
discomfort—with Hanse, for one, whose smallish size meant a temper backed with knives, a
bad reputation for every kind of mischief.

And his sullen, headachy stare passed right
round to a stranger in the territory—to one
Mradhon Vis; to a new and frequent patron at the

Unicorn. "You," Hanse said. "You left about the same time last night. You see anything?"

A shrug. A useless question. No one in the Maze saw anything. But Vis looked too thin-lipped about the shrug and Hanse looked back with a blacker stare still—had sudden awareness of the silence of the crowd when he spoke, of eyes on him; and he unfolded his arms and thought of how they had jostled in a doorway last night, Sjekso and Mradhon Vis, and Sjekso had laughed and acted his usual flippant self at Vis' expense. Hanse drew quiet conclusions—quiet because he cut a mean figure at the moment, having gotten off with a dead man's last cash and last pleasure . . . he swept a glance about at faces dour with their own private conclusions. No love lost on him or dead Sjekso; but Sjekso being local and dead was the focus of pity, while regarding himself—there was quite another thing in the air.

Vis started to leave, edging away through the crowd. "That's the one to look at," Hanse said. "Hey, you! You don't like the questions, do you? The garrison threw you out, hey? You come back here, whoreson coward, you don't turn your back on me."

"He's crazy," Vis said, stopped behind an un-willing screen of onlookers who were trying to melt in all directions, but Mradhon kept with the migrating cover. "Figure who got his money and his woman, you figure that and wonder who did for him, that's who . . . ."

Hanse went for the knives. "Wasn't no mark on him," a youngish voice was shrilling. The crowd was swinging wildly out of the interval Vis was busy preserving. Minsy yelled, and several strong and larger arms wound themselves into Hanse's elbows and about his middle. He heaved and kicked to no use while Mradhon Vis, in the clear, straightened his person and his clothing.

"Crazy," Vis said again, and Hanse poured invective on him and most especially on those holding him from his knives—cold, sweating afraid, because Vis might do anything, or the crowd might, and the knives were all he had. But Vis walked off then, at an increasing pace, and Hanse launched another kick and a torrent of abuse on those holding him.

"Easy." The grip on his left was Cappen Varra's, an arm tucked elbow to elbow into his arm and a hand locked on his wrist; he had no grudge with the minstrel. It was a calm voice, a cultivated, better-than-thou voice: Hanse hated Varra at the moment, but the grip persuaded and the object of his rage was off down the street. He took his weight on his own feet and slowly, brushing off his clothes while he stood fairly shaking with his anger, Varra eased up and let him go. Igan on the other side, big, not very bright Igan, let go his other arm, and claps on his shoulders and sympathy offered . . . started to settle his stomach and persuade him he had some credit here. "Let's have a drink," Varra said. "The corpsetakers will get the rumor—do you want to be standing here conspicuous? Come on inside."

He went as far as the door of the *Unicorn*, looked back, and there was Minsy standing over Sjekso sniffling; and Sjekso lying there a great deal sadder, open-eyed, while the crowd started away under the same logic.

Hanse wanted the drink.

Mradhon Vis turned the corner, none following, stopped against an alley wall and let the
tremors pass from his limbs. Ugly, that back
there. Corpses, he had seen—had created his
share, in and out of mercenary service. He had no
wish to take on useless trouble . . . not now, not
with gold in his boot and a real prospect of more.
A bodyguard sometimes, but he was not big
enough for hired muscle; and with a surly and
foreign look—even guard jobs were hard come
by. He meant to be on time for this one. A patron
who could come up with a fistful of gold on a
whim was one to cultivate—if only her throat
was still uncut. And that thought worried him:
that was what had drawn him, against his
natural and wary instincts, to that noisy scene
outside the *Vulgar Unicorn*—a body he had last
seen alive and escorting the patron who was his
latest and most fervent hope. He was more than
concerned.

Other alarums sounded in his mind, warnings
of greater complexity, but he refused them, because they led to suspicions of traps and connivances; he had a knife in his belt, his wits about
him, and no little experience of employers of all
sorts, no few of whom had had notions of refus-
ing him his pay at the end . . . one way and the
other.

3

The *Vulgar Unicorn* still thumped with com-
ings and goings, an untidy lot of early-morning
patrons and irregulars. For his own part Hanse
drank down his ale and nursed his head back to
size, across the table from Cappen. He had no
inclination to talk or to be the center of anything
at the moment.

"They've got him off," the potboy said from
the door. So the corpse was gone. That cleared
out some of the traffic. Inquiry and snoopery
might be close behind the corpsetakers. "Excuse
me," Cappen Varra said, likewise discreet, and
left his place at the table, bound for the door.
Hanse recovered his equilibrium and stood up
from the bench amid the general flow of bodies
outward.

Someone touched his arm, a feathery light
hand. He looked back, expecting Minsy, in no
mood for her—and looked up instead into eyes
like a statue's eyes, as unfocused and as vague,
in a male face old/young and beardless. The man
was blind.

"Hanse called Shadowspawn?" The voice was
like the man, smooth and sere.

"What's my business with you?"

"You lost a friend."

"Ha. No friend. Acquaintance. What's it to you
and me?"

The groping hand caught his arm and directed
it to the other hand, which caught his fingers—

he began to resist this eerie familiarity, and then
felt the unmistakable metal heaviness of a coin.

"I'm listening."

"My employer has more for you."

"Where?"

"Not here. Do you want a name? Come outside."

The blind man would have taken him out the
front, among the others, following the crowd.
Hanse pulled him instead to another door, out
into the back alley where few had gone and those
already vanished. "Now," Hanse said, taking the
blind man by the arm and backing him against
the wall. "Who?"

"Enas Yorl."

He dropped his hand from the blind man's
arm. "*Him.* For what?"

"He wants to talk to you. You come—
recommended. And you'll be paid."

Hanse took in his breath and fingered his coin,
looked down at it a space, found it new minted
and heavy silver, and reckoned uneasily in what
quarters he was recommended. Coin of that de-
nomination was not so easily come by . . . but
Enas Yorl—the wizard took few visitors . . .
and there were things lately amiss in Sanctuary.
Things larger than Hanse Shadowspawn.
Rumors filtered down into the Maze.

Sjekso dead, unmarked, and Enas Yorl—
offering money to talk to a thief: the world was
mad. He walked it for the narrow lane it was.

"All right," he said, because Yorl had a long
reach and because ignorance scared him. "You
show me."

The blind man took his hand, and they went,

down the alley and out again. It was so unfalter-
ing a progress, so lacking a blind man's moves,
that Hanse inevitably suspected some sham,
such as beggars used—an actor and a good one,
he thought, appreciating art.

Mradhon Vis fretted, paced below the balcony
at the wooden stairs he had found last night. It
was a place as sordid as any in the Maze, un-
painted boards and age-slimed stone, a place
atilt toward the alley and propped on boards and
braces. It breathed decrepitude.

And more and more as he waited in this unlikely place, he gnawed on the thought of his
hoped-for patron . . . dead, it might be, victim
along with Sjekso, lying unfound as yet in some
other alleyway. He had been mad to have gone
off and left a woman in the backways of the
Maze; a cat among hounds, that piece . . . and
gone, snatched up, swallowed up—with friends,
gods, more than likely money like that had
friends and enemies. His mind built more and
grimmer fancies . . . of princes and politics and
clandestine meetings, this Sjekso perhaps more
than he had seemed, this woman casting about
money to be rid of a witness too much for the
man she was with, an expedience—

He built such fancies, paced, stalked finally
halfway up the creaking length of the stairs and
came back down in indecision—then up again,
gathering his courage and his resolve. He
reached the swaying balcony, tried the door.

It swung inward, never locked or barred. That
startled him. He slipped the knife from his belt
and pushed the door all the way open—smelled

incense and spices, perfumes. He walked in, pushed the door very gently shut again. A dim light came from a milky parchmented casement, cast color slantwise on a couch spread with russet silk, on dusty draperies and stacks of cloth and oddments.

Wings snapped and rustled. He spun about into a crouch, found only a large black bird chained to a perch against the wall in which the door was set. His heart settled again. He straightened. He should have smelled the creature: no large bird lived in a place without some fetor . . . but the perfume and the incense were that strong, that he had not. He ignored the creature, poked about amid the debris on a table, feminine clutter of small boxes and brocade.

And the steps creaked, outside. He cast about him in a sudden fright, knife at the ready, slid in amongst the abundant shadows of the room. The steps reached the top, and the bird stirred and beat his wings in gusts as the door opened.

Black robes cast a silhouette against the daylight; the lady turned unerringly in his direction, took no fright at him or the knife, merely closed the door and reached up and dropped her hood from a tumble of midnight hair about a somber face. "Mradhon Vis," she said quietly. She *belonged* in the dark of this place, amid the clutter of worn and beautiful things. It was incredible that she could ever have walked through sunlight.

"Here," he said, "lady."

"Ischade," she named herself. "Do you make free of my lodgings?"

"The man you were with last night. He's dead."

"I've heard, yes." The voice was unreadable and cool. "We parted company. Sad. A handsome boy." She walked to the slight illumination of the parchment panes, drew an incense wand from others in a dragon vase and added it to the one which was dying, a curl of pale smoke in the light. She looked back then. "So. I have employment for you. I trust you're not fastidious."

"Not often."

"You'll find rewards. Gold. And it might be— further employment."

"I don't shy off at much."

"I'll trust not." She walked near him, and he recalled the knife and flipped it into its sheath. Her eyes followed the move and looked up at him . . . grave, so very grave. Women of quality he had seen tended to flutter the eyes; this one stared eye to eye, and he found himself inclined to break the contact, to look down or elsewhere. She extended her hand, close to touching him, a move he thought might be an invitation to take liberties of his own.

And then she drew the hand back and the moment passed. She walked over and offered the bird a morsel from the cup at the side of the stand. The creature took it with a great flapping of wings.

"What do you have in mind?" he asked, vexed at this mincing about, with so much at stake. "It's not legal, I'll guess."

"It might involve powerful enemies. I can

guarantee—equally powerful protections. And the reward. Of course that."

"Who's to die? Someone else . . . like that boy last night?"

She looked about, lifted a brow, then turned her attentions back to the bird, stroked black feathers with a forefinger. "Priests, perhaps. Does that bother you?"

"Not unduly. A man wonders—"

"The risk is mine. So are the consequences. Only I need someone to take care of physical difficulties. I assure you I know what I'm about."

There was more than the scent of incense about the place. Of a sudden there was quite another thing . . . the smell of wizardry. He gathered that, as he had been picking up the pieces all along. It was not a thing a man expected to find—everywhere. But it was here. And there were crimes done in the Maze, by that means and others. Spells, he had dealt with, at least at distance . . . had a hint then of more rewards than gold. "You have protections, do you?"

A second time that cool look. "I assure you it's well thought out."

"Protections for me as well."

"They'd be far less interested in you." She walked back to the table, to the light, a shadow against it. "This evening," she said, "you'll earn the gold I gave you. But perhaps, just perhaps, you ought to go out again. And come back again when I tell you. To prove you know that my door isn't yours."

Heat surged to his face, words into his mouth. He thought of the money and it stifled the rest.

"Now," she said. "About the other thing you have in mind . . . well, that might come later, mightn't it? But you choose, Mradhon Vis. There's gold . . . or other rewards. And you can tell me which you'd like. Ah. Both, perhaps. Ambition. But know me better, Mradhon Vis, before you propose anything aloud. You might not like my terms. Take the gold. The likes of Sjekso Kinzan is commoner than you. And far less to regret."

So she had killed the boy. Markless, and cold and stiff within sight of the doorway which might have saved him. He thought about it . . . and the ambition persisted. It was power. And that was more than the money, much more.

"You'll go now," she said very, very softly. "I wouldn't tempt you. Consider we have a bargain. Now get out."

No one talked to him after that fashion . . . at least not twice. But he found himself silenced and his steps tending to the door. He stopped there and looked back to prove he could.

"I've needed a man of your sort," she said, "in certain ways."

He walked out, into the sun.

4

It was one of those neighborhoods less fre- quented by the inhabitants of the Maze, and Hanse had a dislocated, uncomfortable feeling in this guide and this place, creeping as they did through the cleaner, wider back ways of

Sanctuary at large. It was not his territory or close to any of his known boltholes.

And in the shadows of an alley far along the track, his guide paused and shed an inner and ragged cloak from beneath the outer one, proffering it. "Put it on. You'll not want to be noticed hereabouts for yourself."

Hanse took it, not without distaste: it was gray and a mass of patches. He swung it about his shoulders and it was long enough to hide him down to midcalf.

His guide held out a dingy bandage as well. "For your eyes. For your own safety. The house has . . . protections. If I told you only to shut your eyes, you'd forget at the worst moment. And my master wants you whole."

Hanse stared at the offered rag, liking all of this less and less; and very softly he drew the dagger from his arm sheath and extended the blade toward the guide's face.

Not a flinch or blink. That sent a prickling up his spine. He brought the point of the blade very close to the blind eyes and, truth, the man did not react. He flipped the blade into its sheath.

"If you have doubts," the blind man said, "accept my master's assurances. But don't under any account look from beneath the bandage once inside. My blindness . . . has reasons."

"Huh." Hanse took the dirty bandage, feeling far from assured; but he had dealt with nervous uptowners before, and under conditions and precautions more bizarre and hazardous. He wound it about his eyes and tied it firmly: it was true—about Enas Yorl's doorway there were rumors, and bad ones.

And when the blind man grasped his sleeve
and began to guide him a quiet panic set in: he
had no liking of this helplessness—they entered
a street, he guessed, because he heard a change
in the sound of their footsteps; he sensed watch-
ers about, stumbled suddenly on an unevenness
in the paving and heard the blind man hiss a
warning, wrenching at his sleeve: "Three steps
up."

Three steps to the top and a moment waiting
while his guide opened a door. Then a tug at his
sleeve drew him inside, where a cold draft blew
on his face until the door boomed solidly shut
behind him. Instinctively he put a hand on his
wrist sheath, keeping the knife hilt comfortingly
under his fingers. Again a tug at his sleeve drew
him on . . . the guide; it must still be the guide
and no stranger by him. He wanted a voice.
"How much further with this?" he asked.

Claws scrabbled on stone on his left, a heavy
body slithered closer in haste. He made a frantic
move to get the knife out, but the guide jerked
him to a standstill. "Don't offend it," the guide
said. "Don't try to look. Come on."

A reptile hissed; and by that sound it was a big
one. Something flicked over the surface of his
boot and coiled about his ankle, instantly with-
drawing. The guide drew him on, away from the
touch and down a hall which echoed more
closely on either hand, where the distance was
all in front of them . . . and into a place which
smelled of coals and hot metal and a strange,
musky incense.

The guide stopped, on his right. "Shadowspawn," a new voice said, a throaty sigh,

low, and to his left. He reached for the blindfold,
hesitated. "Go ahead," the new voice invited
him, and he pulled it down.

A robed and hooded form sat in this narrow
marble hall—fine robes, in midnight blue and
bright silver, in deep shadow, beside a heating
brazier. Hanse blinked in the recent pressure on
his eyes—the robes seemed to swell and sink in
the vicinity of the chest, and the right arm, the
hand resting visible . . . it went dark, that hand,
and then, a deception of his abused eyes, went
pale and young. "Shadowspawn." The voice too
was clearer, younger. "You lost a friend last
night. Do you want to know how?"

That unnerved him, a threat on a level he understood. His hand fidgeted toward his sheath-
bearing wrist, his mind conjuring more and un-
blinded servants in the shadows.

"Ischade is her name," the voice of Enas Yorl
continued, rougher now . . . and was the figure
itself smaller and wider? "She's also a thief. And
she killed Sjekso Kinzan. Do you want more?"

Hanse assumed a more careless stance, flipped
the hand outward, palm up. "Money got me
here. If you want more of my time to listen to this,
it costs."

"She's in your own neighborhood. That information might be worth even more than money
to you."

"What, this name of yours?"

"Ischade. A thief. She's better than you,
Shadowspawn. Your knives might not stop her."
The voice roughened further. "But you're good
and you're smart. I've heard so. From—no matter. I have my sources. I'm told you're extraordi-

narily discreet." He moved the fingers, a gesture sideways. "Darous, give him the amulet."

The blind man drew something from the heart of his robes; Hanse's eyes darted nervously from the wizard he was trying to watch to that distraction, a gold teardrop that spun and dazzled on a chain.

"Take it," Enas Yorl said. A degree rougher yet. A sigh like the sea, or like hot iron plunging into water. "This Ischade—steals from wizards. Steals spells and suchlike. Her own abilities are small in that regard . . . but she made a mistake once, and the spell on Ischade is nothing small or harmless. A man who—shares her bed, shall we say? discovers that. He dies . . . of no apparent cause. Like your friend Kinzan. Like a number of others I know of. The curse affects her humor. Imagine—to pursue lover after lover and kill them all. If I hire you, Shadowspawn, you might be glad of such protections as I offer you. Take it."

"Who says I'm to hire?" Hanse looked unhappily from servant to master. The hand which now peeped from the shifting robe was woman-delicate. "Who says that a dozen Sjeksos are any of my concern? I'm my concern. Me. Hanse. I don't have any interest in Sjekso. So I just stay out of the whole business. That's what interests me."

"Then you'll run, will you, and find some safer place to steal." The voice ground like rocks tumbling. "And you'll ignore my gold and protection. Both of which you may need.—It's no great thing I ask, simply a matter of spying out where she is. Did I ask you to go against her yourself?

No. A small favor, well paid. And you've done favors like that before. Would you have that known—that you've worked in high places? Your past patron wouldn't appreciate that publicity. He wouldn't retaliate against me, no. But you—how long do you think you'd live, thief, if your connections went public?"

Hanse had sucked in his breath. He forced a grin then, struck a lighter pose, hand on hip. "So, well, paid in gold, you said?"

"After."

"Now."

"Darous, give the man sufficient as earnest. And give him the amulet."

Hanse turned from the wizard, whose voice had acquired a hissing quality; and the hand—had vanished into one of those blinks of the eye that deceived the mind and memory that anything had—a moment earlier—been there. Hanse took the chain and put it over his head. The amulet itself hit his bare throat and it was bitter and burning cold. The servant held out a purse. Hanse took that, felt the weight in his hand, opened the neck of it and looked at the gold and silver abundance inside. His heart beat wildly, while against his neck the metal failed to be warmed as metal ought, stayed there like lump of ice. It sent a vague malaise through him, which changed character from moment to moment like—

"So what am I supposed to do?" he asked. "And where do I look?"

"A house," a woman's voice said to his right, and he looked, blinked, found only the hooded form in the chair. "Seventh in the alley called

Snake. On the right as you go from the Serpentine at Acban's Passage. She lodges there. Mark what she does and where she goes. Don't attempt to prevent her. I only want to know the business that brought her to Sanctuary."

Hanse let go a sigh, relief, for all that the robes shifted again—felt a wild confidence in himself (it might have been the money) that he could get out of this easily, and with still more money, and an employer satisfied, who was powerful and rich. Hanse Shadowspawn, Hanse the thief, small Hanse the knife . . . had friends in high places, a condition unexpected. He expanded in this knowledge and stood loose, dropped the purse into his shirt, ignoring the chill at his neck. "So, then, and I come here from time to time and report to you."

"Darous will find you from time to time," the same voice said. The changing seemed to have settled for the moment. "Depend on that contact. Good day to you. Darous will show you out."

Hanse made a flourish of a bow, turned to the servant and indicated they should go.

"The blindfold," the blind servant said. "Use it, master thief. My master would regret an accident, especially now."

Hanse put his hand on the metal droplet that hung like ice at his throat, turned to glower at the wizard. "I thought this was supposed to take care of things like that."

"Did I say so? No, I didn't say. I wouldn't be rash in relying on it. Against some things it has no protection at all. My guardians in the hall, for instance, would never notice it."

"Then what good is it?"

"Much . . . in its right place. Afraid, thief?"

"Huh," Hanse said critically. Laughed and swung on his heel, caught the blind servant by the arm and started out with him. But remembering the movements in the outer hall, the thing which had brushed at his leg—"All right, all right," he said suddenly, and let go the man's arm to put the blindfold back in place. "All right, rot you, wait."

The thief went, and Enas Yorl rose from his chair. His shape had settled again into a form far more pleasant than most. He walked to a hall more interior to his house, examined hands delicate and fine, that were purest pleasure to touch—and all the worse when they would begin . . . next moment or next day . . . to change.

It was a revenge, a none too subtle revenge, but then the wizard who had cursed him had never been much on subtleties, which was why his young wife had had Enas Yorl in her bed in the first place—a younger Enas Yorl in those days, but age meant nothing now. The forms his affliction cast on him might be old or young, male or female, human or—not. And the years frightened him. All the time he had had, to become master of his arts, and his arts had no power to undo another's spell. No one could. And some of his forms, still, were young, which suggested that he did not age, that there was no end to this torment—forever.

Yet wizards died, lately, in Sanctuary. Tell the thief that was the name of the game, and even threats might not persuade him. But in these deaths, Enas Yorl was desperately, passionately interested. Ischade . . . Ischade: the name tasted of vile rumor; a wizardous thief, a preyer upon wizards, a conniver in shadows and dark secrets, this Ischade, with reason to hate the prey she chose.

And all her lovers died, softly, gently for the most part; but Enas Yorl was not particular in that regard.

He paused a moment, hearing the great outer doors boom shut. The thief was on his way, thief to take a thief. And Enas Yorl felt a sudden cold. Wizards died, in Sanctuary, and this possibility fascinated him, taunted him with hope and fear: with fear—because shapes like this he wore turned him coward, reminding him there were pleasures to be had. He feared death at such times . . . while the thief he had sent out went to find it for him.

Darous came back, softly stopped on the marble paving. "Well done," Enas Yorl said.

"Follow him, master?"

"No," Enas Yorl said. "No need. None at all." He looked distractedly about again, with the queasiness of impending change upon him. He fled suddenly, his steps quicker and quicker on the pavings. Darous could see nothing—Darous sensed, but that was another matter. There was, however, pride.

And within the hour, in a dark recess of the house with the basilisks prowling the halls unchecked, something gibbered within a pile of midnight robes, and with keen sense of beauty imprisoned in that moaning heap, longed toward oblivion.

Darous, who saw nothing, sensed the essence
of this change and kept himself to other halls.

The basilisks, whose cold eyes saw very well,
writhed scaly-lithe away in haste, outstared and
overwhelmed.

5

Not many women came to the *Unicorn*, not
many at least of the elevated sort, and this one
took a table to herself and held it. One of the
Unicorn's muddled regulars brushed by, and
leaned close, and offered to sit down . . . but a
long hand from beneath those black robes waved
an idle and disinterested dismissal. A ring
glinted there, a silver serpent, and the bully's
bleared eyes stared at that, at immaculate long
nails, into dark almond eyes beneath the
shadowy hood. And a fog of alcohol seemed to
grow thicker then, so that he forgot all the witti-
ness he had meant to say, forgot for a moment to
close his mouth. A second wave of the thin,
olive-skinned hand and he forgot everything and
stumbled away in confusion.

"Acolyte," Cappen Varra thought in his own
counsel, slouched on a bench in the nook nearest
the back door. There was somewhat of chaos in
the *Unicorn* of late, a certain lack of the authority
which had held the peace, and *that* sort moved
in, cheap muscle. But the woman—that was
something extraordinary, like the *Unicorn* before; a woman, a stranger in the neighborhood
. . . He was intrigued by the dark robes and the

fineness of them, and his fingers moved rest-
lessly on the moisture-ringed tabletop, thinking of a song, fingering imaginary strings of the
harp he had pawned (again) and thinking—
oddly—on Hanse Shadowspawn, in another and
quite irrelevant train of thought, as Hanse had
ridden his mind all day. Sjekso gone, Hanse vanished utterly, and night falling outside . . .
Hanse was up to no good, it was certain. There
had been neither sight nor sound of him all day
long and certain whispers passed in the *Unicorn*,
with more and more credibility: of revenge, of
Hanse, about the likelihood of survival of one
Mradhon Vis—or Hanse, should the two meet.
And about a certain blind man who had found
his way without aid into the *Unicorn* and out
again, with Hanse in tow . . . a blind man and no
beggar, for all his looks—but a man of darker
rumor.

It was curious business, and more than mildly
unpleasant. Cappen was not sanguine. Hanse
stalking Vis—it was quite unlikely. Hanse was
all temper and bluster. If anyone was doing the
stalking it was likeliest to be Vis, and Hanse was
ill-advised to have prodded that surly-
countenanced bastard . . . far more trouble than
Hanse really wanted, that was sure. Likely it was
Hanse in hiding, if Vis had not yet got him.
Cappen picked up his cup again, and of a sudden
his eyes hooded and while his hand carrying his
cup to his lips never faltered, the sip he took was
slow and studied: he watched a second man
make attempt on the lady's table.

And that was Mradhon Vis himself . . . who
went up quietly, and met no rebuff at all. The

lady lifted her face and her eyes to him—a face
certainly worth a song, although a dark and
somber one. And when her eyes lit on Mradhon
Vis, very quietly the lady got to her feet and in
Vis' still silent company . . . walked toward the
back door of the tavern. Only a few heads turned,
of those at the other tables, and those only casually. There was at the same time the faintest of
pricklings at Cappen's nape, a feeling he knew:
he touched the amulet at his throat, a silver
coiled serpent . . . a gift, a protection against
spells, more efficacious than most priest-blessed
gimcrack tokens . . . under its own terms. He
saw, with a touch of unease the greater because
no one else in the room seemed to see . . . how
Mradhon Vis and his dark companion moved,
with common purpose and peculiar menace.

Strangeness enough progressed in Sanctuary
. . . deaths which made a man naturally think
on protections of the sorcerous kind, and to be
glad of them if he had them, because where the
powerful died, wizardry was about, selective of
its victims thus far, but not—perhaps—exclusive
of them. There was Sjekso Kinzan, who had been
no one. Cappen wondered did such protection as
he possessed . . . protect or mark him; and as the
lady and Mradhon Vis came past his table by the
door—

A moment Cappen was looking up and the
lady looked down at him, more familiar in that
stare than he would have liked. The prickling
about the amulet became strong indeed while he
stared, lost in those dark eyes with a sense of
deadly peril, of his whole life resting loose and

endangered, as if some small nudge on anyone's part might tumble it. "You're beautiful," he murmured, because three truths was the rule of the amulet if it was to work at all—"You're dangerous—and foreign here."

She lingered, and reaching down picked up his cup where it sat; lifted it, sipped and set it down again, all with an eerie hint of humor or menace flaunted at him, at him who alone in the room but Mradhon Vis—or was he exempt?—Alone of all the others, Cappen stared back at her with his mind clear and with knowledge, with something gut-wrenching telling him that everything about this woman was askew.

She smiled at him, a parting of the lips on white teeth, a flash of dark eyes, an impression that she admired what she saw . . . and all the fineness he kept so studiously, his elegance, different from others about him, his talents, his—if streetworn—finery. . . was suddenly perilous to him, marking him out among all the rest. And most of all . . . she knew he resisted her.

She left then, swept out the door which Mradhon Vis held open, a gust of wind and a sudden thud of the door closing. Cappen wanted wine . . . but his hand stopped short of the cup she had just set down again, the metal she had had her lips to and the wine her mouth had tasted. He pushed back from the table and the bench scraped loudly over the noise of the other patrons. He hesitated looking at the door which led out to the backways, not wanting to go out there, in the gathering dark.

But Mradhon Vis, linked with that, and Sjekso

cold dead with no mark on him; and Hanse out-
right disappeared, hunting Mradhon Vis, as all
the Maze surmised . . . .

Hanse had involved himself in something
which was likely to be the death of him, and
what concern that was to Cappen Varra was unclear to Cappen himself, only that he had drunk
with Hanse of late, with a short and lately successful thief and ruffian who had wanted—
almost pathetically—to acquire style, who spent
most that came into his hands on the finer things,
a cloak—o gods! that cloak!— Cappen's aristo-
cratic soul shuddered. But of the unassuming
ruffians in the lot, of what quality there was to be
had in the Maze, in Hanse there existed at least
the hankering after something else.

The business had marked Hanse down—and
now stopped and stared at himself. It was always
safer, he reckoned, to walk at a thing than to have
it walking up at his back—later and unforeseen.
Cappen opened the door carefully, went out into
the back ways, his hand on his rapier hilt, recalling that Sjekso had used the same door last
night. But there was only the dark outside, amid
the litter of old barrels and used bottles. The
woman in black had vanished, and Vis with her,
vanished, and in what direction Cappen was in
no wise certain.

Patience was rewarded. Vis, by the gods, and
this Ischade . . . in company; and Hanse
crouched lower in the shadows of the alley, a
chill up his back, his fingers rubbing at the well
polished hilt of his left boot knife. That promised
a revenge within his own grasp: so Yorl wanted

the woman, and if Yorl settled with her, then Vis went in the same bargain. Hanse evened his breathing, calmed himself with wild hopes, first of getting out of this Yorl business and then of having Yorl to settle Vis—the means by which the street might be safe again for Hanse Shadowspawn. Report, Yorl had said, and by the gods, he was anxious to have it done, if only they went to earth for the night. . . .

They turned, not the way he had anticipated, toward the lodgings he had been watching, but the other way, toward the Serpentine. Hanse swore and slipped out from his concealment, shadowed them most carefully in their course through the debris of the alley and out onto the street. The moon was not yet up; the only light came from the city itself, a vague glimmering on a bank of fog toward the harbor which diffused across the sky and promised one of those nights in which light spread through milky mist, from whatever sources—a thieves' night, and a worse to come.

The pair tended on up the Serpentine, bold as dockside whores . . . but odd sights were common enough in the Maze by night, masks, cloaks, bright colors flaunted by night when the kindly dark masked the signs of wear and their thread-bare condition. Man and woman, they were only conspicuous by their plainness, the woman shrouded by the robe and hood so that she might be instead some night-prowling priest with an unlikely and rough guard.

Hanse followed, in and out amongst the occasional walkers on the street, a kind of stalking at which he had some skill.

•   •   •

. . . So, well, it answered, at least, what Hanse
had been up to, and upset all Cappen Varra's
calculations about Hanse as bluster and no
threat. Cappen stopped at the corner with the trio
in view, glanced over his own shoulder with a
touch of mad humor and the desperate thought
that the whole was getting to be a procession in
the dark streets . . . the woman and Vis, and
Hanse, and now himself—but at least there was
no fifth person that he could see, following
him.

Hanse moved off, slipping casually down the
street amid the ordinary traffic with a skill Cappen found amazing . . . he had never seen
Hanse work, not after this fashion; had never
particularly wanted to think at depth on the essence of the smallish thief, that there was in fact
something more than the temper and the knives
and the vanity which made this man dangerous.
Having seen it, he reckoned to himself that the
only sensible course for him now was to go back
into the *Unicorn*, work his way into whatever
game   might   start—his   current   hope   of
prosperity—and forget Hanse entirely, never
minding a moment when Hanse turned up as
stiff and cold as Sjekso had, which was assuredly
where he was headed at the moment. But
perhaps it was the poetry of the matter, the sus-
picion that there might be something worth the
witnessing . . . perhaps it was the assurance
that Hanse was into far more than he knew, and
that somewhere up there, without untidy re-
course to the rapier that swung at his side . . . he
might overtake the revenge-bound lunatic and

talk him out of it. Hanse—was the only likely ally
in a situation of his own; the woman had *looked*
at him back there, and there was nagging at him
an unwelcome vision, Hanse lying at the
doorstep in the morning and himself there the
day after—macabre fancy it might be, but the
wind still blew up his back. There was only the
matter of catching Hanse to stop him, and that
was like putting one's hands on a shadow. Cappen was not accustomed to feel awkward in his
moves, looked down on the louts and ne'er-do-
wells who walked the Maze; possessed a grace
surpassing most—in any situation.

But not in walking the Maze by dark and unseen. Hanse was in his element, and Cappen
followed him artlessly, down the length of the
Serpentine, and into territory of the city at
large—where the law came, and where a wanted
thief was less than safe. The houses and shops
here were more sturdy, and finally magnificent,
and those latter existed behind walls, and most
with bars on the windows. Walkers grew scarce
for a time, and Cappen hung further back, afraid
that he himself might attract the notice of the
pair Hanse followed . . . which he earnestly did
not want.

One street and another, and sometimes a passage through narrower ways where Cappen
found Hanse going more carefully, where they
four were virtually alone and where a false move
could alert the pair ahead. Cappen stayed far
back then, and once he thought he had lost them
all . . . but a quick move around a corner put
them all in view again. Hanse looked back in that
instant, while Cappen tried to stay inconspicu-

ously part of a stack of barrels, recalling Hanse's
knives, and the murk of the night. The fog was
coming on and the light played tricks; a light
mist slicked the stones . . . and still the pair kept
moving, out of the merchant quarter and into the
quarter of the gods, past the square of the Promise of Heaven, where prostitutes, bedraggled in
the mist, sat their accustomed benches like rain-
soaked birds—They swung past this place and
into the Avenue of Temples itself; and Cappen
shrugged his cloak about him with a genuinely
wretched chill and marvelled at the trio ahead,
who moved, pursued and pursuer, with such a
tireless purpose.

And then another alley, a sudden move aside,
which almost caught Hanse himself by surprise,
near the magnificence of the dome of the temple
of Ils and Shipri.

There Hanse tucked himself away into shadow
and Cappen quite lost sight of him, among the
buttresses and the statuary of the outthrust wing
of the temple . . . vanished.

Then the woman in black went out into the
street, ascended the plain center of the steps of
Ils and Shipri, toward the temple guards who
warded the constantly open doors in these uneasy times . . . four men and well armed, setting
hands on hilts at once as they were approached.
The woman cast back her hood: swords stayed
undrawn, hands unmoving, numb as the patrons
of the Unicorn.

Then another shadow began to move, from the
unwatched side of the steps, a man from out of
the shadows, knife in hand, a swift stalking . . .

which afforded Cappen even less of comfort and
made him think that a wayward minstrel
perhaps should have spent a safer, drier night in
the *Unicorn*.

Follow, the wizard had said, and Hanse
pressed himself close against the wall, in the
scant shadow afforded by a bit of brickwork,
pressed himself there and watched in chill
discomfort—blinked in horror while it happened, and four men died with swords still in
sheath—only the last attempted a defense, and
Mradhon Vis cut his throat in one quick and
unmistakable move. Hanse blinked again and
discovered to his consternation that the dark
one, the woman, was gone, Mradhon Vis crouching now in sole possession of that bloody thresh-
old. Hanse fingered his belt knife like a warding
talisman; and wanted only to stay put, but all the
while the icy cold at the pit of his neck, more
biting than the cold of the mist, reminded him
what he was there to do—what other power there
was to offend. And he waited, reckoning every
small move Mradhon Vis made, crouched over
the bodies of the guards—every small shifting of
a man busy at corpse-looting, every glance about
as some hardy passerby noised along the main
avenue—but none saw, none came near.

The woman delayed about her business inside: it might have been a moment, or far
longer—time did tricks in his mind. Hanse
shifted uneasily, finally gathered his nerve,
slipped out of that safe concealment and, in the
turning of Vis' head toward a distraction on the

street . . . he eased past a gap in cover and into
the alley Vis and the woman had left, along the
temple itself.

He reached the first of three barred windows,
and with utmost silence took the chance and
seized the bars, hoisted himself up to see. The
breath passed silently over his teeth and his gut
knotted up—a robber of wizards, Enas Yorl had
said: and now a thief who preyed on gods.

That struck hard . . . not that he darkened the
doorway of his city gods with his presence or
practiced alms; but there were territories, there
were limits to a thief's audacity . . . or it went
hard for all. It was his *craft*, by the gods, his *art*
the woman involved; and they were old, those
gods, and belonged in Sanctuary, as the Rankan
emperor's new lot never would. And the woman,
the foreigner, the witch-thief, climbed up to the
lap of bearded Ils himself and lifted the fabled
necklace of Harmony from about the marble
neck.

"Shalpa," Hanse swore silently, and with
chilling appropriateness—let himself ever so
carefully down from his vantage with one chill
throbbing about his neck and another one travelling his backbone. So Enas Yorl wanted a report.
And the gods of old Ilsig were plundered by a
foreign witch while the Rankans moved in with
their new lot of deities down the block, with
scaffolds and plans and the evident intent of
overshadowing the gods of Ilsig. Prince
Kithakadis and the Rankan gods; and: "recommended," Enas Yorl had said, sending a thief out
to keep watch on this god-thievery.

Hanse flattened himself back into his concealment with a sense of a world amiss, of matters under way no mere thief wanted part of. He had mixed in Kitty-cat's connivances once to his discomfort . . . but now, now it was possible Enas Yorl had a side of his own.

And hired help.

A footstep toward the temple front warned him: he crouched low and held his breath—Ischade, rejoining Mradhon Vis. "Done," he heard her say; and "here's an end. Let's be gone, and quickly."

Of course an outsider like Mradhon Vis—of course a man not Ilsig, who would have no scruples in killing Ilsig priests or robbing Ilsig gods.

In the emperor's hire? Hanse wondered, which was far too much and too clear wondering for a thief; the sweat was coursing down his ribs despite the misty chill of the air. He was not sure at all now what side Yorl was . . . and it occurred to him to tear the amulet from his neck, drop it in the alley and run.

But how far? And how long? He thought a second and chilling time of the wizard and his connections; recalled Sjekso; and Kithakadis himself . . . a prince of some small gratitude for services a thief had rendered; but more than dangerous if certain rumors started, that Yorl could spread . . . effortlessly.

The pair headed back the way they had come, and he set out after them, seeing no other course.

More and more bizarre, this midnight wander-

ing. Cappen went rigid in his hiding place first
as the quarry passed, and then as he caught sight
of Hanse again, padding after them as before.

So there was no encounter. They went out and
they did murder and came back, while Hanse
followed after having seen what Hanse had seen
. . . very unlike Hanse. Cappen suspected motives ill-defined, gave shape to nothing, only
sure it was something more than Hanse's private
impulses that moved him now. He recalled the
way in which the woman had passed a roomful
of patrons at the *Unicorn,* in which she and her
companion went where they liked on the street,
in which guards died like slaughtered cat-
tle. . . .

The relief Cappen felt at seeing Hanse mobile
and not lying stiff in the alley further on, gave
way to a horror at the silence of all that was done,
the neatness of it; and a subtle dread of this
pacing about the streets. The procession which
had started to be humorous and might have become yet more so on the return . . . now assumed a thoroughly macabre character, such
that he forbore to contact Hanse when he had, for
one instant, the chance. Hanse's face too, in the
small glimpse he had had of it as he passed, had
the wan, set look of terror.

They went back very much the way they had
come, and long before they came close to the
alley behind the *Unicorn,* Cappen had a sure
idea that such was their destination.

6

The pair of them went well enough where
Hanse had figured they would go, in the alley
behind the Unicorn. He held back as he had been
doing and kept them in sight . . . wished anew
that he had had the chance during the day to
creep up to Ischade's lodgings and have a closer
look, but she had been there most of the day, and
daylight and the fact that it was the second story
gave him no easy options. When she had left,
toward evening, he had been obliged to follow,
having no real idea of her motives and habitual
movements . . . and well that he had followed,
since this evening had turned out as it had.

But there was still, as there had been, a presence on his trail—and that was Cappen. Hanse
knew that much, had caught sight of the minstrel
out of his own territory and seen him more than
once on streets where Cappen had no business
being.

And who had hired Cappen?

It was not Cappen's custom to take employment; he diced and he sang songs; but never this
kind of work. He was not suited for it. Enas Yorl
could have hired better. Far better.

But this Ischade—

Hanse refused the idea. And yet constantly
nagging at him in that small nook of his mind
where he tucked coincidences, was Cappen's
presence that morning. But Cappen had been in
the game too, like Mradhon Vis and Sjekso; and

Cappen had gotten off with some profit, as Cappen usually did.

Cappen bought him a drink; and that was uncommon, that Cappen had that much to spare. But it was in Cappen's nature to play the lord and throw about what he had.

Cappen had ducked out of the *Unicorn* a scant moment before the blind man came, having assured Hanse's presence there with that drink . . . but that then circled the matter back to Yorl, where it made least sense.

Hanse forbore another glance over his shoulder, reckoning that even Cappen's unskilled stalking might pick that up. He kept his attention toward the pair in front of him, kept moving where necessary—watched them reach the steps and both of them start up the stairs toward the lady's lodgings, without any exchanged movement which might mean the passing of the loot.

Now . . . now while the noise of the creaking stairs gave him sound to rely on in tracking them—he had his chance, and took it, a path he had marked out that afternoon. He carefully set his hands on a barrel, levered himself up into a tuck and sought the next level of debris, noiselessly, one after the other, holding his breath as one foothold rocked and the next proved stable.

He made the roof as the pair made the door and opened it; he edged along it with the greatest care—a wooden roof at least, and not the tiles some fancied uptown. Even now he would have preferred to be rid of the boots and to go barefoot, as he had worked in the days before prosperity, but he figured there was no time for such. He edged his way around the ell of the roof on wet shingles and out onto that section over the room itself.

There was noise inside, a sharp, animal sound which lifted his nape hairs and made him less certain he wanted near this place at all. He edged closer to the very edge of the eaves, put his head over, viewing upside down where only parchment covered the window and formed a scant barrier to sounds and voices from inside. He heard footsteps clearly, heard a flapping sound . . . and suddenly a jolt and crack as an aged shingle snapped in two under his hand on the edge. It flung him overbalance, but he caught himself on his belly, spread-eagled on the roof. "Hssst!" he heard from inside, and he swore silently by appropriate gods and began to work his way hastily back from the vulnerable edge.

His hands, his legs went numb; his breath grew short and the talisman at his throat became a lump of ice and fire. Magic, he thought, some warding spell flung his way . . . he dealt with wizards; and it was a trap. He strove to make his limbs do what they well knew how to do: carefully he put a knee on a wet and worn row of shinkles on the slant.

One broke; he slipped, a rattling loud career down the layered face of the shingles, his feet swinging into empty air, his wild final thought that if he fought the fall now he might go head downward or onto his back. He let go, slid, expecting a dizzying long drop—the barrels, maybe, the debris of the alley might break his fall and save his back and legs—

He hit the edge of the porch unprepared, a

shock that sent him tumbling a further few feet down the stairs backward—a ridiculous lot of noise, his battered mind was thinking through the pain, an embarrassing lot of noise . . .

And then the door was open above him, and he was lying sprawled on his back head downward on the narrow steps, looking up through his feet at Mradhon Vis, who came with the metal flash of a dagger in his fist.

Hanse went for the belt knife, curled up and threw it with all he had: Mradhon Vis staggered back with an oath, spun half about by the cast as Hanse twisted to get up, his feet higher than his head with a railing on his left and a wall at his right, which hindered more than helped. He got as far as his knee when the bravo's foot caught him under the jaw and hurled him back into the wall; and a knife followed—further humiliation—up against his throat while Mradhon Vis grabbed his hair and twisted. Hanse fought to get loose; he thought that he struggled, but the messages were slow getting to his limbs and the burning of the amulet at his throat distracted him with the feeling that he was choking—or was it the knife?

"Bring him up," a female voice said from the light of the doorway; and Hanse looked blurrily up into it, while a hand twisted into his hair jerked him up and the dagger shifted a keen point to his back under the ribs. He went up the stairs, and followed the blackrobed figure which retreated inside. There seemed little else at the moment that he could do, that he wanted to do, bruised as he was and with his wits leaden weighted. He blinked in the interior light, stared dully at the russet silks, at the clutter of objects separately beautiful, but which lay disarrayed—like bones in a nest, he thought distantly, thinking of something predatory; and he jerked at the sudden racket and flutter of wings, a fluttering of the lamplight in the commotion of a great black bird which sat on its perch over against the wall.

"You can go," the woman said, and Hanse's heart lifted for the instant. "You've been paid. Come back tomorrow." And then he knew she spoke to Mradhon Vis.

"Tomorrow."

"Then."

"Is that all there is? And leave this here?" A jab at Hanse's back. "I took a knife, woman; I've got a hole in my arm and you keep this and turn me out in the wet, do you?"

"Out," she said, in a lower tone.

And to Hanse's bewilderment the knife retreated. Hanse moved then, turned in the instant, thinking of a quick stab from behind, his own hand to his wrist sheath . . . and he had the blade out, facing Mradhon Vis—but somehow the rest of the move failed him, and he watched dully as Mradhon Vis turned away and sulked his way to the open door.

"Close it behind you," the woman said, and Mradhon Vis did so, not slamming it. Hanse blinked, and the amulet at his neck hurt more than any bruise he had taken. It burned, and he had no sense left to get rid of it.

Ischade smiled abstractedly at her guest, left him so a moment, having greater business at hand. "Peruz," she said softly, shook back her hood, and taking from her robes the necklace, she drew near the huge raptor . . . or the guise it wore. With the greatest of care she slipped the necklace into a small case which hung from the side of the stand and fastened the case in its turn to the scaly leg of the bird. Peruz stood still too, uncommonly so, his great wings folded. A last time she teased the breast feathers, the softness about the neck—she had grown fond of the creature in recent weeks, as anything that shared her life. She smiled at the regard of a cold topaz eye.

"Open the window," she instructed her intruder/guest, and he moved, slowly, with the look of a man caught in a bad dream. "Open it," and he did so. She launched Peruz and he flew, with a clap of wings, a hurtling out toward the dark, a lingering coolness of wind.

So he was sped. Her employer had all he had paid to have—and well paid. And she was alone. She let go her mental grip on the ruffian . . . and at once his face showed panic and he whipped up the knife he had in hand. She stopped that. He looked confused, as if he had quite forgotten what the dagger was doing in his hand. And that effort would cost her, come the morning: on the morrow would be a fearful headache and a mortal lassitude, so that she would want to do nothing for days but drowse. But now the blood was still quick in her veins, the excitement lingered, and in the threat of ennui and solitude which followed any completed task . . . she felt another kind of excitement, and looked on her uninvited visitor knowing, quite knowing that at such times she was mad, and what it cost to cure such madness for the time. . . .

Attractive. Her tastes were broad, but in that
curiously compartmented mind of hers, it
pleased her . . . the mission done . . . that there
was room for Mradhon to go. Here stood instead
an unmissable someone—he had all the marks of
that condition. It was justice owed her for her
pains . . . twice as sweet when it all came together just as it did now, her satisfaction and the
last untidy threads of a business, tied together
and nipped short.

She held out her hand and came closer, feeling
that sweet/sad warmth that sex set into her blood
. . . and had felt it, at every weakening moment,
from the time she had robbed the wrong wizard
and left him living. In the morning she would
even feel some torment for it, a tangled regret:
the handsome ones always left her with that, a
sense of beauty wasted. But for the moment
reason was quite gone.

And there had been so many before.

Hanse still held the knife and could not feel it;
then heard the distant shock it made hitting the
floor. There was no pain of the bruises, no sensation but of warmth and of the woman's nearness,
her dark eyes regarding him, her perfume en-
veloping him. And the amulet at his throat,
which gave off a bitter cold: that was the one last
focus of his discomfort. She put her arms about
his neck and her fingers found the chain. "You
don't want this," she said, lifting it ever so gently
over his head. He heard it fall, far, far away.
Truth, he did not want it. He wanted her. It came
to him that this was the way that Sjekso had
gone, before he had ended up dead and cold

outside the *Unicorn,* and it failed to matter. Her lips pressed his and oh, gods, he wanted her.

The floor wavered, and a wind swept in, laden with sweetish incense . . .

"Pardon me," Enas Yorl said, and the couple on the verge of further intimacies broke apart, the woman staring at him wide-eyed and Shadowspawn with a hazy desperation. The russet silks in the room still billowed with the draft he had set up.

"Who are *you?*" the woman Ischade asked, and at once Enas Yorl felt a small trial of his defenses, which he shrugged off. Ischade's expression at once took on a certain wariness.

"Let him go," Enas Yorl said with a backhanded wave toward Shadowspawn. "He's admirably discreet. And I'd take it kindly.—Go on, Shadowspawn. Now. Quickly."

Shadowspawn edged toward the door, hesitated there with a look of violated sanity.

"Out," Enas Yorl said.

The thief spun about and opened the door, a fresh gust of wind.

And fled.

Hanse hit the stairs running, hardly pausing for the steps, never saw the figure loom up at the bottom until he was headed straight down at the knife that aimed up at his gut.

He knocked the attacking blade aside and grabbed for arms or clothes, whatever he could hold, fell, in the shock of the collision, tumbled with the attacker and the blade, and lost his purchase in the impact with the ground. He hit on his back, desperately got a grip on the descending knife hand with Mradhon Vis' face coming down on him with a weight of body a third again his own. It was his left hand he used on the descending arm, left hand, knife hand, involved with that, and his battered muscles shook under the strain while he plied his unaccustomed right hand trying to reach the knife strapped to his leg. His left arm was buckling.

Suddenly Vis' weight shifted rightwards and came down on him, pinning his other arm—a limp weight, and in the space Vis' grimace had occupied, most improbably, Cappen Varra stood with a barrel stave in both his hands.

"Did you want rescue?" Cappen asked civilly. "Or is it all some new diversion?"

Hanse swore, kicked and writhed his way from under Vis' inert weight and went for his dagger in fright. Cappen checked his arm and the heat of anger went out of him, leaving only a sickly shiver. "Hang you," he said feebly, "couldn't you have hit him easier and given me a go?"

And then he realized the source of the light which was streaming down on them by way of the stairs, and that above them was the open door in which two wizards met. "Gods," he muttered, and scrambling up, grabbed Cappen by the arm.

And ran, for very life.

"Not my doing."

"No?" Enas Yorl felt his shoulders expand ever so slightly, his features shift, and in his pride he refused to look down at his hands to

know. Perhaps it was not too terrible, this form:
Ischade's eyes flickered, but seemed unappalled.

"None of the killings that interest you," she
said, "are mine. They're not my style. I trust I'm
somewhat known in the craft. As you are, Enas
Yorl."

He gave a small bow. "I have some unwilling
distinction."

"The story's known."

"Ah." Again he felt the shift, a wave of terror.
He bent down and picked up the amulet which
lay on the floor, saw his hand covered with a
faint opalescence of scales. Then the scales faded
and left only a young and shapely male hand. He
tucked the amulet into his robes and
straightened, looked at Ischade somewhat more
calmly. "So you're not the one. I don't ask you
then who hired you. I can guess, knowing what
you did—ah, I do know. And by morning the
priests will have discovered the loss and made
some substitution—the wars of gods, after all,
follow politics, don't they? And what matter a
riot or two in Sanctuary? It interests neither of
us."

"Then what is your interest?"

"How did they die, Ischade—your lovers? Do
you know? Or don't you wonder?"

"Your curiosity—has it some specific grievance?"

"Ah, no grievance at all. I only ask."

"I do nothing. The fault's their own . . . their
luck, a heart too fragile, a fall . . . who am I to
know? They're well when they leave me, that's
the truth."

"But they're dead by morning, every one."

She shrugged. "You should understand. I have nothing to do with it."

"Ah, indeed we have misfortunes in common. I know. And when I knew you'd come to Sanctuary—"

"It took me some few days to acclimate myself; I trust I didn't inconvenience you . . . and that we'll avoid each other in future."

"Ischade: how am I— presently?"

She tilted back her head and looked, blinked uncertainly. "Younger," she said. "And quite handsome, really. Far unlike what I've heard."

"So? Then you can look at me? I see that you can. And not many do."

"I have business," she declared, liking all of this less and less. She was not accustomed to feel fear . . . hunted the sensation in the alleys of cities in the hope of discovering a measure of life. But this was far from comfortable. "I have to be about it."

"What, some new employer?"

"Not killing wizards, if that's your worry. My business is private, and it need not intrude on yours."

"And if I engaged you?"

"In what regard?"

"To spend one night with me."

"You're mad."

"I might become so—I don't age, you see. And that's the difficulty."

"You're not afraid? You're looking to die? Is that the cause of all this?"

"Ah, I'm afraid at times. At times like this, when the shape is good. But it doesn't last. There are other times . . . and they come. And I never grow old, Ischade. I can't detect it if I do. And that frightens me."

She regarded him askance . . . he was handsome, very. She wondered if this had been his first shape, when he was young, that brought his trouble on him. It was a shape fine enough to have done that. The eyes were beautiful, full of pain. So many of her young men of the streets were full of that pain. It touched her as nothing else could.

"How long has it been," he asked, setting his hands on her shoulders, touching ever so gently, "since you had a lover worth the name? And how long since I've had hope of anything? We might be each other's answer, Ischade. If I should die, then that's one way out for me; or if I don't—then you're not doomed to lose them all, after all, are you, Ischade? Some of my forms might not be to your taste, but others—I have infinite variety, Ischade. And no dread of you at all."

"For this you hunted me down? That was it, wasn't it—the amulet, a way to draw yourself to me—"

"It costs you nothing. No harm. So small a thing for you, Ischade . . . ."

It tempted. He was beautiful, this moment, this one moment, and the nights and the years were long.

And then the other chance occurred to her and she shivered, who had not shivered in years. "No. No. Maybe you're set to die, but I'm not. No.

Oppose two curses the like of ours—half the city could go in that shock, not to mention you and me. The chance of that, the merest chance—No. I'm not done living . . . ."

He frowned, drew himself up with the least tremor about his lips, a look of panic. "Ischade. . . ." The voice began to change, and of a sudden the features starting with the mouth wavered, as if the strain had been too much, too long and dearly held. The scales were back; and "No," he cried, and plunged his face into hands which were not quite still hands. The draperies billowed, the very air rippled, and "No . . . ." the air sighed after him, a vanishing moan, a sob.

A second time she shivered, and looked about her, distracted, but he was quite gone.

So, well, she thought. He had had his answer, once for all. Her business took her here and there about the empire, but she discovered a liking for Sanctuary as for no other place she had known . . . and it was well that Yorl took his answer, and that it was settled. New tasks might come. But at the moment she thought of the river house. This lodging was too well known for the time; and she might walk to the river . . . might meet someone—along the way.

The wine splashed into the cup and such was Hanse's state of mind that he never looked to see who served, only hoisted the cup and drank a mouthful.

"That's good," he said; and Cappen Varra across the table in the *Unicorn* watched him shake off the ghosts and lifted his own cup, thinking ruefully of a song abandoned, a tale best not sung at all, even in the safe confines of the *Unicorn*. The city would be full of questions tomorrow, and it was well to know nothing at all . . . as he was sure Hanse planned to know least of all.

"A game," Cappen proposed.

"No. No dicing tonight." Hanse dug into his purse and came up with a silver round, laid it carefully on the table. "That's for another pitcher when this is done. And for a roof tonight."

Cappen poured again, topping off the cup—a wonder, that Hanse bought drinks. Hanse flinging money about as if he wished to be rid of it.

"Tomorrow on the game," Cappen said, in hope.

"Tomorrow," Hanse said, and lifted the cup.

Blind Darous poured, the cup held just so for his finger to feel the coolth of the liquid . . . measured it carefully and extended the filled goblet toward his seated master. The breathing was hoarse tonight. A hand took the stem of the cup most delicately, not touching his fingers at all, for which Darous was deeply grateful.

And toward the river, a house apart from others . . . which seemed oddly discontinuous from its surrounds: in squalor, it had a garden, and a wall; and yet had a quaint decrepitude. Mradhon Vis stood outside the gate—sore and much out of sorts. *She* was there: she had found herself a young man much the image of Sjekso, who presently held the warmth and the light inside.

He had walked that far.

And finally, knowing what he knew, he did the harder thing, and walked away.

A GIFT IN PARTING

Robert Asprin

The sun was a full two handspans above the horizon when Hort appeared on the Sanctuary docks; early in the day but late by fishermen's standard. The youth's eyes squinted painfully at the unaccustomed brightness of the morning sun. He fervently wished he were home in bed . . . or in someone else's bed . . . or anywhere but here. Still, he had promised his mother he would help the Old Man this morning. While his upbringing made it unthinkable to break that promise, his stubbornness required that he demonstrate his protest by being late.

Though he had roamed these docks since early childhood and knew them to be as scrupulously clean as possible, Hort still chose his path care-

fully to avoid brushing his clothes against anything. Of late he had been much more attentive to
his personal appearance; this morning he had
discovered he no longer had any old clothes
suitable for the boat. While he realized the futility of trying to preserve his current garb through
an entire day's work in the boat, newly acquired
habits demanded he try to minimize the damage.

The Old Man was waiting for him, sitting on
the overturned boat like some stately sea-bird
sleeping off a full belly. The knife in his hand
caressed the stray piece of wood he held with a
slow, rhythmic cadence. With each pass of the
blade a long curl of wood fell to join the pile at
his feet. The size of the pile was mute testament
to how long the Old Man had been waiting.

Strange, but Hort had always thought of him as
the Old Man, never as Father. Even the men who
had fished these waters with him since their
shared boyhoods called him Old Man rather than
Panit. He wasn't really old, though his face was
deceptive. Wrinkled and crisscrossed by
weather lines, the Old Man's face looked like
one of those red clay riverbeds one saw in the
desert beyond Sanctuary: parched, cracked,
waiting for rain that would never fall.

No, that was wrong. The Old Man didn't look
like the desert. The Old Man would have nothing
in common with such a large accumulation of
dirt. He was a fisherman, a creature of the sea and
as much a part of the sea as one of those weathered rocks that punctuated the harbor.

The old man looked up at his son's approach
then let his attention settle back on the whittling.

"I'm here," Hort announced unnecessarily, adding, "sorry I'm late."

He cursed himself silenced when that remark slipped out. He had been determined not to apologize, no matter what the Old Man said, but when the Old Man said nothing . . .

His father rose to his feet unhurriedly, replacing his knife in its sheath with a gesture made smooth and unconscious by years of repetition.

"Give me a hand with this," he said, bending to grasp one end of the boat.

Just that. No acceptance of the apology. No angry reproach. It was as if he had expected his reluctant assistant would be late.

Hort fumed about this as he grunted and heaved, helping to right the small boat and set it safely in the water. His annoyance with the whole situation was such that he was seated in the boat, accepting the oars as they were passed down from the dock, before he remembered that his father had been launching this craft for years without assistance. His son's inexpert hands could not have been a help, only a hindrance.

Spurred by this new irritation, Hort let the stern of the boat drift away from the dock as his father prepared to board. The petty gesture was in vain. The Old Man stepped into the boat, stretching his leg across the water with no more thought than a merchant gives his keys in their locks.

"Row that way," came the order to his son.

Gritting his teeth in frustration, Hort bent to the task.

The old rhythms returned to him in mercifully

few strokes. Once he had been glad to row his
father's boat. He had been proud when he had
grown enough to handle the oars himself. No
longer a young child to be guarded by his
mother, he had basked in the status of the Old
Man's boy. His playmates had envied his association with the only fisherman on the dock who
could consistently trap the elusive Nya—the
small schooling fish whose sweet flesh brought
top price each afternoon after the catch was
brought in.

Of course, that had been a long time ago. He'd
wanted to learn about the Nya then—he knew
less now; his memories had faded.

As Hort had grown, so had his world. He
learned that away from the docks no one knew of
the Old Man, nor did they care. To the normal
citizens of Sanctuary he was just another fisherman and fishermen did not stand high in the
social structure of the town. Fishermen weren't
rich, nor did they have the ear of the local aris-
tocrats. Their clothes weren't colorful like the
S'danzo's. They weren't feared like the soldiers
or mercenaries.

And they smelled.

Hort had often disputed this latter point with
the street urchins away from the docks until
bloody noses, black eyes and bruises taught him
that fishermen weren't good fighters, either. Besides, they did smell.

Retreating to the safety of the dock community
Hort found that he viewed the culture which had
raised him with a blend of scorn and bitterness.
The only people who respected fishermen were
other fishermen. Many of his old friends were

drifting away—finding new lives in the crowds and excitment of the city-proper. Those that remained were dull youths who found reassurance in the unchanging traditions of the fish-craft and who were already beginning to look like their fathers.

As his loneliness grew, it was natural that Hort used his money to buy new clothes which he bundled and hid away from the fish-tainted cottage they called home. He scrubbed himself vigorously with sand, dressed and tried to blend with the townsfolk.

He found the citizens remarkably pleasant once he had removed the mark of the fishing community. They were most helpful in teaching him what to do with his money. He acquired a circle of friends and spent more and more time away from home until . . .

"Your mother tells me you're leaving."

The Old Man's sudden statement startled Hort, jerking him rudely from his mental wanderings. In a flash he realized he had been caught in the trap his friends had warned him about. Alone in the boat with his father he would be a captive audience until the tide changed. Now he'd hear the anger, the accusations and finally the pleading.

Above all Hort dreaded the pleading. While they had had their differences in the past, he still held a lingering respect for his father, a respect he knew would die if the Old Man were reducing to whining and begging.

"You've said it yourself a hundred times, Old Man," Hort pointed out with a shrug, "not everyone was meant to be a fisherman."

It came out harsher than he had intended, but Hort let it go without more explanations. Perhaps his father's anger would be stirred to a point where the conversation would be terminated prior to the litanies of his obligations to his family and tradition.

"Do you think you can earn a living in Sanctuary?" the Old Man asked, ignoring his son's baiting.

"We . . . I won't be in Sanctuary," Hort announced carefully. Even his mother hadn't possessed this last bit of knowledge. "There's a caravan forming in town. In four days it leaves for the capital. My friends and I have been invited to travel with it."

"The capital?" Panit nodded slowly. "And what will you do in Ranke?"

"I don't know yet," his son admitted, "but there are ten jobs in Ranke for every one in Sanctuary."

The Old Man digested this in silence. "What will you use for money on this trip?" he asked finally.

"I had hoped . . . There's supposed to be a tradition in our family, isn't there? When a son leaves home his father gives him a parting gift. I know you don't have much, but . . ." Hort stopped; the Old Man was shaking his head in slow negation.

"We have less than you think," he said sadly. "I said nothing before, but your fine clothes, there, have tapped our savings; the fishing's been bad."

"If you won't give me anything, just say so!"

Hort exploded angrily. "You don't have to rationalize it with a long tale of woe."

"I'll give you a gift," the Old Man assured him. "I only wanted to warn you that it probably would not be money. More to the left."

"I don't need your money," the youth growled, adjusting his stroke. "My friends have offered to loan me the necessary funds. I just thought it would be better not to start my new life in debt."

"That's wise," Panit agreed. "Slow now."

Hort glanced over his shoulder for a bearing then straightened with surprise. His oars trailed loose in the water.

"There's only one float!" he announced in dumb surprise.

"That's right," the Old Man nodded. "It's nice to know you haven't forgotten your numbers."

"But one float means . . ."

"One trap," Panit agreed. "Right again. I told you fishing was bad. Still, having come all this way, I would like to see what is in my one trap."

The Old Man's dry sarcasm was lost on his son. Hort's mind was racing as he reflexively maneuvered the boat into position by the float.

One trap! The Old Man normally worked fifteen to twenty traps; the exact number always varied from day to day according to his instincts, but never had Hort know him to set less than ten traps. Of course the Nya were an unpredictable fish whose movements confounded everyone save Panit. That is—they came readily to the trap if the trap happened to be near them in their random wanderings.

One trap! Perhaps the schools were feeding elsewhere; that sometimes happened with any fish. But then the fishermen would simply switch to a different catch until their mainstay returned. If the Old Man were less proud of his ability and reputation he could do the same . . .

"Old Man!" The exclamation burst from Hort's lips involuntarily as he scanned the horizon.

"What is it?" Panit asked, pausing as he hauled his trap from the depths.

"Where are the other boats?"

The Old Man returned his attention to the trap. "On the dock," he said brusquely. "You walked past them this morning."

Open-mouthed, Hort let his memory roam back over the docks. He had been preoccupied with his own problems, but . . . yes! there had been a lot of boats lying on the dock.

"All of them?" he asked, bewildered. "You mean we're the only boat out today?"

"That's right."

"But why?"

"Just a minute . . . here!" Panit secured a handhold on the trap and heaved it onto the boat. "Here's why."

The trap was ruined. Most of the wooden slats which formed its sides were caved in and those that weren't dangled loose. If Hort hadn't been expecting to see a Nya trap he wouldn't have recognized this as something other than a tangle of scrap-wood.

"It's been like this for over a week!" the Old Man snarled with sudden ferocity. "Traps smashed, nets torn. That's why those who call themselves fishermen cower on the land instead of manning their boats!" He spat noisily over the side of the boat.

Was it also why his mother had insisted Hort give the Old Man a hand?

"Row for the docks, boy. Fishermen! They should fish in buckets where it's safe! Bah!"

Awed by the Old Man's anger, Hort turned the boat toward the shore. "What's doing it?" he asked.

There was silence as Panit stared off to the sea. For a moment Hort thought his question had gone unheard and was about to repeat it. Then he saw how deep the wrinkles on his father's face had become.

"I don't know," the Old Man murmured finally. "Two weeks ago I would have said I knew every creature that swam or crawled in these waters. Today . . . I just don't know."

"Have you reported this to the soldiers?"

"Soldiers? Is that what you've learned from your fancy friends? Run to the soldiers?" Panit fairly trembled with rage. "What do soldiers know of the sea? Eh? What do you want them to do? Stand on the shore and wave their swords at the water? Order the monster to go away? Collect a tax from it? Yes! That's it! If the soldiers declare a monster tax maybe it'll swim away to keep from being bled dry like the rest of us! Soldiers!"

The Old Man spat again and lapsed into a silence that Hort was loath to break. Instead he spent the balance of the return journey mentally speculating about the trap-crushing monster. In a way he knew it was futile; sharper minds than his, the Old Man's for example, had tried and failed to come up with an explanation. There wasn't much chance he'd stumble upon it. Still, it occupied his mind until they reached the dock. Only when the boat had been turned over in the late morning sun did Hort venture to reopen the conversation.

"Are we through for the day?" he asked. "Can I go now?"

"You can," the Old Man replied, turning a blank expression to his son. "Of course, if you do it might cause problems. The way it is now, if your mother asks me: 'Did you take the boat out today?' I can say yes. If you stay with me and she asks: 'Did you spend the day with the Old Man?' you can say yes. If, on the other hand, you wander off on your own, you'll have to say 'no' when she asks and we'll both have to explain ourselves to her."

This startled Hort almost more than the discovery of an unknown monster loose in the fishing grounds. He had never suspected the Old Man was capable of hiding his activities from his wife with such a calculated web of half-truths. Close on the heels of his shock came a wave of intense curiosity regarding his father's plans for a large block of time about which he did not want to tell his wife.

"I'll stay," Hort said with forced casualness. "What do we do now?"

"First," the Old Man announced as he headed off down the dock, "we visit the Wine Barrel."

The Wine Barrel was a rickety wharf-side tavern favored by the fishermen and therefore shunned by everyone else. Knowing his father to be a nondrinker, Hort doubted the Old Man had ever before been inside the place, yet he led the way into the shadowed interior with a firm and confident step.

They were all there: Terci, Omat, Varies; all the fishermen Hort had known since childhood plus many he did not recognize. Even Haron, the only woman ever accepted by the fishermen, was there, though her round, fleshy and weathered face was scarcely different from the men's.

"Hey, Old Man? You finally given up?"

"There's an extra seat here."

"Some wine for the Old Man!"

"One more trap-wrecked fisherman!"

Panit ignored the cries which erupted from various spots in the shadowed room at his entrance. He held his stride until he reached the large table custom reserved for the eldest fisherfolk.

"I told you, you'd be here eventually," Omat greeted him, pushing the extra bench out with his long, thin leg. "Now, who's a coward?"

The Old Man acknowledged neither the jibe nor the bench, leaning on the table with both hands to address the veterans. "I only came to ask one question," he hissed. "Are all of you, or any of you, planning to do anything about whatever it is that's driven you from the sea?"

To a man, the fishermen moved their gazes elsewhere.

"What can we do?" Terci scowled. "We don't even know what's out there. Maybe it will move on . . ."

" . . . And maybe it won't," the Old Man con-

cluded angrily. "I should have known. Scared
men don't think; they hide. Well, I've never been
one to sit around waiting for my problems to go
away on their own. Not planning to change
now."

He kicked the empty bench away and turned
toward the door only to find Hort blocking his
way.

"What are you going to do?" Terci called after
him.

"I'm going to find an answer!" the Old Man
announced, drilling the room with his scorn.
"And I'll find it where I've always found answers—in the sea; not at the bottom of a wine-
cup."

With that he strode out the door. Hort started
to follow when someone called his name and he
turned back.

"I thought that was you under those city-
clothes," Omat said without rancor. "Watch over
him, boy. He's a little crazy and crazy people
sometimes get killed before they get sane."

There was a low murmur of assent from those
around the table. Hort nodded and hurried after
his father. The Old Man was waiting for him
outside the door.

"Fools!" he raged. "No money for a week and
they sit drinking what little they have left. Pah!"

"What do *we* do now, Old Man?"

Panit looked around then snatched up a Nya
trap from a stack on the dock. "We'll need this,"
he said, almost to himself.

"Isn't that one of Terci's traps?" Hort asked
cautiously.

"He isn't using it, is he?" the Old Man shot

back. "And besides we're only borrowing it. Now, you're supposed to know this town— where's the nearest blacksmith?"

"The nearest? Well, there's a mender in the Bazaar, but the best ones are . . ."

The Old Man was off, striding purposefully down the street leaving Hort to hurry after him.

It wasn't a market-day; the bazaar was still sleepy with many stalls unopened. It was not necessary for Hort to lead the way as the sharp, ringing notes of hammer striking anvil were easily heard over the slow-moving shoppers. The dark giant plying the hammer glanced at them as they approached, but continued his work.

"Are you the smith?" Panit asked.

This earned them another, longer, look but no words. Hort realized the question had been ridiculous. A few more strikes and the giant set his hammer aside, turning his full attention to his new customers.

"I need a Nya trap. One of these." The Old Man thrust the trap at the smith.

The smith glanced at the trap, then shook his head. "Smith; not carpenter," he proclaimed, already reaching for his hammer.

"I know that!" the Old Man barked. "I want this trap made out of metal."

The giant stopped and stared at his customers again, then he picked up the trap and examined it.

"And I'll need it today—by sundown."

The smithy set the trap down carefully. "Two silvers," he said firmly.

"Two!" the Old Man snorted. "Do you think you're dealing with the Kitty-Kat himself? One."

"Two," the smithy insisted.

"Dubro!"

They all turned to face the small woman who had emerged from the enclosure behind the forge.

"Do it for one," she said quietly. "He needs it."

She and the smithy locked eyes in a battle of wills, then the giant nodded and turned away from his wife.

"S'danzo?" the Old Man asked before the woman disappeared into the darkness from which she'd come.

"Half."

"You've got the sight?"

"A bit," she admitted. "I see your plan is unselfish but dangerous. I do not see the outcome—except that you must have Dubro's help to succeed."

"You'll bless the trap?"

The S'danzo shook her head. "I'm a seer, not a priest. I'll make you a symbol—the Lance of Ships from our cards—to put on the trap. It marks good fortune in sea-battles; it might help you."

"Could I see the card?" the Old Man asked.

The woman disappeared and returned a few moments later bearing the card which she held for Panit. Looking over his father's shoulder, Hort saw a crudely drawn picture of a whale with a metal-sheathed horn proceeding from its head.

"A good card," the Old Man nodded. "For what you offer—I'll pay the two silvers." She smiled and returned to the darkness, Dubro stepped forward with his palm extended. "When

I pick up the trap," Panit insisted. "You needn't fear. I won't leave it to gather dust."

The giant frowned, nodded and turned back to his work.

"What are you planning?" Hort demanded as his father started off again. "What's this about a sea-battle?"

"All fishing is sea-battle," the Old Man shrugged.

"But, two silvers? Where are you going to get that kind of money after what you said in the boat this morning?"

"We'll see to that now."

Hort realized they weren't returning to town but heading westward to the Downwinder's hovels. The Downwinders or . . . "Jubal?" he exclaimed. "How're you going to get money from him? Are you going to sell him information about the monster?"

"I'm a fisherman, not a spy," the Old Man retorted, "and the problems of the fishermen are no concern of the land."

"But . . ." Hort began then lapsed into silence. If his father was going to be closed-mouthed about his plans, no amount of brow-beating was likely to budge him.

Upon reaching Jubal's estate, Hort was amazed at the ease with which the Old Man handled the slaver's underlings who routinely challenged his entry. Though it was well known that Jubal employed notorious cut-throats and murderers who hid their features behind blue-hawk masks, Panit was unawed by their arrogance or their arms.

"What do you two want here?" the grizzled gate-keeper barked.

"We came to talk to Jubal," the Old Man retorted.

"Is he expecting you?"

"I need an appointment to speak with the slaver?"

"What business could an old fisherman have with a slaver?"

"If you were to know, I'd tell you. I want to see Jubal."

"I can't just . . ."

"You ask too many questions. Does *he* know you ask so many questions?"

That final question of the Old Man's cowed the retainer, confirming Hort's town-refined suspicions that most of the slaver's business was covert rather than overt.

They were finally ushered into a large room dominated by a huge, almost throne-like, chair at one end. They had been waiting only a few moments when Jubal entered, belting a dressing-gown over his muscular, ebony limbs.

"I should have known it was you, Old Man," the slaver said with a half-smile. "No other fisherman could bluff his way past my guards so easily."

"I know you prefer money to sleep," the Old Man shrugged. "Your men know it too."

"True enough," Jubal laughed. "So, what brings you this far from the docks so early in the day?"

"For some the day's over," Panit commented dryly. "I need money: six silver pieces. I'm offering my stall on the wharf."

Hort couldn't believe what he was hearing. He opened his mouth to speak, then caught himself. He had been raised to know better than to interrupt his father's business. His movement was not lost on Jubal, however.

"You intrigue me, Old Man," the slaver mused. "Why should I want to buy a fish-stall at any price?"

"Because the wharf's the only place your ears don't hear," Panit smiled tightly. "You send your spies in—but we don't talk to outsiders. To hear the wharf you must be on the wharf—I offer you a place on the wharf."

"True enough," Jubal agreed. "I hardly expected the opportunity to fall my way like ripe fruit . . ."

"Two conditions," the Old Man interrupted. "First: four weeks before you own my stall. If I repay the money—you don't own my stall . . ."

"All right," the slaver nodded, "but . . .

"Second: anything happens to me these next four weeks you take care of my wife. It's not charity; she knows the wharf and the Nya—she's worth a fair wage."

Jubal studied the Old Man a moment through hooded eyes. "Very well," he said finally, "but I sense there is much you are not telling me." He left the room and returned with the silver coins which rattled lightly in his immense palm. "Tell me this, Old Man," he asked suspiciously, "all these terms—why don't you just ask for a loan?"

"I've never borrowed in my life," Panit scowled, "and won't start now. I pay as I go—if I don't have enough I do without or I sell what I must."

"Suit yourself," the slaver shrugged, handing over the coins. "I'll be expecting to see you in thirty days."

"Or before."

The silence between father and son was almost habitual and lasted nearly until they had reached the town again. Strangely, it was the old man who broke the silence first.

"You're being quiet, boy," he said.

"Of course," Hort exploded. "There's nothing to say. You order things we can't pay for, sell your life-work to the biggest crook in Sanctuary and then wonder why I'm quiet. I know you don't confide in me—but Jubal! Of all the people in town . . . And that talk about conditions! What makes you think he'll stand by any of them? You don't trust soldiers but you trust Jubal!"

"He can be trusted," the Old Man answered softly. "He's a hard one when he's got the upper hand—but he stands by his word."

"You've dealt with him before? Nothing can surprise me now," Hort grumbled.

"Good," his father nodded. "then you'll take me to the Vulgar Unicorn?"

"The Vulgar Unicorn!" He was surprised.

"That's right. Don't you know where it is?"

"I know it's in the Maze somewhere, but I've never been there."

"Let's go."

"Are you sure you want the Vulgar Unicorn, Old Man?" Hort pressed. "I don't think a fisherman's ever set foot in there. The people who drink at the Unicorn are mercenaries, cut-throats and a few thieves thrown in for good measure."

"So they say," the Old Man nodded. "Wouldn't be going there if they weren't. Now, you leading or not?"

All conversation stopped as they entered that infamous tavern. As he struggled to see in the darkness, Hort could feel the eyes of the room on his, sizing them up, deciding if he was a challenge or a victim.

"Are you gentlemen looking for someone?" The bartender's tone implied he didn't think they should stay for a drink.

"I want some fighting men," the Old Man announced. "I've heard this is the place."

"You heard right," the bartender nodded, suddenly a bit more attentive. "If you don't know who you want, I'll be glad to serve as your agent—for a modest fee, of course."

Panit regarded him as he'd regarded his fellow fisherfolk. "I judge my own people—go back to your dishes."

The bartender clenched his fists in anger and retreated to the other end of the bar as the Old Man faced the room.

"I need two, maybe three men for a half-day's work," he called loudly. "A copper now and a silver when it's over. No swords or bowmen— just axes or pole-arms. I'll be outside."

"Why are we going to talk to them outside?" Hort asked as he followed his father into the street.

"I want to know what I'm getting," the Old Man explained. "Couldn't see a thing in that place."

It took most of the afternoon but they finally

sorted out three stalwarts from the small pack
that had followed them. The sun was dipping
toward the horizon as Panit gave his last man the
advance coin and turned to his son.

"That's about all we can do today," he said.
"You run along and see your friends. I'll take
care of the trap."

"Aren't you going to tell me your plan?" Hort
pleaded.

"Haven't got it all worked out yet," the Old
Man admitted, "but if you want to see what hap-
pens, be on the dock at first light tomorrow.
We'll see how smart this monster is."

Unlike the day before, Hort was at the dock
well before the dawn. As the first tendrils of
pre-dawn light began to dispel the night he was
pacing impatiently, hugging himself against the
damp chill of the morning.

Mist hung deep over the water, giving it an
eerie, supernatural appearance which did nothing to ease Hort's fears as he alternately cursed
and worried about his absent father. Crazy old
man! Why couldn't he be like the other fishermen? Why take it on himself to solve the mystery
of the sea-monster? Knowing the best way to
combat the chill was activity he decided to
launch the family's boat. For once, he would be
ready when the Old Man got here.

He marched down the dock, then slowed, and
finally retraced his steps. The boat was gone.
Had Sanctuary's thieves finally decided to ply
their trade on the wharf? Unlikely. Who would
they sell a stolen boat to? The fishermen knew

each other's equipment as well as they knew their own.

Could the Old Man have gone out already? Impossible—to be out of the harbor before Hort got there, the Old Man would have had to take the boat out at night—and in these waters with the monster . . . .

"You there!"

Hort turned to find the three hired mercenaries coming down the pier. They were a sullen crew by this light and the pole-arms two of them carried gave them the appearance of Death's own oarsmen.

"We're here," the leader of the trio announced, shifting his battle-axe to his shoulder, "though no civilized man fights at this hour. Where's the old man who hired us?"

"I don't know," Hort admitted, backing down from this fierce assemblage. "He told me to meet him here same as you."

"Good," the axe-man snarled. "We've appeared, as promised. The coppers are ours—small price for a practical joke. Tell that old man when you see him that we've gone back to bed."

"Not so fast," Hort surprised himself with his sudden outspoken courage as the men turned away. "I've known the Old Man all my life and he's no joker. If he paid you to be here, you'll be needed. Or don't you want the silver that goes with those coppers?"

The men hesitated, mumbling together darkly.

"Hort!" Terci was hurrying toward them. "What's going on? Why are there cut-throats on the dock?"

"The Old Man hired them," Hort explained. "Have you seen him?"

"Not since last night," the lanky fisherman replied. "He came by late and gave me this to pass to you." He dropped three silver coins into the youth's palm. "He said if he wasn't here by mid-day that you were to use this to pay the men."

"You see!" Hort called to the mercenaries as he held up the coins. "You'll be paid at midday and not before. You'll just have to wait with the rest of us." Turning back to Terci he lowered his voice to a conspiratorial whisper. "What else did the Old Man say—anything?"

"Only that I should load my heaviest net this morning," Terci shrugged. "What's going on?"

"He's going to try to fish for the monster," Hort explained as the Old Man's plan came clear to him. "When I got here his boat was gone."

"The monster," Terci blinked. "The Old Man's gone out alone after the monster?"

"I don't think so. I've been here since before first light. No, even the Old Man wouldn't take a boat out in the dark—not after the monster. He must be . . ."

"Look there! There he is!"

The sun had finally appeared over the horizon and with its first rays the mist began to fade. A hundred yards offshore a small boat bobbed and dipped and in it they could see the Old Man pulling frantically at the oars.

As they watched he suddenly shipped the oars, waiting expectantly. Then the boat was jerked around, as if by an unseen hand and the Old Man bent to the oars again.

"He's got it! He's got the monster!" Terci shrieked, dancing with delight or horror.

"No!" Hort disagreed firmly, staring at the distant boat. "He doesn't have it. He's leading it, baiting it into shallow water."

It was all clear to him now. The metal trap! The monster was used to raiding the Old Man's traps, so he fed it one that couldn't be crushed. Now he was teasing the unknown creature toward shore, dragging the trap like a child drags a string before a playful kitten. But this kitten was an unknown, deadly quantity that could easily attack the hand that held the string.

"Quick, Terci," Hort ordered, "get the net! It won't follow him onto the shore."

"The lanky fisherman was gaping at the scene, his mind lost in his own thoughts. "Net the monster?" he mumbled. "I'll need help, yes, help . . .HELP!" He fled down the dock screaming at the still-dark, quiet huts.

This was not the Maze where cries for help went unheeded. Doors opened and bleary-eyed fishermen stumbled out to the wharf.

"What is it?"

"What's the noise?"

"*Man your boats! The Old Man's got the monster!*"

"The monster?"

"Hurry, Ilak!"

"The Old Man's got the monster!" The cry was passed from hut to hut.

And they came, swarming over their boats like a nest of angry ants: Haron, her sagging breasts flopping beneath the nightdress she still wore; Omat, his deformed arm no hindrance as he

wrestled his boat onto the water with one hand,
and in the lead, Terci, first rowing, then standing, in the small boat to shout orders at the
others.

Hort made no move to join them. They were
fishermen and knew their trade far better than
he. Instead he stood rooted on the dock, lost in
awe of the Old Man's courage.

In his mind's eye Hort could see what his
father saw: sitting in a small boat on an inky sea,
waiting for the first tug on the rope—then the
back-breaking haul on the oars to drag the metal
trap landward. Always careful not to get too far
ahead of the invisible creature below, yet keeping its interest. The dark was the Old Man's
enemy as much as the monster was; it threatened
him with disorientation—and the mist! A blind-
ing cloud of white closing in from all sides. Yet
the Old Man had done it and now the monster
was within reach of its victims' nets.

The heavy net was spread now, forming a wall
between the mystery beast as it followed the Old
Man and the open sea behind them. As the boats
at either end of the net began to pull for shore, the
Old Man evened his stroke and began to move
steadily through the water . . . but he was tired
now; Hort could see that even if no one else
could.

"There!" Hort called to the mercenaries, he
pointed toward the shore-line. "That's where
they'll beach it! Come on!"

He led their rush down the dock. He heard
rather than saw the nets scoop up its prey; a
cheer went up from the small boats. He was waiting waist-deep in the water when the Old Man's

boat finally reached the shallows. Grabbing onto the cleats, Hort dragged the boat to the beach as if it were a toy while his father sagged wearily between the oars.

"The trap," the Old Man wheezed through ragged gasps, "pull it in before those fools get it tangled in their nets!"

The rope was cold and hard as cable, but Hort dragged the trap hand-over-hand away from the sea's grip. Not surprisingly, it was full of Nya that shimmered and flopped in the morning sun. Without thinking, Hort reached behind his father and dumped the fish into the boat's live-well.

All the boats were ashore now, and there was splashing and thrashing around the net in the shallows.

"What is it like?" the Old Man gasped; he could scarcely raise his head. "What's the monster like?"

"It looks to be a large crab," Hort announced, craning his neck. "The mercenaries have got to it."

And they had; waving the crowd back they waded into the water to strike at the spidery giant even before the net was on the shore.

"I thought so," the Old Man nodded. "There weren't any teeth marks on the traps. Some damn sorceror's pet run loose," he added.

Hort nodded. Now that he could see the monster it fit the rumors he had heard from time to time in the town. The Purple Mage had kept large crabs to guard his home on the White Foal River. Rumor said he was dead now, killed by his own magic. The rumor was confirmed by the

crab; it must have wandered downstream to the
sea when its food no longer appeared.

"Whose catch is that?"

Hort turned to find two Hell-Hounds standing
close beside him. Simultaneously he noticed the
crowd of townsfolk which had gathered on the
streets.

"Everybody's," the Old Man declared, getting
his strength back. "They caught it. Or anybody's.
Maybe it's Terci's—it's mangled his net."

"No, Old Man," Terci declared, approaching
them. "It's your catch. There's none on the wharf
who'd deny that—least of all me. You caught it.
We netted and gaffed it for you after the fight."

"It's yours then," the Hell-Hound decided,
facing the Old Man. "What do you plan to do
with it?"

It flashed across Hort's mind that these soldiers might be going to fine his father for dragging the crab to the beach; they might call it a
public nuisance or something. He tightened his
grip on the Old Man's arm, but he'd never been
able to hold his father.

"I don't know," Panit shrugged. "If the circus
was still in town I'd try to sell it to them. Can't
sell it for food—might be poisonous—wouldn't
eat it myself."

"I'll buy it," the Hell-Hound announced to
their surprise. "The Prince has tasters and a taste
for the unknown. If it's poisonous it will still
make table-talk fit for an Emperor. I'll give you
five silvers for it."

"Five? Ten—times're hard; I've got debts to
Jubal for my fish-stall," the Old Man bargained,

no more awed by the Hell-Hounds than he had been by Jubal himself.

At the mention of the slaver's name, the tall Hell-Hound scowled and his swarthy companion sucked air noisily through his teeth.

"Jubal?" the tall man mumbled as he reached for his pouch.. "You'll have your ten silvers, fisherman—and a gold piece besides. A man should have more than a slaver's receipt for this day's work."

"Thankye," Panit nodded, accepting the coins. "Take your watch to the marshes and swamps; there's never one crab but there's ten. Corner'em on dry land an' Kitty-Kat'll eat crab for a month."

"Thanks for your information," the Hell-Hound grimaced. "We'll have the garrison look into it."

"Not a bad day's catch," the Old Man chortled after the retreating soldiers, "and Nya besides. I'll send two in luck-money to the blacksmith and the S'danzo and get new traps besides." He cocked his head at his son. "Well," he tossed the gold coin in the air and caught it again, "I've got this too, to add to your other gift."

"Other gift?" Hort frowned.

The smile fell from the Old Man's face like a mask. "Of course," he snarled. "Why do you think I went after that thing anyway?"

"For the other fishermen?" Hort offered. "To save the fishing ground?"

"Aye," Panit shook his head. "But in the main it was my gift to you; I wanted to teach you about pride."

"Pride?" Hort echoed blankly. "You risked your life to make me proud of you? I've always been proud of you! You're the best fisherman in Sanctuary!"

"Fool!" the Old Man exploded, rising to his feet. "Not what you think of me; what you think of yourself!"

"I don't understand," his son blurted. "You want me to be a fisherman like you?"

"No, no, no!" the Old Man leaped to the sand and started to march away, then returned to loom angrily over the youth. "Said it before—not everyone can be a fisherman. You're not—but be something, anything, and have pride in it. Don't be a scavenger, drifting from here to yon. Take a path and follow it. You've always had a smooth tongue—be a minstrel, or even a storyteller like Hakiem."

"Hakiem?" Hort bristled. "He's a beggar."

"He lives here. He's a good storyteller; his wealth's his pride. Whatever you do, wherever you go—take your pride. Be good with yourself and you'll be at home with the best of 'em. Take my gift, son; it's only advice, but you'll be the poorer without it." He tossed the gold coin to the sand at Hort's feet and stalked off.

Hort retrieved the coin and stared at the Old Man's back as he marched away.

"Excuse me, young sir?" Old Hakiem was skuttling along the beach, waving his arms frantically. "Was that the Old Man—the one who caught the monster?"

"That's him," Hort agreed, "but I don't think this is a good time to be talking to him."

"Do you know him?" the storyteller asked,

holding fast to Hort's arm. "Do you know what happened here? I'll pay you five coppers for the story." He was a beggar, but he didn't seem to starve.

"Keep your money, Hakiem," the youth murmured, watching the now-empty beach. "I'll give you the story."

"Eh?"

"Yes," Hort smiled, tossing his gold coin in the air, catching it and putting it in his pocket. "What's more, I'll buy you a cup of wine to go with it—but only if you'll teach me how to tell it."

THE VIVISECTIONIST

Andrew Offutt

A minaret topped the Governor's Palace, naturally. The narrow, eventually pointed dome resembled an elongated onion. Its needle-like spire thrust up to pierce the sky. That spire, naturally, flaunted a pennon. It bore the device of Imperial Ranke (*Ranket Imperatris*). Below, the dome was clamped by a circular wall like upended herbivorous teeth. If ever the palace were attacked, that crenelated wall promised, beware archers in the embrasures between the merlons! Beware dumpers of boiling oil.

Every bit of it was haughty and imperious, insultingly imperial. And high.

Even from the top of the (lower) wall of the granary across the avenue from the wall surrounding the Governor's Palace complex, no grapnel could be hurled, for no human was so strong.

An arrow, however, could be shot.

On a night when the moon over Sanctuary was not a maiden's pale round breast but a niggling little crescent hardly worthy of the business end of a scythe, a bow twanged like a dying lute. An arrow rushed at the pennon spire of the Governor's Palace. After it, like the web-trail of an industrious spider or a wind-blown tent caterpillar, sped a silken cord so slim as to be invisible.

And then it was laboriously and time-consumingly drawn and dragged back, for the archer had missed his shot.

He aimed anew, face set for curses rather than prayers. Elevating his bow a bit, he drew to the cheek and, daringly endangering the springy wood, drew even farther. Uttering not a prayer but a curse, he released. Away sped the arrow. It trailed its spidery line like a strand of spittle in the pallid moonlight.

It proved a night for the heeding of curses, if not the answering of prayers. That was appropriate and perhaps significant in Sanctuary called Thieves' World.

The shaft streaked past the spire and reached the end of its tether if not its velocity. It snapped back. The line forced it into a curving attempt to return. It snapped around the spire. Twice, thrice, four times. The archer was dragging hard. Keeping taut the silken line bought at the expense of a pair of lovely ear pendants of gold and amethyst and chrysoprase stolen from—never mind. The archer pulled his line, hard. That maintained and increased tension, tightened the arrow's whipping about the spire which was, naturally, gilded.

Then all motion ceased. A mourning dove spoke to the night, but no one believed that dolorous call presaged rain. Not in Sanctuary! Not at this time of year. The archer leaned into his line, and braced his heels to lean his full weight on it. The cord was a taut straight-edge of immobility and invisibility under the unimposing one-ninth moon.

Teeth flashed in the dimness. The archer's, standing atop the granary behind the Governor's Palace of Sanctuary. His mop of hair was blacker than shadowed night and his eyes nearly so, under brows that just missed meeting above a bridged nose that just missed being falcate.

He collected his other gear, collected himself, swallowed hard, choked up all he could on his line until he was straining, stretched, on tiptoe.

Then he thought something rather prayer-like, and out he swung.

Out above the street made broad enough to accommodate several big grain wagons abreast he swung, and across it. The looming wall rushed at him.

Even with the bending of his knees until they were nearly at his chest, the jar of his impact with the unyielding wall was enough to rattle teeth and turn prayers to curses. Nothing broke, neither legs nor silken line. Certainly not the wall, which was of stone, quarried and cut to form a barrier four feet thick.

He went up the rope in a reverse rappel, step after step and hand over hand. Dragging himself up the wall, walking up the fine perfectly set stones, climbing above death, for that was the penalty for slipping. The street was far below and farther with each pulling step.

He never considered that, or death, for he never considered the possibility of slipping.

A mighty warrior he was not. As an archer he had many peers and many betters. As a youth he was perfect, lean and wiry and strong. He was a highly competent thief in a citylet named for thieves. Not a cutpurse or a street-snatcher or an accoster; a thief. A burglar. As such, he was a superb climber of walls, without better and possibly without peer. He was good at slipping in by high-set windows, too.

His coloring and clothing were for the night, and shadows. They were old friends, he and shadows.

He did not slip. He ascended. He muscled himself atop the broad wall of the Governor's Palace, of Sanctuary. Unerringly, he stepped through the crenel, the embrasure between two merlons like blunt lower teeth. And he was at home, in shadow.

Now he gazed upon the palace itself; the palace of the golden prince sent out from Ranke to (pretend to) govern Sanctuary. The thief smiled, but with his mouth closed. Here there were tigers in the form of guards, and young teeth would flash even in this most wan of moonlight. That precaution was merely part of his competence.

At that, he had lived only about a score of years. He was not sure whether he was nineteen or twenty or a bit older. No one was sure, in this anile town the conquering Rankans called

Thieves' World. Perhaps his mother knew—
certainly not the father he had never known and
whom she had known casually, for this thief was
a bastard by birth and often, even usually, by
nature—but who knew who or where his mother
was?

Below, within the wall lay ancillary buildings
and a courtyard the size of a thoroughfare or a
small community common, and guards. Across,
just over there, rose the palace. Like him it was a
shadow, but it loomed far more imposing.

He had broken into it once before. Or rather he
had previously gained nocturnal entry in manner clandestine, for that other time he had help.
A gate had been left unlocked for him, and a door
ajar.

Entering that way was far easier and much
preferable to this. But that time the opener of the
gate had been bent on the public embarrassment
and downfall of the Governor, and the thief was
not.

Prince-Governor Kadakithis was no enemy, as
a matter of fact, to this youth spawned in the
shadows of the wrong end of town. The thief had
rendered the Rankan prince two considerable
services. He had been rewarded, too, although
not in such a manner that he could live happily
ever after.

Now, on this night of the most niggling of
crescent moons, he stood atop the wall and took
in his line from behind and below. It stretched
upward still, to the pennon-spire. It remained
taut. He had to believe that it would continue to
do. Elsewise he was about to splatter onto the
pave below like a dropped pomegranate, a fruit

whose pulp is plentiful and whose juice is red.

When the line was again taut he yanked, dragged, braced, yanked, swallowed hard, and kicked himself off the wall into space. His stomach fell two storeys to the pave; he did not. His soft-booted but padded feet struck another wall of cut fulvistone. Impact was no fun and he had to stifle his grunt.

Then he went up.

"D'jou hear something, Frax?" A voice like a horse-drawn sledge gliding over hard earth. Not stone, or sand, but packed dry earth.

"Mmm? Hm? Huh? Wha'?" A deeper voice.

"I said: Frax, did you hear something?"

Silence. (At sound of the voices the thief had frozen. Hands-forearms-torso atop the very palace; tail in space and legs adangle.)

"Uh-huh. I heard something, Purter. I heered her say 'Oh Frax you han'some dawg, you're the best. Now suck on thisun awhile, darling.' and then you woke me up, you bastard."

"We're supposed to be on guard duty not sleeping, Frax, damn it. —Who was she?"

"Not gonto tell you. No I din't hear nothing. What's to hear? An army of Downwinders comin' over the friggin' walls? Somebody riding in on a hootey-owl?"

"Oh," Purter's higher voice said, with a shiver in it. "Don't say that. It's dark and creepy enough tonight."

"Stuporstishus rectum," Frax accused, with more austerity than skill, and lowered his head again onto his uplifted knees.

During their exchange the thief had got his rangy self onto the wall. He made hardly any

sound, but those idiots would have drowned out
something even as loud as snapping fingers. He
wiggled through another embrasure and onto
the defense gallery that ran around the top of the
palace, below the dome and spire that rose on up,
higher than the outer wall. Men trusted with
guard duty, he was thinking contemptuously,
heard something and blabbered. He shook his
head. Idiots! He could teach these stupid soft-
butted "soldiers" a thing or three about security!
It took a civilian to know about the best security
measures, in such a town as this. For one thing,
when you thought you heard something, you
shut the hell up and listened. Then you made
just a little noise to pretend unconcern, and froze
to catch the noisemaker in another movement.

The shadow of a shadow, he moved along the
gallery, between the smooth curve of the dome
and the crenelations of a wall. After thirty-one
paces he heard the scuffing footsteps and tap-
tapping pikestaff butt of a careless sentry. That
persuaded him to squat, get as close to the wall as
he could, and lie down. Flat, facing the wall,
whose merlons rose above the gallery. He lay
perfectly still, a shadow in shadow.

A spider wandered over his shoulder and up
his cheek and began struggling in his black mop
of hair, and was unmolested. The spider felt
warmth, but no movement, not so much as a
twitch. (If mental curses could have effect, the
spider was a goner.)

The sentry ambled by, scuffing and tapping.
The thief heard him yawn. Dumb, he thought,
dumb. How nice it was of sentries to pace and
make noise, rather than be still and listen!

The sentry having moved on leftward along
the perimeter of the wall, the thief moved on
rightward; northwestward. He'd an armlet of
leather and copper well up his right upper arm,
and a long bracer of black leather on that wrist.
Each contained a nasty leaf-bladed throwing
knife of dull blue-black. There was another in his
left buskin, where sheath and hilt were mere
decoration. He wore no other weapons, none that
showed. Certainly he bore neither sword nor ax,
and the bow lay at the base of the granary wall.

. He stopped. Stepped into a crenel just above
two feet deep. Stared, off into the darkness. Yes.
There was the spire of the Temple of Holy Alles-
tina Ever Virgin, poor thing. It was the first of the
markers he had so carefully spotted and chosen,
this afternoon.

The thief did not intend to enter the palace by
just any window. He knew precisely where he
was going.

The task of regaining line and arrow was more
difficult than he had anticipated. He silenced
snarls and curses. Knot a rope ten times and try
swinging on it and the accursed thing might well
work itself loose. Shoot an arrow to wrap a cord
slimmer than a little finger around a damned
gilded brass flagpole, and he had to fight to get
the damned thing to let go!

Within four or six minutes (with silenced
snarls and curses) he had sent enough loops and
twitches ripple-writhing up the line to loosen
the arrow. It swung once around the spire, twice,
encountered the line, and caught. More curses, a
sort of prayer, and more twitches and ripples
riding up the line. Reluctantly the arrow ended

its loving embrace of the pennon spire. The line fluttered loose. Down came the arrow. It fell with a clatter that, to a shadowy thief in shadows, sounded like thunder on a cloudless day.

Sleepy sentries heard no thunder. Only he noticed. He reeled in line and arrow. In a crouch, he reached behind him into his snugly fitted backpack. From it he drew two cylinders of hardwood wrapped with black cloth. Around them he looped his line, arrow detached. He held silent for a time, listening. A fly hummed, restless and loud. The thief heard nothing to indicate that any of his actions had been noticed with anything approaching alarm.

Rising, he went on his way. Along the perimeter of the palace, along the flagged walkway betwixt dome and toothy wall.

Moving with a cat suppleness that would have been scary to any observer, he reached his second marker. Nicely framed between two merlons, he could see it, away off in the distance. The purple-black shape of Julavain's Hill. Again he smiled, tight of lip.

A merlon became a winch, aided by the two wooden cylinders brought for the purpose. They would pay out the silken cord and prevent the stone from slicing it. Its other end he secured to his ankles. And froze, waiting while the sentry clumped by. He was not importantly thumping his pike's butt, now. He no longer cared to keep himself awake. The thief gritted his teeth against the ghastly noise of the hardest of wood grating over harder flagstones. The porker was dragging his pike!

Then silence was thick enough to cut with a

knife, of which the thief owned an abundance.
He waited. And waited.

At last he stepped, still crouching, into the
crenel. Turning, he carefully winched himself,
backward, down the wall. Down and down, until
he came to a particular window. It was cut in the
shape of a diamond. That decision had involved
more than esthetics; the damned thing was
harder to enter.

Most carefully indeed, he turned. He paid out
the cord with his hands until he was quite upside
down outside that window. Blood flowed into
his head while he strained muscles and vision
until he was assured that the chamber was unin-
habited.

Then, grinning, Hanse the thief flipped down
and dropped lightly into the bedchamber of
H.R.H. Kadakithis, Prince-Governor of Sanctuary.

He had done it again! And this time all on his
own and without aid. He had breached the wall,
eluded the guards, broken into the palace, and
was in the very privatemost chamber of the
Prince-Governor himself!

*Well, lord Prince, you wanted to see
Shadowspawn—here he is, awaiting you!* Thus
he thought while he freed his ankles of expensive silken line and removed his gloves. At least
this time no bedmate waited here for her youthful lord.

It was all Hanse could do to keep from laughing aloud in sheerest prideful delight.

"A nice-looking girl left this here for you,
Hanse," Moonflower the Seer had told him. "She

got it from another—along with a coin for her trouble—who got it from still another."

Hanse raised his dark, dark brows and hooked a thumb in the shagreen belt he wore over a screamingly red sash. From one side of the belt was slung a dagger. An Ilbarsi knife, long as his whole arm, hung down his other leg.

"This you . . . *Saw*, Passionflower?"

She smiled, a hugely fat and grossly misnamed woman who overflowed two cushions atop a low stool. She saw him as a boyish boy and had ever let him turn her head with his charm, which she was almost alone in seeing.

"Oh no," Moonflower said almost archly, "I needed to go to no such trouble. I know things, you know."

"Oh, I know you know things, you clever darling," he told that gross dumpling in her several skirts, each of more than one unrepeated color. "And this time you're going to let me know how you know, I know."

She nodded at the wax-sealed walnut shell he was idly tossing in his left hand. "You know me too well, don't you, you naughty scamp! Smell it."

Up went his close-snuggling brows again, and he brought the shell to his nose. He rolled his eyes. "Aha! Perfume. A good one. Times are good for the only true mage of Sanctuary, then."

"You know that is not my perfume," she said, not without a sideward turn of her blue-tressed head to give him an arch look.

"*Now* I know that," Shadowspawn said, jocular and easygoing and almost cute in the sunlight, "because you tell me so. The walnut was

given you by a well-off girl wearing good perfume, then. Betwixt her breasts, I'll bet, where
she bore this charming charm."

She lifted a dimpled finger. "Ah! But that is
the point. The scent on that charm is not mine,
and the girl who gave it me wore none at all."

"Oh Moonflower, pride of the S'danzo and of
Sanctuary! By Ils if the P-G knew of your genius,
he'd not have that ugly old charlatan at court, but
you, only you! So. By the perfume you know that
there was a third woman, who gave this and a
coin to another to give to you to give to me." He
wagged his head. "What a game of roundabout!
But what makes you think this thing was given
her by still another, to begin with?"

"I saw the coin," Moonflower said, all kit-
tenish inside a body to block a door or bring
groans to a good steed.

"It bore still another scent?"

Moonflower laughed. "Ah Hanse, Hanse. I
know that. Soon you will know too, surely, once
you open the walnut shell. Surely it contains a
message from someone who wanted no one to
know he sent it to you."

"He?"

"Do you care to make a wager?"

He who was called Shadowspawn clutched
the walnut to him in mock terror. With his other
hand he clutched his purse theatrically. "Wager
with you about your wisdom? Never! No one has
accused me of being stupid." *Well, almost no
one,* he mentally added, thinking of that burly
strangel, Tempus the Hell Hound . . . Tempus
the . . . what?

"Be off with you and open it privily then.

You're standing between me and paying clients!"

There were none present, Hanse assured himself before he said, "In a moment," and thumbnailed the brownish wax along the lip-like closure of the walnut shell. He knew Moonflower was frowning, believing that he should be more secretive, but he also knew what he wanted to do. A gesture, merely a gesture. The scrap of extra fine leaf-paper he took out and poked, still folded, into his sash. Pressing the shell closed and thumbing the wax into a semblance of seal, he proffered it to the S'danzo seer who consistently proved that she was no charlatan.

"For Mignureal," he said, pretending shyness. "To scent her . . . her clothing, or something?"

For a moment the flicker of a frown appeared on Moonflower's doughy face, for her big-eyed daughter was quite taken with this dangerous youth from Downwind, whose means of income was no secret. Then she smiled and accepted the scented shell. It swiftly vanished into the vast cleavage of what she called her treasure chest, under her shawl.

"You're such a nice boy, Hanse. I'll give it to her. Now you git, and inspect your message. Maybe some highborn lady wants a bit of dalliance with your handsome self!"

The rangy young man called Shadowspawn had left her then. Smile and even pleasant expression left his face and he swaggered like a Mrsevadan gamecock. Face and walk were part of his image, which none would dare say might stem from insecurity. Still, Moonflower's words would not have made him smile anyhow. He was not handsome and knew it, as he knew that his height was no more than average. The biggest thing about him was his ego—although his lips, which some thought were sensuous, were to him too full. His nickname others had given him. He did not dislike it; his mentor Cudget Swearoath had told him a nickname was good to have— even such a one as "Swearoath." Hanse was just a name; *Shadowspawn* was dramatic, with a romantic and rather sinister sound that appealed to the youth.

He left Moonflower remembering how he had indeed dallied with a beauty of means. Highborn she was not, though she had been from the palace, and richly garbed. Hanse had been touched both in his ego and in his greed, by her attentions. Only later had he discovered that it was not truly he she was interested in. She and a fellow plotter were in the employ of someone back in Ranke—the emperor himself, perhaps envious or wary of Kidakithis's good looks?— who wanted to discredit and destroy the new Prince-Governor, him they called Kitty-cat. They had elected to use Hanse in their plot; Hanse had been their dupe! —for a while.

But that was done with, and on this later day he left Moonflower and swaggered along the streets. His eyes were hooded and the weapons all too obvious on him. Some stepped off the narrow planking of the sidewalk for him, and (quietly) cursed themselves for it. Still, they would do it again. In appearance, all tucked in behind his eyes and abristle with sharp blades, he was "about as pleasant as gout or dropsy," as a certain merchant had once described him.

Well, he was alive. Both the lovely plotter and her traitorous Hell-hound co-conspirator were not. Further, Kadakithis was grateful. And now, as Hanse discovered to his astonishment back in his quarters, the Prince-Governor had actually sent him a note!

Hanse recognized the seal and the scrawl at the bottom from other documents. Since Prince Kadakithis knew that Hanse could not read, the bit of fine paper contained not writing, but clever drawings. The Governor's seal, with a hand extending from it, beckoning to a dark splotch. It was man-shaped—a shadow. Under that was an untidy jumble of (turnip slices?) with straight lines raying up from them. Shadowspawn's frown was a momentary thing. Then he was nodding in comprehension—he hoped.

"The P-G wants me to come calling on him, and here's a promise of reward: shiny coins. He sealed up the message in the walnut shell and gave it to one of his harem, with instructions. No one should see Hanse the thief receive a message from the Prince-Governor, else Hanse's name become Plague and he be avoided the same. So that girl found another, and passed on the walnut and a coin, with her lord's instructions: 'Take this to Moonflower for Hanse.' "

And she had actually done it, without prying open the shell in an attempt to gain greater treasure than one coin! Well, miracles had happened before, Hanse mused, gazing pensively at the strange message. Had she opened the shell, she'd likely have discarded the note.

Or nervously pressed it back into the shell to

scuttle to Moonflower with it. *Maybe someone
does know that Hanse received a message that
shows a beckoning hand from the Rankan seal,
and a pile of coin. I hope she's the quiet sort! If I
knew who she is, I'd scare her into silence. But
then maybe she didn't open it at all . . .*

*The point is, I hate to walk into the palace, day
or night. How would that look? Me!*

*Besides, someone inside probably spies for
someone out here, and the word would be
passed. Hanse just walked right up and in, and
he was passed, too! Better watch him; maybe
he's a spy for that golden-haired Rankan boy in
the palace!*

And so Hanse had thought on that, and begun
to grin, and then to plan, and out he went to
reconnoiter and plan, and now he had broken in,
all unseen and unknown, to await his summoner
in the latter's own privy apartment!

And now, sitting there waiting, Hanse reflected and contemplated the more, and his face
clouded. The prickling in his arms started
slowly, and grew.

Unwittingly the tool of that pretty Lirain who
had so cleverly seduced or "seduced" him (with
no trouble at all!), he had gained this apartment
before, also by night and secretly. That time he
had stolen the very symbol of Rankan, power
that wand called the Savankh. Eventually all that
had turned out, and governor and thief reached
an understanding. By way of reward, Hanse was
granted pardon for all he might have done—once
he had assured the royal youth that he had never
slain. (He had, since. It afforded him little enjoyment or pride.) Hanse also came out of that

painful adventure with a nice little fortune. Unfortunately it was in two saddlebags currently reposing at the bottom of a well. He hoped those saddlebags were of good leather.

Now he had broken in here twice. This time he had proven that he could enter this apartment without help from inside or out. What then, when Kadakithis gave thought to that?

Hanse had respect for the youthful Rankan's mind. It even possessed a devious quality. Hanse had seen and felt proof of that, when as Kadakithis's unwilling agent he had participated in the ruin of the two plotters, Bourne and Lirain.

Suppose, the frowning Hanse mused, that Kadakithis pondered, and kept thinking.

There existed in Sanctuary one who could gain his chambers and thus his royal and gubernatorial self, at will. At any time, and never mind guards and sentries! Suppose that one chose to come again, as thief?—or was hired to do, as assassin? Would such a possibility not tend to prey on Kadakithis's good mind? Might he not decide that he was less than wise to trust him called Shadowspawn, a thief and ruthless besides? Might he not go even further in his thinking, and decide—wisely, as he would see it— that all things considered, Hanse was more dangerous than valuable?

In that case, the Prince-Governor might very well conclude, he and thus Sanctuary and thus Ranke were better off without such worries, such a possibility. In that event, it might occur to him that the world were better off without Hanse's continued presence in it. Nor would the world take heed of the timely demise of a cocky young thief.

Hanse swallowed, blinked. Sitting stiffly on a divan in the luxurious apartment, he put it all through his mind again and chased its tail. He came to his own conclusion.

I have been a fool. I did all this for my pride, to be such a clever fellow. I am a clever thief, but a stupid fellow! Being here thus when he comes in could gain me another signature on another document from him—this time my death-order! Oh damn plague and pox, what have I Done!?

Nothing, he thought as he rose with a great sigh, that could not be undone . . . he hoped. All he had to do was betake himself from here so that neither Kadakithis nor anyone else would ever know he had broken in. He glanced around and swallowed hard. It certainly was hard and against the grain not to steal something!

And so Shadowspawn went to the window, and wearily began the process of breaking out of the Governor's Palace and its grounds.

2

"It develops that I need help," Prince-Governor Kadakithis said, "and I cannot see a way to threaten it out of anyone."

"Including me?"

"Including you, Hanse. Furthermore, if you won't help, I can't see how I can punish you either."

"I'm glad to hear it. But I didn't know there were things a governor couldn't do, much less a prince."

"Well, Shadowspawn, now you know. Even Kittycat isn't all powerful."

"You need help and the Hell Hounds can't provide it?"

"That is close, Hanse. The *Imperial Elite Guardsmen* cannot help me with this. Or so I perceive it."

"I sure do wish you would sit down, Highness, so I can."

Kadakithis walked across the rich carpet of his privatemost chamber and sat on the edge of the peacock spread of his bed. He gestured. "Do take that divan, Hanse, or those cushions as it pleases you."

Hanse nodded his thanks. He sank among the cushions, curbing a grin at their luxury. Last night he had sat on the divan, and only he knew it. This day he chose the luxury of the jumble of stuffed Aurveshan silk. (Quag the Hell Hound had been on duty at the gate. He had recognized the hooded blind beggar, who winked at him. Having been secretly apprised that Hanse was invited, Quag conducted the blind beggar to His Highness. The hooded robe lay on the bed beside the prince now, who had congratulated Hanse on the cleverness of his entry. Hanse forbore to tell him how much more clever he had been last night.)

Now he decided that he could afford a modicum of daring: "Either I'm hearing sideways or you just told me you need me for something the

Hell Hounds I mean Imperial Elites can't do. Or
that your Highness can't trust them with? Or that
you don't want them to know about." Revela-
tion: "Or . . . something illegal?"

"I will not affirm or deny anything that you
have said." That said, the prince merely gazed at
him. The boy did a good job of looking enigmatic, Hanse mused, overlooking the fact that they
were about the same age.

"If the prince will forgive my saying it . . . his
Chief of Security is surely not one to balk at such
a . . . mission."

The prince continued to stare. One pale eyebrow rose slightly under that disgustingly handsome shock of yellow hair. And then Hanse was
staring.

"Tempus! It's *about* Tempus, isn't it! I haven't
seen him for weeks."

Kadakithis turned his gaze on an ornate
Yenizedish tapestry. "Hanse: neither have I."

"He is not on a mission for your Highness?"

"Just use the pronoun for me, Hanse, and we
can save whole days of our lives. No. He is not.
He is missing. Who might wish him to be missing?"

Hanse was wary of being used as informant,
but saw no reason not to answer that one. "Oh,
half the people in town. Maybe more. About the
same number that would wish the governor to be
missing. Your pardon of course, Governor. Or
the Emperor. Or Ranke."

"Hmm. Well, Empire is built on conquest, not
love, however often they are the same. But I have
striven to be decent here. Fair."

Hanse considered. "It is possible that you have been fairer than we might have expected."

"Nicely put. Carefully chosen words. You may well become a diplomat yet, Shadowspawn. And the *Hell Hounds*? What of them?"

Hanse smiled briefly at the slim noble's calling his elite guards by the people's name for them; indeed, even the Hell Hounds called themselves Hell Hounds these days. It was a dramatic name with a romantic and rather sinister sound that appealed to their sort.

"Shall I answer that, to one from Ranke, with all the power there is? What power have I?"

"You have influence with the Prince-Governor, Hanse, and with his Chief of Security. You uncovered the plot against me and helped break it up.[1] You regained that awful fear-rod, and it cost you.[2] Recently you helped Tempus in a matter, too. Now we are even in one area at least, aren't we?"

"Even? I? Me? Hanse of Sanctuary and the Emperor's brother?"

"Stepbrother," the prince corrected, and fixed Hanse with a wide-eyed gaze, all blue. It reminded Hanse of his own ingenuous pose. "Yes. Now we have both killed. I, Bourne. You . . . the night Tempus lost his horse."

"The Prince-Governor is not without knowledge," Hanse observed.

"Another careful, diplomat's phrasing! Now: Tempus set himself to destroying the minions of

1 In *Thieves' World*; Ace Books, 1979
2 In *Tales from the Vulgar Unicorn*; Ace Books, 1980

that Jubal fellow. Do you know why?"

"Maybe Tempus is a racist," Hanse said, trying to look wide-eyed and ingenuous.

It didn't appear to be working. Damn. This golden-locked boy was smarter than Moonflower, despite her extra-human ability. Hanse sighed. "You know. Jubal is a slaver and those weird-masked employees of his are feared. He has respect, and power. Tempus works for you, for Ranke's power."

"Let's don't go making wagers on that. Would you say his killing of those in the blue bird-masks might be called murder, Hanse?"

"It might if it was one of us," Hanse said, to the gleaming top of a low table. "Surely not for him that calls us Wrigglies, though."

The prince failed to disguise his little start. "Strong words, Hanse of Sanctuary. And to one who does not call the Children of Ils 'Wrigglies'!"

"Yes, and I really wish I hadn't said it. As a matter of fact I wish I wasn't here at all. How can I share confidences here? How can I say my mind to you, when you aren't a you, but both prince and governor?"

"Hanse: we have been through some things together."

In a manner of speaking, Hanse thought. You weren't poked with that damned terror-stick, and you didn't spend half the night down a well and the other on a torturer's table!

"I might even consider myself in your debt," Kadakithis went on.

"I am getting awfully uncomfortable, my lord

of Ranke," Hanse said elaborately. "Will my lord Prince tell me why I am here?"

"Damn!" Kadakithis regarded the carpet and heaved a great sigh. "I've an idea it would be a waste of time to offer you wine, my friend. So I—"

"*Friend!*"

"Why yes, Hanse," Kadakithis said, all large of eye and open-looking. "I call you friend. We are even of an age."

Hanse erupted to his feet in a jerk that was still admirably sinuous. He paced. "Oh," he said, and paced. "Oh gods, Prince—don't call me friend! Don't let anyone else hear that!"

The prince looked very much as if he wanted to touch him, and was sure that Hanse would shrink away. "How lonely we both are, Hanse. You *won't* have any friends, and I can't! I dare trust no one, and you who could trust—you reject even an extended hand."

Hanse was almost stricken. Friends? He thought of Cudget, dead Cudget. Of Moonflower. Of Tempus. Was Tempus a friend? Who could trust Tempus? Who could trust anyone wearing the title "governor?"

"Ranke and Sanctuary are not friends," he said slowly, quietly. "You are Ranke. I am of Sanctuary, and . . . more. Not, uh, noble."

"Trusted friend of the governor? The thief Shadowspawn?"

Hanse caught himself about to say "Thief? Who, me, Governor?" and stopped the words. Kadakithis knew. Nor was he Moonflower or that melon-peddler Irohunda, to be taken in by

Hanse's cultivated (and seldom used) boyish act.
But . . . *friend?* It was a frightening word, to
Shadowspawn from Downwind and the Maze.

"Let's try to be bigger than Ranke and
Sanctuary. Let's *try,* Hanse. I am reaching out.
Speaking plainly: Tempus declared war on
Jubal—*not on my orders*—and Jubal retaliated or
tried to. You were there and you didn't run.
Tempus lost a horse and gained a friend. You
defended Tempus, helped him. More
Hawkmasks died. Are you in danger for that,
from Jubal?"

"Probably. I've been trying not to think about
that."

"And me?"

"The Empire's governor in Sanctuary knows
to go forth armed and with guards, because he is
governor," Hanse said, not so enigmatically.

"Diplomatic, careful words again! —And
Tempus?"

It was then that Hanse knew why he was here.
"You . . . you think Jubal has Tempus!"

The prince regarded him. "Hanse, some
people don't try to be particularly likable. Tempus seems to try *not* to be. I cannot imagine
calling him friend." Kadakithis paused to be certain Hanse grasped his implication. "Still, I rep-
resent the Empire. I govern for Ranke, subject to
the Emperor, Tempus serves and represents me,
and Ranke. I do not have to love him, or like him.
But! How can I tolerate anyone's taking action
against any of my people?" Kadakithis made a
two-handed gesture while Hanse thought: *How
strange that I think more of Tempus—Thales—
than the Prince-Governor he serves!* "I cannot,

Hanse! Nor can I use the Hell Hounds to investigate, not in a really sensitive matter such as this. Nor can I launch attack on Jubal, or even arrest him—not and govern the way I wish to do."

He really does want to do well, to be friends with Sanctuary! What a strange Rankan! "You could call him in for questioning." Hanse was hopeful.

"I had rather not." The young Rankan called Kittycat shot to his feet with admirable use of legs alone, if not with a thief's sinuous grace. "I had rather acknowledge his existence, can you see that?" He waved a hand in a rustle of aquamarine silk sleeve, took a pace, turned his earnest face on Hanse. "I am governor here. I am Empire. He is—"

"Gods, Prince, I'm only a damned thief!"

Kadakithis frowned and glanced around, ignoring Hanse's look of horror at his blurted words. "Did you hear someone say something, just then?"

"No."

"Neither did I. As I was saying. Tempus doesn't mean that much to me and I don't mean that much to Tempus. Tempus, I fear, serves Tempus and whatever he fancies is his destiny. I might not even miss him. Still, there are some things I dare not allow, dare not tolerate. Oh how I wish you could understand a bit of how difficult it is, being born royal, and holding this job!"

Hanse, who had never held any job, tried. And without trying, he looked earnest and sympathetic. With a prince!

"Now I think that you are Tempus's friend,

Hanse. Would Jubal torture him?"

Hanse felt himself about to develop a taste for strong drink. Looking at the other very young man's sash—an Ilsigi sash—he nodded. Abruptly he wanted to curse. Instead he felt an unwonted and unwanted prayer come catsidling into his mind: *O Ils, god of my people and father of Shalpa my patron! It is true that Tempus-Thales serves Vashanka Tenslayer. But help us, help us both, Lord Ils, and I swear to do all I can to destroy Vashanka Sister-wifer or drive him hence, if only You will show me the way!*

And Hanse blinked, and hurled that ridiculous and unwelcome thought bodily from his mind. Prayers indeed!

"Hanse . . . consider the limits to my power. I am not a man named Kadakithis; I am governor. I *cannot* do anything about it. I cannot."

Hanse looked up to meet those cerulean eyes. "Prince, if someone broke in here to kill you right now, I'd probably defend you. But I would not try to sneak into Jubal's keep for half your fortune and all your women."

"Alone against Jubal? Lord, neither would I!" Kadakithis came to him then, and laid hands on a thief's shoulders. His eyes were intense and large. "My only request of you, Hanse, is . . . I just wish you'd agree to try to learn where Tempus is. That's all. Your way, Hanse, and for a lot less reward than half my fortune and the women I brought here."

Hanse backed from under those hands, from those staring eyes so full of sincerity. He paced to the bed, and the hooded robe of a blind beggar.

"I wish to leave by the fourth window down, Prince. That way I can let myself onto the roof of your smokehouse. If you were to call in your sentinels for review, I'd be out of here by the time they reached your presence."

Kadakithis nodded. "And?"

"And I—I don't want any reward but don't dare ever tell anyone I said that, or remind me! You'll hear from me—" he whirled and skewered the other very young man with a gaze like an accusation—"*friend.*"

Kadakithis was wise enough to nod without smile or comment. Besides, he looked more as if he wanted to cry, or reach out.

"I understand your reason, Hanse. But, are you sure you can manage to break out of here . . . the *palace*?"

Hanse turned away to roll his eyes. "With your help, Prince I *may* be able to do it. I'd hate to have to try to break *in*, though!"

3

It might have taken a trained investigator from Ranke a week, or a lifetime. It might have taken a Hell Hound a month or two lifetimes (a Tempus lifetime?), or a couple of days with the aid of shining ugly instruments of suasion. It took a thief of Sanctuary less than a full day to collect the information. Had he had letters, he'd have made a list.

Since he was unlettered, he must reckon and account in his head, once he had talked with this one and that one and some others. Only one

realized that he was actively seeking information, and that was because Hanse let her know.
Now he made his list, in his head, while he
sprawled on his own bed and stared at nothing in
particular.

Tempus did not get on with the other Hell
Hounds.

Tempus waged private war on Jubal. It was his
own decision. (Not a good one; Jubal's business
profited Thieves' World and Empire as well.)

Jubal was a merchant who dealt in human
merchandise. He provided some few to that
scrawny Kurd fellow of whom even hardened
Sanctuarites spoke susurrantly and with glances
cast uncomfortably this way and that.

In the barracks, Tempus had had serious trouble with Razkuli and that snarly-growly Zalbar.
(Quag had mentioned that to a certain woman
under the most intimate of circumstances. A bad
but common time for the imparting of confidences.)

Stulwig Northborn had spent a shining coin
bearing the Emperor's likeness. Such coinage
was not all that common here, although it was
welcome. People of the governor's staff occasionally spent such coins. Likely then someone
had bought something of Stulwig; someone from
the palace. Stulwig dealt in potions and drugs
and worse.

Harmocohl Dripnose had most recently seen
two men conveying a sizable burden to the
lovely gardened home of Kurd. Harmocohl's impression was that the two were hood-cloaked
Hell Hounds.

Hell Hounds were elite Imperial guardsmen

and did not deal with such as Stulwig or Kurd.
Indeed, at least one of them hated Kurd. Hardly
likely that Hell Hounds would deliver a human
package to him. Unless there was someone they
hated more than the dark experimenter.

Tempus was missing.

The word was out that Jubal heroically sold no
more human merchandise to Kurd the vivisectionist . . . a man with a Rankan accent.

Why would such as Jubal cut off such a source
of revenue? For moral reasons, because Kurd did
evil things to people? Hardly. Because Jubal had
made a deal with other enemies of Tempus? Zalbar and Razkuli, perhaps? Because Tempus was
now in the mysterious experimenter's foul and
reeking hands, perhaps?

In an ugly dark stenchy room Hanse learned
more of Kurd and his business. Kurd claimed to
be dedicated to the god Science. Medicine. That
required experimentation. But Kurd was not
content to experiment with the wounded and
victims of accidents. The pallid fellow created
his own. And, Hanse thought with rather more
than distaste, Kurd could occupy himself for a
lifetime with one whose wounds—Hanse suspected and thought he knew—healed with in-
human speed and completeness. Make that
superhuman, or preternatural. Tempus-call-
me-Thales was a man of war who had participated in many battles. Yet there were no scars on
the man. Not one.

Tempus/Thales.

"You, I own, can call me anytime," he had told
Hanse, and "my friend," he had called Hanse,
and "Just tell me not to call you friend," he had

dared Hanse. And Hanse had not been able to tell
him that, thus revealing and silently replying
that he was close onto desperate for friends, a
friend; for someone to care about him. For someone to care about.

Hanse sprawled supine on his bed in an upstairs room in the heart of the Maze, and he
pondered what he had learned. He rose to pace
and chew his full lower lip and ponder, with his
soul and heart and longing all naked in his eyes
so that it was good no one was there to see, for
Hanse wanted others to see only what he deliberately projected.

*All I need do is report all this to Kitt—to
Kadakithis*, he thought. The Prince-Governor
who had begun his term here by announcing that
there would be law and order and safety for citizens and had hanged, among others, one Cudget
Swearoath, mentor (and father image?) to Hanse.
The P-G did not like Tempus (and father image?)
to Hanse.

It was all Hanse need do. Just report what he
had learned and now suspected. Then it was up
to Kadakithis. He had the power and the re-
sources. The men and the swords. The savankh.

Surely that was as far as Hanse's responsibility
extended, to Kadakithis and to Tempus. If he had
any responsibility to that krff-snorting bully.

And . . . suppose H.R.H. Kadakithis, P-G, did
nothing? Or if his Hell Hounds, the charming
Razkuli and Zalbar, received their orders but
only pretended to act. Did not Rankans protect
their own? Did not soldiers obey authority? Was
there not honor among those thieving over-
Lords?

If not, then Hanse's world would be a-teeter.
Despite his pretenses there had to be trust and
some sort of order, didn't there, and trustworthi-
ness? Hanse frowned and looked about almost
wildly. An animal in a cage it feared but could
not escape, yet also feared what lay beyond the
bars. Even the spawn of shadows did not want to
live in a world that askew and a-teeter. If it
existed, if the world was truly a thing of Chance
and Chaos, he preferred not to know. Fighting it,
he had learned to trust Tempus. He had been
forced to trust Kadakithis, because he was down
a well up at Eaglenest. Later, disbelieving and
resisting, he had learned that he *could* trust the
Rankan. That disturbed his haven of cynicism
and was hard to admit. But was not cynicism
merely a mask on an idealist seeking more, seeking perfection, seeking disproof of his cynical
assumptions?

*Far better just to report what I know and leave
it at that and go on about my business.* That
would be enough. Tempus already owed him a
debt, anyhow, and had promised him a service.

Shadowspawn began collecting his materials
for a night of stealth, of breaking and entering. It
was a thief's business and these were the tools.
Yet he knew that he was not preparing for theft.

You are a fool, Hanse, he told himself with a
curse in Shalpa's name, and he agreed. And he
continued with what he was doing.

At the door he stopped, blinking. He looked
back with a frown. Only now did he remember
the look Mignureal had given him just two hours
ago, and her strange words. They meant nothing
and connected to nothing. "Oh, Hanse," she had

said with a strange intensity on her girlish face.
"Hanse—take the crossed brown pot with you."

"With me where?"

But she had to flee, for her glowering mother
was calling.

Now Hanse stared at the brown crock with the
etched pair of X's. Mignureal did not know about
it. She could not. Mignureal had mentioned it
specifically! She was Moonflower's daughter
. . . Name of the Shadowed One, she must have
some of the power too!

Hanse turned back to pick up that well-
stoppered container, a fired pot a bit larger than a
soldier's canteen. *Why, Mignureal? Why, Lord
Ils?*

He had acquired it months ago, easily and
quickly, without knowing what it contained.
Mignureal had never seen it and could not know
about this container of quicklime. She could not
know where he was going this night for he had
only just decided (and that without quite admit-
ting it to himself); she was Moonflower's daughter . . .

Stupid, cumbersome, senseless, he thought
while he slipped the crock into a good oilskin
bag he had lifted in the bazaar. He secured it to
his belt so that it rested high on one buttock. And
he touched the sandal of Thufir tacked above the
door, and went forth.

The white blaze of the sun had hours since
become yellow in its daily waning, and then
orange. Now it quatted low and seemed to spray
streamers of crimson across the darkening sky. It
did not look at all like blood, Hanse told himself.

Besides, soon it would be dark and his friends would be everywhere, in black and indigo and charcoal. The shadows.

I could use a good sword, the shadow thought, blending into another shadow. An eerie feeling still lay on him, from that business with Mignureal. Surely not even Kurd deserved quicklime! *This long "knife" from the Ilbarsi Hills is a good tool,* he thought, to keep his mind on sensible, practical matters. *But it's time I had a good sword.*

I'll have to try and steal one.

"Thou shalt have a sword," a voice said sonorously inside his head, a lion within the shadowed corridors of his mind, *"if thou free'st my valued and loyal ally. Aye, and a fine sheath for it, as well. In silver!"*

Hanse stopped. He was still and dark as the shadow of a tree or a wall of stone. He was good at it; six minutes ago four cautious people had passed close enough to touch him, and never knew he was there.

I want nothing of you, incestuous god of Ranke, he thought, almost speaking while a thousand ants seemed at play along his spine. *Tempus serves you. I do not and will not.*

Yet you do this night, seeking him, that silent voice that was surely the god Vashanka's said. And a cloud ate the moon.

No! I serve—I mean . . . I do not . . . No! . . . Tempus is my . . . my . . . I go to aid a fr—man who might help me! Leave me and go to him, jealous god of Ranke! Leave Sanctuary to my

patron Shalpa the Swift, and Our Lord Ils. Ils, Ils
O Lord of a Thousand Eyes, why is it not You
who speaks to me?

There was no reply. Clouds rolled and they
seemed dark men astride dark horses that loped
with manes and long tails aflow. Hanse felt a
sudden chill absence of that presence in his
mind. In a few seconds he was praying not to
gods but cursing himself for giving heed to the
delusions of a dark night, a night badly ruled by a
moon pale as a Rankan concubine and now covered like the whore she was. The Swift-footed
One ruled this night.

And Hanse went on, not in shadows now for
there were no shadows; all the land was one vast
shadow. Out of Sanctuary. Past lovers who
neither saw nor heard this son of Shalpa the
Shadowed One. On, to the beautifully tended
gardens surrounding the house of a pasty-faced
walking skeleton called Kurd and worse. The
little crescent of moon pretended to return. It
was only a ghost struggling weakly against
clouds like restless shadows blotting the sky.

The well-tended, scented gardens provided a
pleasant if unneeded cover. A gliding anthro-
pomorphic shadow amid herbaceous shapes
like looming shadows. Hanse went right up to
the house. It too was dark.

No one wants to visit Kurd. No one considers
trying to steal from Kurd. Why should it not be
easy, then? Kurd must think he needs no precau-
tions or defenders!

Still, he kept his lips over his teeth when he
smiled. He glided into the fragrant shrubs, odd
deciduous shrubs with long thin branchlets, set

up close against Kurd's house exulting in how simple it was, and then the bush's trailing tendrils moved, rustling, and turned, and twined, and clutched. And clamped. And Shadowspawn understood then that Kurd was not without exterior defenses.

Even as he struggled—fruitlessly, against frutescence—he knew that the knowledge was gained too late. Whether this thing was bent on strangling him or twisting his limbs until they broke or merely holding him until someone came, it was more horribly effective than human guards or three watchdogs. Amid silent rustling horror Hanse tugged at the tendril more slender than a brooch-pin, and only cut his fingers. His knife he only dulled, sawing at a purposeful tendril that gave but refused to be cut. And they moved, twining, rustling, insinuating themselves between his arms and body and around his legs and arms and torso and—throat!

That one he fought until his fingers bled. It was relentless. *O ye gods, no, no, not like this—* he was going to die, silently strangled by a damned skinny plant's tendril!

He was, too. His "N—" disposed of his last breath. He could not draw another. As his eyes started to bulge and a dull hum commenced to invade his ears on the way to becoming a roar and then eternal silence, it occurred to him that Kurd's garden could do more than strangle him. If it continued to tighten, it would slice in and in until it beheaded a strangled corpse.

Hanse fought with all his strength and the added power of desperation. As well have resisted the tide, or the sand of the desert. His movements became more restricted as his limbs were more and more constricted. Dizziness began to build like storm clouds and the hum rose to the roar of a gale.

So did the clouds above, and great big drops of water commenced to fall from the laden sky. That was just as eerie and impossible, for rain in Sanctuary fell in accord with the season, and this was not that season. The land was weeks away from the time called Lizard Summer, when lizards fried or were said to fry in their own juices, out on the desert.

What matter? Plants loved rain. And this one loved to kill. And it was killing Hanse, who was losing consciousness and feeling while his hearing became restricted to the roar inside his head. More rain fell and Hanse, dying, tried to swallow and could not and did what he thought he could never do: he began to give up.

Memory came like a white flash of late summer lightning. He heard her words as clearly as he had hours ago. *"Hanse—take the crossed brown pot with you."*

Even that blazing flare of hope seemed too late, for how could his bound arms detach the bag from his belt, open it, open the crock inside, and give this predatory plant a message it might understand?

Answer: he could not.

He could, however, dying, jerk his forearm four or five inches. He did, again and again, breathless, dying, losing consciousness but still moving, puncturing the leather bag again and again and banging the point of his knife off the pot which was smooth, glazed, well made, and O damn it all too damned *hard!*

It broke. Shards punched through knife holes and widened them to let quicklime spill down in a candent stream. Hanse was sure it hissed in the moist grass about the moist base of the strangler plant—but Hanse could not hear that hissing or anything else save the roar of a surf more powerful than life could withstand.

He slumped, dead now with streamers of caustic stream rising above his legs—and a suddenly frenetic shrub began waving and snapping its tendrils about as if caught by the very Compass Bag itself, whence issues the wind of every direction at once. In those whipping throes it not only released its prey, it hurled him several feet backward. He lay sprawled, away from the plant and clear of the smoking corrosive death about its base, and the soles of his buskins smoked. Rain pelted his face and he lay still, still, while the killer plant died.

It was not raining in Sanctuary but out of a clear night sky came a sizzling bolt that hardly rocked the structure that grounded it. The graven name VASHANKA, *however, abruptly disappeared from the facade of that structure, which was the Governor's Palace.*

4

Oh damn, but my damned head aches!
Pox and plague, that's rain on my face and I'm getting soaked!

Holy cess—I'm alive!

None of those thoughts prompted Hanse to move, not for a longish while. Then he tried opening his mouth to let rain assuage a sore throat, and choked on the fifth or sixth drop. He sat up hurriedly. His grunt was not from his head, which felt fat and swollen and stuffed to bursting. He rolled swiftly leftward off a source of sharper pain. He had been lying on his back. Under him, thonged to his belt, had been the ruins of a nice leathern bag of broken pottery.

If I don't bleed to death I'll be picking pieces of pottery out of my tail for a week!

That thought made him angry and with a low groan he rose to glare triumphantly on the faintly smoking remnant of a destroyed shrub. Its neighbor looked almost as bad. Shadowspawn took no chances with it. Avoiding shrubs and indeed anything herbaceous that was larger than a blade of grass, he went to the nearest window. Just as he completed his slow slicing of the sheet of pig's bladder stretched over the opening, he heard the awful sound from within. A groan, long and wavery and hideous. Hanse went all over gooseflesh and considered heading for home.

He did not. He peeled aside the ruined window and peered into a dark room containing neither bed nor person. Mindful of his punctured and lacerated buttock, he went in. There was nothing to do about his head. He had, after all, been strangled to death. Or come so close that the difference wasn't worth considering—save that he was alive, which was absolutely all the difference that mattered.

After a long measured while of standing frozen, listening, staring in effort to make his eyes see, he moved. He heard nothing. No groan, no movement, no rain. The moon was back. It was not in line with the window, but it was up there and a little light sneaked in to aid a thief.

He found a wall, a jamb. Squatted, then went lower, wincing at rearward pain, to ensure that no light showed under the door. The latch was a simple press-down hook. He took his time depressing it. He took more time in slowly, slowly pulling open the door. It revealed a corridor or short hall.

While he wondered whether to go right or leftward, that ghastly sound of agony came again. This time a pulpy mumble underlay the moaning groan, and once again Hanse felt the icy, antsy touch of gooseflesh.

The sound came from his right. He slipped his knife back into its sheath, patted other sheathed knives, and undid the thong at his belt to get the bag off. That hurt, as a shard of pottery emerged from his clothing, and him. That hand he moved very slowly, mindful of the clink of broken pottery. He squinted before he glanced back, because he did not want his enlarged pupils to shrink.

The window showed a pretty night, small-mooned but dark of sky, without clouds or rain. Without even knowing that the rain had been confined to Kurd's grounds, Shadowspawn shivered. Did gods exist? Did gods help?

Hanse took a long step into the corridor and turned right. The bag swung at the end of its thong from his right hand. Just in case someone

popped up, that might make him look less
deadly: anyone sensible would assume him to be
normally right-handed.

As he reached the end of the hall with a big
door ahead and another on his left, someone
popped up. The side door opened and light
rushed forth. It flared from the oil lamp in the
hand of a gnome-like man who wore only a long
ungirt tunic; a nightshirt.

"Here—" he began and Hanse said "Here
yourself" and hit him with the wet, rent bag of
broken pottery. Since it struck the fellow in the
face, he moaned and let go the lamp to rush both
hands to his bloodied face. "Damn," Hanse said,
watching hot oil slosh onto the man's tunic and
bare legs and feet. It also splashed wall and door
and ran along the floor, burning. At the same
time, a third groan of unendurable agony rose
behind the other door, the big one still closed.

"Master!" Hanse screeched, high-voiced.
"FIRE!" And he shoved the squatty fellow backward, kicked the burning lamp in after him, and
yanked the door shut. Instantly he attacked the
other one, and soon entered Hell.

Part of a man lay on a table, a short skinny
fellow. He was even shorter and skinnier now,
bereft of both legs and both arms, all his hair, and
his left nipple with part of the pectoral. Even as
Hanse shuddered, he knew there was only one
form of rescue for this wretch. Ignoring the shining sharp instruments Kurd used, Hanse drew
the arm-long blade those crazies up in the Ilbars
Hills called a knife, got his best two-handed grip,
and struck with all his might. Blood gushed and
Hanse clamped his teeth against vomit. He had

to strike again to complete the job. Now only a
torso lay on the table, and a shuddering
Shadowspawn clung to the weapon as he
squinted around a chamber full of tables and
thoughtfully provided with graded runnels in
the floor, for the carrying off of blood.

"Thales?"

Two groans replied. One of them ended with
"help," weak as a kitten. It was not Tempus's
voice, but Hanse went to that table.

"He—he—he's cut off my right arm and . . .
and three fingers of my my l-l-le-eft hannnd . . .
just to . . . just to . . ." An enormous bodyshak-
ing shudder refused to let the man finish.

"You do not bleed. Your legs? Feet?" Hanse
was squinting without really wanting to see.

"I—I—they . . . there . . ."

"Think," Shadowspawn said, swallowing
hard. "I can cut these straps or your throat.
Think, and choose." He started to turn away.

"I am . . . ali-i-ive . . . I can wa-a-alk . . ."

Hanse sliced off the man's restraining straps.
"I seek Tempus."

"You seek death here, thief!" a voice said, and
light flooded the chamber.

Hanse didn't pause to reply or look to see who
bore the light. He turned, plucking forth a guard-
less knife like a leaf of steel, and threw. Only
then did he really look at the man in the doorway; throw once to disconcert, the second time
with aim. Lean and more than lean the man was,
pallid skin taut. A man in a voluminous nightshirt, a man to get a chill from a south wind in
June. A man who held a cocked crossbow in one
hand, awkwardly, and a closed lamp or lanthorn

in the other, sleeve sliding back to show an arm
of bone plated with parchment. Kurd.

He was ducking the whizzing knife that
missed by several inches. The lanthorn swung
wildly, splashing lunatic flashes of yellow light
off walls and floor and tables with ghastly stains.
The doke should have put the light down first,
Hanse thought, plucking out another sliver of
sharp steel. With both hands on that little
crossbow Kurd might be dangerous. Instead his
arm was nailed to the door by a knife that caught
cloth but only raked skin—there was no flesh—
so that the monster cried out more in fear than in
pain. The crossbow hit the floor, thunked, and
sent its bolt thunk-twanging into a wall or a table
leg or—Hanse didn't care.

"I'm here for Tempus, butcher. Just stand there
and provide light. Move and I'll throw again."
He showed Kurd a third bright blade, sheathed
it. "You'd look good with another navel, anyhow." Then he went to the source of the third
groan. "Oh, oh gods, oh, oh gods why is this
allowed?"

No god answered the anguished query torn
from Shadowspawn by the sight of Tempus.

Big blond Tempus answered, scarless and
armless, and the answer came from a mouth
without a tongue. He managed to make Hanse
understand that three pins were stuck into each
stump. Hanse steeled himself to pull them out
before turning to gush vomit onto the grooved
floor of Kurd's laboratory of torment, and
whirled back to send such a glare at the vivisectionist that Kurd shivered and stood still as a
statue, lanthorn held high.

Hanse cut Tempus loose and helped him sit up. The big man did not bleed. He bore various cuts, all of which looked old. They were not. He made stomach- and heart-wrenching sounds, ghastly noises that Hanse interpreted as *"I'll heal,"* which was just as ghastly. What *was* this man?

"Can you walk?"

More noises. Repeated. Again. Hanse thought he understood, and bent to look. Yes. Minus some toes, Tempus had said. He was. Three. No, four. The middle one was gone from the left foot.

"Thales, there's only me and I can't carry you. I freed another and he can't help. What shall I do?"

It took Tempus a long while to make him understand, trying to form words without a tongue, and once Kurd moved. Hanse turned to see the other freed wretch fleeing past the vivisectionist. Hanse threatened and Kurd froze. He held the lantern in a quivering hand at the end of a wavering arm.

Strap Kurd to a table, Tempus had said. *Where's servant?*

Kurd answered that one, once he had a knife at his flat gut. His gardener and sole retainer was unconscious.

"Oh," Hanse said, "he'll want to be bound, then," and worked the blade out of sleeve and door. With a knife in either hand, he gestured. "Hang the lanthorn."

"You can't—"

Hanse poked him with sharp steel. "I can. Run complain to the Prince-Governor as soon as you can. You can also die now, which would be a shame. But I'll try to stick you in the belly, low, just deep enough so you'll be a day or three about dying. Of gangrene, maybe. *Hang that lanthorn, monster!*"

Kurd did, on the hook that was, naturally enough, beside the door. He turned to meet Hanse's foot driving straight up between his skinny shanks. It impacted with a jar.

"Something for your balls, if you have one," Hanse said, and didn't even glance at the man who sank all bulge-eyed and gasping to his knees, with both hands in the predictable position. Hanse hurried to where the gardener lay, not even covered by the blanket his master had used to smother the fire. By the time Hanse finished trussing him with strips of his nightshirt, the gnomish fellow would starve before he freed himself.

Minutes later his master was strapped to one of his own tables. Hanse gagged him, because Kurd had left off threatening to plead and make the most ridiculous promises. Hanse returned to Tempus.

"They couldn't get loose for a roomful of gold, Thales. Now how in the name of every god am I to get you out of here and back to town, friend?"

Tempus required five minutes and more to make himself understood. *Don't. Lay me back. I'll heal. The toes first. Tomorrow I'll be able to walk. Wine?*

Hanse laid him back. Hanse fetched wine and blankets and some sort of gruelly pudding. Knowing that Tempus hated his helplessness, Hanse fed him, helped him guzzle about a gallon of wine, arranged him, covered him, checked

Kurd and his servant, made sure the house was locked, and roamed it.

Surgeon's tools, a bag of coins, and a pile of bedding he piled outside the door to the chamber of scientific experimentation. He would not lie in a monster's bed, or on one of those tables! He slept, at last, on the floor. On bedding from the gardener's chamber, not Kurd's. He wanted nothing of Kurd's.

Valuable knives and the bag of money were different.

He awoke at dawn, looked in on three sleeping men, marveled, and left that place that was nine times more horrible by day. He found a sausage, considered, and chose flatbread instead. Only the gods and Kurd knew what sort of meat comprised that sausage. In a shed Hanse found a cart and a mule. He had to do some chopping and some sweating. At last he got Tempus out of the ruined house and into the cart padded with hay. Hanse covered him amid shudders. Tempus's cuts looked days older, nearly healed.

"Would you like a few fingers or nose or something of Kurd to accompany you out of here, Thales?"

Almost, Tempus frowned. " 'O," he said, and Hanse knew it was a no. "You want to, uh, leave them for . . . later?" Tempus's reply was almost a yes, for me.

Hanse got him out of there. He used much of Kurd's money to buy the place and services of a tongueless, nearly blind old woman, along with some soft food, wine, blankets and cloak, and he went away from them with a few coins and hideous memories. The coins bought him expensive treatment from a leech who dared not chuckle or comment as he cleaned and bandaged a buttock with multiple lacerations, which he said would heal beautifully.

After that Hanse was sick in his room for the better part of a week. The remaining three coins bought him anesthetic in the form of strong drink.

For another week he feared that he would encounter Tempus on the street or someplace, but he did not. After that, amid rumors of some sort of insurrection somewhere near, he began to fear that he would never see Tempus, and then of course he did see him. Healed and scarless. Hanse went home and threw up.

He traded a few things for more strong drink, and he got drunk and stayed that way for awhile. He just didn't feel like stealing, or facing Tempus, or Kadakithis either. He did dream, of two gods and a girl of sixteen or so. Ils and Shalpa and Mignureal. And quicklime.

THE RHINOCEROS
AND THE UNICORN

Diana L. Paxson

"So why did you come back?" Gilla's shrill
retort interrupted Lalo's attempts to explain why
he had not been home the night before. "Has
every tavern in Sanctuary shown you the door?"
She planted her fists on her spreading hips, the
meaty flesh on her upper arms quivering below
the short sleeves of her shift, and glared at him.

Lalo stepped backwards, caught his heel on
the leg of his easel, and clattered to the floor in a
tangle of splintering wood and skinny limbs.
The baby began to cry. While Lalo gasped for
breath, Gilla took a long stride to the cradle and
clutched the child to her breasts, patting him
soothingly. Echoes of their older children's
quarrels with their playmates drifted from the

street below, mingling with the clatter of a cart
and the calls of vendors hawking their wares in
the Bazaar.

"Now see what you've done!" said Gilla when
the baby had quieted. "Isn't it enough that you
bring home no bread? If you can't earn an honest
living painting, why don't you turn to thievery
like everyone else in this dungheap of a town?"
Her face, reddened by anger and the heat of the
day, swam above him like a mask of the demon-
goddess Dyareela at Festival time.

At least I have that much honor left! Lalo bit
back the words, remembering times, when one of
his merchant patrons had refused to pay, that the
limner had let fall the location of rich pickings
while drinking in the Vulgar Unicorn. And if,
thereafter, one of his less reputable acquaintances chose to share with him a few anonymous
coins, surely honor did not require him to ask
whence they came.

No, it had not been honor that kept him honest,
thought Lalo bitterly, but fear of bringing shame
to Gilla and the children, and a rapidly de-
teriorating belief in his own artistic destiny.

He struggled up on one elbow, for the moment
too dispirited to stand. Gilla sniffed in exasperation, laid down the child and stalked to the other
end of the single room in the tenement which
served as kitchen and chamber for the family,
and, too rarely, as the painter's studio.

The three-legged stool groaned as Gilla sat
down, set a small sack on the table, and began
with ostentatious precision to shell peas into a
bowl. Late afternoon sunlight shafted through
the shutters, lending an illusory splendor to the

tarnished brocade against which his models used to pose, and leaving in obscurity the baskets of soiled clothing which the wives of the rich and respectable (terms which were, in Sanctuary, roughly synonymous) had graciously given to Gilla to wash.

Once, Lalo would have rejoiced in the play of light and shadow, or at least reflected ironically on the relationship between illusion and reality. But he was too familiar with the poverty the shadows hid—the sordid truth behind all his fantasies. The only place he now saw visions was at the bottom of a jug of wine.

He got up stiffly, brushing ineffectually at the blue paint smeared across the old stains on his tunic. He knew that he should clean up the pigments spilling across the floor, but why try to save paint when no one wanted his pictures?

By now the regulars would be drifting into the Vulgar Unicorn. No one would care about his clothing there.

Gilla looked up as he started towards the door, and the light restored her greying hair to its former gold, but she did not speak. Once, she would have run to kiss her husband goodby, or railed at him to keep him home. Only, as Lalo stumbled down the stairs, he heard behind him the vicious splatter of peas hitting the cracked glaze of the bowl.

Lalo shook his head and took another sip of wine, carefully, because the tankard was almost empty now. "She used to be beautiful . . ." he said sadly. "Would you believe that she was like Eshi, bringing spring back into the world?" He peered muzzily through the shadows of the Vulgar Unicorn at Cappen Varra, trying to superimpose on the minstrel's saturnine features the dimly-remembered image of the golden-haired maiden he had courted almost twenty years ago.

But he could only remember the scorn in Gilla's grey eyes as she had glared down at him that afternoon. She was right. He was despicable—wine had bloated his belly as his ginger hair had thinned, and the promises he had once made her were as empty as his purse.

Cappen Varra tipped back his dark head and laughed. Lalo caught the gleam of his white teeth in the guttering lamplight, a flicker of silver from the amulet at his throat, the elegant shape of his head against the chiaroscuro of the Inn. Dim figures beyond him turned at the sound, then returned to the even murkier business that had brought them there.

"Far be it from me to argue with a fellow-artist—" said Cappen Varra, "but your wife reminds me of a rhinoceros! Remember when you got paid for decorating Master Regli's foyer, and we went to the Green Grape to celebrate? I saw her when she came after you . . . Now I know why you do your serious drinking here!"

The minstrel was still laughing. Suddenly angry, Lalo glared at him.

"Can you afford to mock me? You are still young. You think it doesn't matter if you tailor your songs to the taste of these fleas in the armpit of the Empire, because you still carry the *real* poetry in your heart, along with the faces of the beautiful women you wrote it for! Once already you have pawned your harp for bread. When you are my age, will you sell it for the price of a drink, and sit weeping because the dreams still live in your heart but you have no words to describe them anymore?"

Lalo reached blindly for his tankard, drained it, set it down on the scarred table. Cappen Varra was drinking too, the laughter for a moment gone from his blue eyes.

"Lalo—you are no fit companion for a drinking man!" said the minstrel at last. "I will end up as sodden as you are if I stay here!" He rose, slinging his harp case over his shoulder, adjusting the drape of his cloak to a jauntier flare. "The *Esmeralda's* back in port from Ilsig and points north—I'm off to hear what news she brings. Good evening, Master Limner—I wish you joy of your philosophy . . ."

Lalo remained where he was. He supposed he should go too, but where? If he went home he would only have to face Gilla again. Idly he began to draw on the table, his paint-stained forefinger daubing from a little pool of spilt wine. But his memory had sought the past, when he and Gilla were painfully saving the gold pieces that would deliver them from Sanctuary. He remembered how they had planned what they would do with the wealth sure to come once the lords of Ranke recognized his talent, the images of transcendent beauty he had dreamed of creating when he no longer had to worry about tomorrow's bread. But instead, they had had their first child.

He looked down, and realized that his finger had been clumsily outlining the pure profile of the girl Gilla had been so long ago. His fist smashed down on the table, obscuring the lines in a splatter of wine, and he groaned and hid his face in his hands.

"Your cup is empty . . ." The deep voice made a silence around them.

Lalo sighed and looked up. "So is my purse."

Broad shoulders blocked the light of the hanging lamp, but as the newcomer turned to shrug off his cloak his eyes glowed red, like those of a wolf surprised by a peasant's torch at night. Beyond him, Lalo saw the tapster's boy slithering among the crowded tables towards the new customer.

"You're the fellow who did the sign outside, aren't you?" said the man. "I'm getting transferred, and a picture for my girl to remember me by would be worth the price of a drink to me . . ."

"Yes. Of course." answered Lalo. The tapster's boy stopped by their table, and his companion ordered a jug of cheap red wine. The limner reached into his pouch for his roll of drawing paper, weighted it with the tankard to keep it from curling up again. The stopper of his ink bottle had dried stuck, and Lalo swore as he struggled to open it. He picked up his pen.

Swiftly he sketched his first impression of the man's hulking shoulders and tightly curled hair. Then he looked up again. The features blurred and Lalo blinked, wondering if he had already had too much wine. But the hollow in his belly cried out for more, and the tapster's boy was already returning, ducking beneath a thrown knife and detouring around the resulting struggle without spilling a drop.

"Turn towards the lamp—if I'm to draw you I must have some light!" muttered Lalo. The man's eyes burned at him from beneath arched brows. The limner shivered, forced himself to focus on the shape of the head and noted how the lank hair receded across the prominent bones of the skull.

Lalo looked down at his drawing. What trick of the light had made him think the fellow's hair curled? He cross-hatched over the first outline to merge it into a shadowy background and began to sketch the profile again. He felt those glowing eyes burning him. His hand jerked and he looked up quickly.

The nose was misshapen now, as if some drunken potter had pressed too hard into the clay. Lalo stared at his model and threw down his pen. The face before him bore no resemblance to the one he had drawn!.

"Go away!" he said hoarsely. "I can't do what you ask of me—I can't do anything anymore . . ." He began to shake his head and could not stop.

"You need a drink." Pewter clinked against the tabletop.

Lalo reached for the refilled tankard and drank deeply, not caring anymore whether he would be able to earn it. He felt it burn all the way down to his belly, run tingling along his veins to barrier him from the world.

"Now, try again." commanded the stranger. "Turn your paper over, look well at me, then draw what you see as quickly as you can."

For a long moment Lalo stared at the oddly attenuated features of the man before him, then bent over his work. For several minutes only the scratching of swift penstrokes competed with the clamor of the room. He must capture the glow of those strange eyes, for he suspected that when he looked at his companion again, nothing but the eyes would be the same.

But what matter? He had his payment now. With his free hand he reached for the mug and drank again, shaded a final line, then pushed the drawing across the table and sat back.

"Well—you wanted it . . ."

"Yes." The stranger's lips twitched. "Everything considered, it's quite good. I understand that you do portraits." he went on. "Are you free to take a commission now? Here's an earnest of your fee—" He reached into the folds of his garment, laid a gold piece shining on the table, quickly hid his misshapen fingers once more.

Lalo stared, reached out gingerly as if expecting the coin to vanish at his touch. Fortified by the wine, he could admit to himself how very odd this episode had been. But the gold was hard and cool and weighed heavily in his palm. His fingers closed.

The stranger's smile stiffened. He drew back suddenly, away from the light. "Now I must go."

"But the commission!" cried Lalo. "Who is it for, and when?"

"The commission . . ." the man seemed to be having trouble enunciating the words. "If you have the courage, come now . . . Do you think that you can find the house of Enas Yorl?"

Lalo cringed from his snarl of laughter, but the sorcerer did not wait for him to reply. He had cast his cloak around him and was lurching towards the door, and this time the shape the cloak covered was hardly human at all.

Lalo the limner stood in Prytanis Street before the house of Enas Yorl, shivering. With the setting of the sun, the wind off the desert had turned cold, although there was still a greenish light in the western sky. Once he had spent two months trying to capture on canvas the translucent quality of that glow.

The rooftops of the city made a deceptively elegant silhouette against the sky, topped by the lacy scaffolding of the tower of the Temple of Savankala and Sabellia nearby. Insulting to local prejudices though the new temple might be, at least it promised to be magnificent. Lalo sighed, wondering who would paint the murals within—probably some eminent artist from the capital. He sighed again. If he had gone to Ranke it might have been himself, returning in triumph to his birthplace.

But that consideration forced his attention back to the edifice that loomed before him, its shadows somehow darker than those of the other buildings, and the job that he had come here to do.

Terrors coiled like basilisks in the corners of his mind. His legs trembled. A dozen times during his journey across the town they had threatened to buckle or turn in the opposite direction, and the wine had been sweated out of him long ago.

Enas Yorl was one of the darker legends of Sanctuary, although, for reasons which the episode in the Vulgar Unicorn had amply illus-

trated, he was rarely seen. Rumor had it that the
curse of some rival had condemned him to the
existence of a chameleon. But that was said to be
the only limit on his power.

Had the sorcerer's offer been some perverted
joke, or part of some magical intrigue? *I should
take the gold to Gilla,* he thought, *it might be
enough to buy us places in an outward-bound
caravan . . .*

But the coin was only a retainer for a service
he had not yet performed, and there was no place
he could flee that would be beyond the reach of
the sorcerer. He could not return the money
without facing Enas Yorl, and he could not run
away. Shaking so that he could hardly grasp the
intricately-wrought knocker, he let it fall upon
the brazen surface of the door.

The interior of the building seemed larger than
its outside, though the colorless mists that
swirled around him made it hard to be certain of
anything except the glowing red eyes of Enas
Yorl. As the mists curdled and cleared, Lalo saw
that the sorcerer was enthroned in a carven chair
which the artist would have itched to examine
had anyone else been sitting there. He was considering a slim figure in an embroidered Ilsig
cloak who stood twirling a mounted globe.

Seas and continents spun as the stranger
turned, stared at Lalo, then back at Enas Yorl.

"Do you mean to tell me that sot is necessary to
your spell?"

It was a woman's voice, but Lalo had already
noted the fine bones structuring the face beneath
the scarred tanned skin and cropped hair, the
wiry grace of the body in its male attire. So might

a kitten from the Prince's harem have looked if it
had been left to fight its way to adulthood in the
alleys of the town.

Abruptly perceiving himself through the woman's eyes, Lalo straightened, acutely aware of
his stained tunic and frayed breeches, and the
stubble on his chin.

"Why do you need a painting?" she asked
scornfully. "Isn't this enough to purchase the
use of your own powers?" From a bag suspended
around her neck she poured out a river of moonlight which resolved itself into a string of pearls
which she cast rattling upon the stone-flagged
floor.

"I could . . ." said the sorcerer wearily. He
was smaller than he had been, an oddly shaped
mound in the great chair. "If you had been anyone else, I would have given you a spell worth as
much as that necklace, and laughed when your
ship outran the land winds that carry the ener-
gies I use, and your beauty became ugliness
again. The natural tendency of things is towards
disorder, my dear. Destruction is easy, as you
know. Restoration takes more energy."

"And your power is not great enough?" Her
voice was anxious now.

Lalo averted his eyes as the sorcerer's appearance altered again. He was feeling alternately hot
with embarrassment and chill with fear. Risky as
involvement in the public affairs of wizards
might be, to be privy to their personal affairs
could only bring disaster. And whatever the relationship between the figureless sorcerer and the
disfigured girl might be, it was obviously both
extremely personal, and an affair.

"There is a price for everything." replied Enas
Yorl once he had stabilized. "I can transform you
without aids, but not while continuing to protect
myself. Jarveena, would you ask that of me?" His
voice was a whisper now.

The girl shook her head. Suddenly subdued,
she let her cloak slip to the floor and seated
herself. Lalo saw an easel beside him—had it
been there before? He took an involuntary step
towards it, seeing there a set of brushes of perfectly matched camel's hair, pots of pigment
finely ground, a smoothly stretched canvas—
tools of a quality of which he had only been able
to dream.

"I want you to paint her." said Enas Yorl to
Lalo. "Not as you see her now, but as I see her
always. I want you to paint Jarveena's soul."

Lalo stared at him as though he had been
struck to the heart but had not yet begun to feel
the pain. He shook his head a little.

"You read my heart as you see the lady's soul
. . ." he said with a curious dignity. "The gods
alone know what I would give to be able to do
what you ask of me!"

The sorcerer smiled. His form seemed to shift,
to expand, and in the blazing of his eyes Lalo's
awareness was consumed. *I will provide the vision and you will provide the skill* . . . the words
echoed in Lalo's mind, and then he knew no
more.

The stillness of the hour just before dawn
hushed the air when Lalo again became conscious of his own identity. The girl Jarveena lay
back in her chair, apparently asleep. His back

and shoulder ached furiously. He stretched out his arm and flexed his fingers to relieve their cramping, and only then did his eyes focus on the canvas before him.

Did I do that? His first reaction was one he had known before, when hand and eye had cooperated unusually well and he had emerged from an intensive bout of work amazed at how close he had come to capturing the beauty he saw. But this—the image of a face whose finely arched nose and perfect brows were framed by waves of lustrous hair, of a slenderly curved body whose honey-colored skin had the sheen of the pearls on the floor and whose delicately up-tilted breasts were tipped with buds of dusky rose— this *was* that Beauty, fully realized.

Lalo looked from the picture to the girl in the chair and wept, because he could see only blurred hints of that beauty in her now, and he knew that the vision had passed through him like light through a windowpane, leaving him in the darkness once more.

Jarveena stirred and yawned, then opened one eye. "Is he done? I've got to go—the *Esmeralda* sails on the early tide."

"Yes." answered Enas Yorl, his eyes glowing more brightly than ever as he turned the easel for her to see. "The painting holds my magic now. Take it with you and look at it as you would look into a mirror, and after a time it will become a mirror, and all will see your beauty as I see it now . . ."

Shaking with fatigue and loss, Lalo sat down on the floor. He heard the rustle of the sorcerer's robes as he moved to embrace his lady, and after a little while the sound of the painting being removed and her footsteps going to the door. Then Lalo and Enas Yorl were alone.

"Well . . . it is done . . ." The sorcerer's voice was fleshless, like wind whispering through dry leaves. "Will you take your payment now?"

Lalo nodded without looking at him, afraid to see the body to which that voice belonged.

"What shall it be? Gold? Those baubles on the floor?" The pearls rattled as if they had been nudged by the sorcerer's current equivalent of a toe.

Yes, I will take the gold, and Gilla and I will go and never set eyes on this place again . . . The words were on his lips, but every dream he had ever known was clamoring in his soul.

"Give me the power you forced on me last night!" Lalo's voice strengthened. "Give me the power to paint the soul!"

The laughter of Enas Yorl began as the whisper in the sand that precedes the simoom, but it grew until Lalo was physically buffeted by the waves of pressure in the room. And then, after a little, there was silence again, and the sorcerer asked, "Are you quite sure?"

Lalo nodded once more.

"Well, that is a little thing, particularly when you are already . . . when there is such a strong desire. I will throw in a few extras—" he said kindly, "some souls for you to paint, perhaps a commission or two . . ."

Lalo jerked as the sorcerer's hands closed on his head, and for a moment all the colors in the rainbow exploded in his brain. Then he found himself on his feet by the door with a leather satchel in his hand.

"And the painter's gear . . ." continued Enas Yorl. "I have to thank you not only for a great service, but for giving me something to look forward to in life. Master Limner, may your gift reward you as you deserve!"

And then the great brazen door had shut behind him, and Lalo found himself in the empty street, blinking at the dawn.

The desert shimmered glassily with heat, appearing as insubstantial as the mists in the house of Enas Yorl, but the moist breath of a fountain cooled Lalo's cheeks. Dazed by the contrasts, the limner found himself wondering whether this moment, or indeed any of the past three days, were real or only the continuation of some sorcerous dream. But if that were so, he thought as he turned back to the echoing expanse of Molin Torchholder's veranda, he did not want to wake.

Before the first day after his adventure had passed, Lalo had received requests for portraits from the Portmaster's wife and from Jordis the stonemason, newly enriched by his work on the temple for the Rankan gods. In fact the first sitting was to have been this morning. But yesterday's summons had taken precedence; and so it was that Lalo, uncomfortable in worn velveteen breeches that were loose in the shanks and pinched his waist, his embroidered wedding vest, and a shirt which Gilla had starched so that it scraped his neck every time he turned his head, waited to be interviewed for the honor of decorating Molin Torchholder's feasting hall.

A door opened. Lalo heard light footsteps above the plash and gurgle of the fountain, and a young woman with precisely coiled fair hair beckoned to him.

"My Lady?" he hesitated.

"I am the lady Danlis, ancilla to the mistress of this house." she answered briskly. "Come with me . . ."

I should have known, thought Lalo, *after hearing Cappen Varra sing her praises for so long.* But that had been some time ago. As he followed her straight-backed progress along the corridor Lalo wondered what vision had made Cappen fall in love with her, and why it had failed.

A startled slave looked up and hastily began gathering together his rags and jars of wax paste as Danlis ushered Lalo through a door of gilded cedarwood into the Hall. Lalo stopped short, taken aback by the abundance of color and texture in the room. Figured silken rugs littered the parquet floor; gilded grape vines laden with amethyst fruit twisted about the marble columns that strained against the beamed ceiling; and the walls were draped with patterned damask from the looms of Ranke. Lalo stared around him, wondering what could possibly be left to decorate.

"Danlis, darling, is this the new painter?"

Lalo turned at a rustle of silks and saw hastening across the carpets a woman who was to Danlis as an overblown rose is to the bud of the flower. She was followed by a maid, and a fluffy dog spurted ahead of her, yapping fiercely and knocking over the pots of wax which the slave had set aside.

"I'm so glad that my lord has given me permission to get rid of these *dreary* hangings—so bourgeois, and as you see, they are quite faded now!" The lady went on breathlessly, her trailing skirts upsetting the pots which the slave had just finished righting again. The maid paused behind her and began to berate the cowering servant in low fierce tones.

"My Lady, may I present Lalo the Limner—" Danlis turned to the artist, "Lalo, this is the Lady Rosanda. You may make your bow."

"Will you take long to finish the work?" asked the Lady. "I will be happy to advise you— everyone has always complimented me on my excellent taste—I often think that I might have made an excellent artist—if I had been born into another walk of life, that is . . ."

"Lord Molin's position requires a worthy setting—" stated Danlis as her mistress paused for breath. "After the initial . . . difficulties . . . construction of the new temple has proceded smoothly. Naturally there will be celebrations in honor of its completion. Since it would be impious to hold them in the temple, they must take place in surroundings which will demonstrate whose genius is responsible for the achievement which will establish Sanctuary's position in the Empire."

Lady Rosanda stared at her companion, impressed, but Lalo scarcely heard her, already abstracted by consideration of the possibilities of the place. "Has Lord Molin decided on the subjects that I am to depict?"

"*If* you are chosen—" answered Danlis. "The murals will portray the goddess Sabellia as Queen of the Harvest, surrounded by her nymphs. First, of course, he will want to see your sketches and designs."

"I might model for the Goddess . . ." suggested Lady Rosanda, twitching an improbably auburn curl over one plump shoulder and looking arch.

Lalo swallowed. "My Lady is too kind, but modeling is exacting work—I wouldn't consider asking someone of your refinement to spend hours posing in such uncomfortable positions and scanty attire . . ." His panic eased into relief as the lady simpered and smiled. His own vision of the Goddess was characterized by a compassionate majesty which he doubted Lady Rosanda could even visualize, much less portray. Finding a model for Sabellia would be his hardest task.

"Now that you understand the work, how much time will you require?"

"What?" Lalo forced himself to the present again.

"When can you bring us the designs?" Danlis repeated tartly.

"I must consider . . . and choose my models . . ." he faltered. "It will take two or three days."

"Oh Lalo . . ."

The limner jerked, turned, and realized that he had come all the way from Molin Torchholder's well-guarded gatehouse to the Street of the Goldsmiths without conscious direction, as if his feet were under a charm to carry him home.

"My dear friend!" Puffing a little, Sandol the rug dealer drew up beside Lalo, who looked at him in bewilderment. It had not been 'my friend' the last time they met, when Sandol had refused to pay the full price for his wife's portrait because she said it made her look fat.

"I have wanted to tell you how much enjoyment your painting brings us. As they say, a work of art is a lasting pleasure—Perhaps we ought to have a portrait of myself to balance my wife's. What do you say?" He wiped his brow with a large handkerchief of purple silk.

"Well of course I would be happy—but I don't know just when—my time may be occupied for awhile . . ." answered Lalo, confused.

"Yes indeed—" Sandol smiled unctiously. "I understand that your work will shortly grace a much more august residence than my own. My wife was saying just this morning what an honor it was to have been painted by the man who is decorating Molin Torchholder's feasting hall!"

Suddenly Lalo understood. The news of his prospective commission must be all over town by now. He suppressed a grin of triumph, remembering how he had humbled himself to this man to get even a part of his fee. Perhaps he should do the picture—the rug merchant was as porcine as his lady, and they would make a good pair.

"Well, I must not discuss it yet . . ." replied Lalo modestly. "But it is true that I have been approached . . . I fear that an opportunity to serve the representative of the gods of Ranke must take precedence over lesser commitments." Interested commentary followed them like an echo down the busy street, apprentices telling their masters, silk-veiled matrons whispering to each other as they tried on rings.

"Oh indeed I *do* understand." Sandol assured him fervently. "All I ask is that you keep me in mind . . ."

"I'll let you know," said Lalo graciously, "when I have time." He increased his pace, leaving the rug merchant standing like a melting icicle in the sea of people behind him. When he had crossed the Path of Money into the Corridor of Steel, Lalo permitted himself a discreet skip or two.

"Not only my feet but my entire life is charmed now!" he told himself. "May all the gods of Ranke and Ilsig bless Enas Yorl!"

Sunshine glared from the whitewashed walls around him, flashed from polished swords and daggers displayed in the armorer's stalls, glittered in myriad points of light from linked mail. But the brilliance around him was less dazzling than the vistas opening to Lalo's imagination now. He would have not merely a comfortable living, but riches; not only respect, but fame! Everything he had ever desired was within his grasp . . .

Cutpurses flowed around him like shadows as he passed through an alleyway, but despite the rumors, his purse still swung slackly, and they drew back again without his having noticed them. Someone called out to him as he passed the more modest establishments near the warehouses, but Lalo's eyes were blinded by his visions.

It was not until his feet had carried him onto

the Wideway that edged the harbor that he realized that he had been hailed by Farsi the Coppersmith, who had loaned him money when Gilla was sick after the birth of their second child. He thought of turning back, but surely he could visit Farsi another time. He was too busy now.

Plans for the new project were boiling in his brain. He had to come up with something that could transcend the rest of Molin's decor without trying to compete with its vulgarity. Colors, details, the interplay of line and mass, rippled before his mind's eye like a painted veil between him and the sordid streets of the town.

So much would depend on the models he chose for the figures in the design! Sabellia and her nymphs must display a beauty that would uplift the imagination even as it pleased the eye, an air at once both regal and innocent.

Lalo slipped on a fishhead. He flailed wildly for a moment, then regained his balance and stood panting and blinking in the bright sun.

"And where will I find such maidens in Sanctuary?" he asked himself aloud, "Where mothers sell their daughters into whoredom as soon as their breasts begin to show?" Even the girls who retained some outward beauty were swiftly corrupted within. In the past, he had found his models among the street singers and the girls who eked out a weaver's paltry daylight wages on their backs, at night. He would have to look elsewhere now.

He sighed and turned his face to the sea. It was cooler here, and the changing wind brought a fresh sea breeze to compete with the rotting fish odor of the shore. The blue water sparkled like a virgin's eye.

A woman with a child in her arms waved to him, and after a moment Lalo recognized Valira, come to the shore for an hour or two of sunshine with her baby before it was time for her to ply her trade with the sailors there. She lifted the child for him to see, and he noted with a pang that although her eyes were painted, and glass beads glittered in her hennaed hair, her arms were still childishly thin. He remembered when she had been one of his oldest daughter's playmates, and had often come to Lalo's house for supper when there was no food at her own.

He knew about the rape that had started Valira in this profession, the poverty that kept her there, but her cheerful greeting made him uncomfortable. She had not chosen her fate, but she could not escape it now. Her existence clouded the bright future he had been envisioning.

Lalo waved briefly at Valira and then hurried on, at once relieved and ashamed when she did not call out to him.

He continued along the Wideway, past the wharves where the foreign ships were berthed, pulling at their moorings like a nobleman's horses tethered outside a peasant's sty. Some of the merchants had spread out their wares on the docks, and Lalo threaded his way among knots of people bickering over prices, exchanging insults and news with equal good humor. A few City Guards lounged against a piling, weariness and wariness mingling in their faces as they surveyed the motley crowd. They were accompanied by one of the Prince's Hell Hounds, his expression differing from theirs only in that it became, if possible, even more supercilious when he looked at his men.

Lalo passed without stopping the abandoned wharf near Fisherman's Row which had become his favorite place for meditation over the years. He had no need of it now—he had too much to do! Where could he find models? Perhaps he should visit the Bazaar this afternoon. Surely he could find some honest maidens there . . .

He hurried up the Street of Smells towards his home, but stopped short when he saw his wife hanging out laundry in the building's courtyard, talking over her shoulder to someone hidden behind her. He approached cautiously.

"Did the interview go well, dear?" asked Gilla brightly. "I've heard that the Lady Rosanda is most gracious. You're quite favored by the ladies today—see, here's Mistress Zorra come to call on you . . ."

Lalo winced at the edge in her voice, then forgot her as she moved and the caller came towards him. He received in quick succession an impression of a trim figure, a complexion that glowed like the roses of Eshi, copper-bright hair and a pair of dazzling eyes.

He swallowed. The last time he had seen Mistress Zorra was when she had accompanied her father to collect their rent, which was three months overdue. He tried to remember whether they had paid last month's rent on time.

"Oh, Master Lalo—you've no need to look so

apprehensive!" Zorra blushed prettily. "You should know that your credit is good with us after so many years . . ."

After so much gossip about my new prosperity, you mean! He thought, but her smile was infectious, and after all she was not responsible for the stinginess of her sire. He grinned back at her, thinking that she was like a breath of spring in this summer-parched street. Like a nymph . . .

"Perhaps you can help me to maintain my credit, mistress!" he replied. "Would you like to be one of my models for the paintings in Molin Torchholder's Hall?"

How delightful it was to be the dispenser of largesse, thought Lalo as he watched Zorra dance away down the street. She had been painfully eager to break all previous engagements so that she could come to him the next day.

Was that how Enas Yorl felt when he gave me my desire? he wondered, and wondered also (but only for a moment) why, in doing so, the sorcerer had laughed.

"But why can't I pose for you in Molin Torchholder's house?" Zorra pouted, glanced at Lalo to see if he was watching her take off her petticoat, and let the garment slip to the floor.

"If my patrons could detach their walls and sent them here for decoration, I doubt they would let even me in the door . . ." replied Lalo abstractedly, transferring paint from paintpots to palette in the precise order he always used. "Besides, I'll need to make several studies from each model before I decide on the final design . . ."

Morning sunlight shone cheerfully on the clean-swept floor, cleared now of strangers' laundry, gleamed on Lalo's palette knife and glowed through the petals of the flowers he had given to Zorra to hold.

"That's right—" he said, draping a wisp of gauze around her hips and adjusting the angle of her arms. "Hold the flowers as if you were offering them to the Goddess." She twitched as he touched her, but his awareness of her flesh was already giving way to his perception of her body as a form in space. "Generally I would do only a quick sketch or two," he explained, "but this must be complete enough to give Lord Molin an idea of what the finished work will be like, so I'm using color . . ."

He stepped back, seeing the picture as he had visualized it—the fresh beauty of the girl in the sunlight with her bright hair flowing down her back and her arms filled with bright flowers. He picked up his brush and took a deep breath, focusing on what he saw.

His awareness of the murmur of conversation at the other end of the room, where Gilla and their middle daughter were preparing the noonmeal, faded. He did not turn when one of his sons came in, was shushed by his mother and sent outdoors. The sounds slid past him as his mind stilled, as the tensions of the past days slipped away.

Now he was himself at last, serenely confident that his hand would obey his eye, that both would reflect the perceptions of his soul. And he knew that not the commissions, but this confidence in himself, was the true gift of Enas Yorl.

Lalo dipped his brush in the paint and began to work.

The bar of light had moved halfway across the floor when Zorra abruptly straightened and let her flowers fall to the floor.

"This had better be worth it!" she complained. "My back hurts, and my arms are falling off." She flexed her shoulders and bent back and forth to ease the strain.

Lalo blinked, trying to orient himself. "No, not yet—it's not finished—" he began, but Zorra was already moving towards him.

"What do you mean, I can't look? It's my picture, isn't it?" She stopped short, staring. Lalo's eyes followed her gaze back to the picture, and appalled, he let the brush slip from his hand.

The face that looked at him from the easel had eyes narrowed with cupidity, lips drawn back in a predatory grin. The red hair flamed like a fox's brush, and somehow the rounded limbs had been distorted so that she looked as if she were about to spring. Lalo shuddered, looking from the girl to the picture and back again.

"You whoreson maggoty bastard, what have you done to me?" She rounded on him furiously, then turned back to the picture, snatched up his palette knife, and began to stab at the canvas. "That's not me! That's hateful! You hate women, don't you? You hate my father, too, but just you wait! You'll be living with the Downwinders by the time he gets through with you!"

The floor shook as Gilla charged towards them. Lalo staggered back as she thrust between him and the half-naked girl, squeezed Zorra's wrist until the little knife clattered to the floor.

"Get dressed, you hussy! I'll have no such language where my children can hear!" snapped Gilla, ignoring the fact that they heard far worse every time they went into the Bazaar.

"And you too, you bloated sow!" Zorra pulled away, began to struggle into her clothes. "You're too gross for even Amoli to hire—I hope you end on the streets where you belong!" The door slammed behind her and they heard her clatter down the rickety stairs.

"I hope she breaks her neck. Her father still hasn't fixed those stairs." said Gilla calmly.

Lalo bent stiffly to pick up his palette knife. "She's right . . ." He took a step towards the mutilated picture. "Damn him . . ." he whispered. "He tricked me—he knew that this would happen. May all the gods damn Enas Yorl!"

Gilla looked at the picture and began to laugh. "No . . . really," she gasped, "it's an excellent likeness. You only saw her pretty face. I know what she's been up to. Her fiancé killed himself when she threw him over for that gorilla from the Prince's guard. The vixen is out for all she can get, which the picture makes abundantly clear. No wonder she hated it!"

Lalo slumped. "But I've been betrayed . . ."

"No. You got what you asked for, poor love. You have painted that wretched girl's soul!"

Lalo leaned on the splintery railing of the abandoned wharf, staring with unfocused eyes into the golden dazzle cast upon the waters by the setting sun as if by wishing hard enough he could become one with that beauty and forget his despair. *I have only to climb over this flimsy barrier and let myself fall* . . . He imagined the feel of the bitter waters closing over him, and the blessed release from pain.

Then he looked down, and shuddered, not entirely because of the cooling wind. The murky waters were littered with obscene gobbets that had once been part of living things—offal flushed down the gutters from the shambles of Sanctuary to the sea. Lalo's gorge rose at the thought of that water touching him. He turned away, sank down with his back against the wall of a shanty the fishermen sometimes used.

Like everything else I see, he thought, *whatever seems fairest is sure to be most foul within!*

A ship moved majestically across the harbor, passed the lighthouse and disappeared around the point. Lalo had thought of shipping out on such a vessel, but he was too unskilled for a sailor, too frail for a common hand. Even the solace of the taverns was denied to him. In the Green Grape they would congratulate him on the success that was impossible now, while the clients at the Vulgar Unicorn would try to rob him, and beat him senseless when they discovered his poverty. How could he ever explain, even to Cappen Varra, what had happened to him?

The planks on which he was sitting shook beneath a heavy tread. Gilla . . . Lalo tensed, waiting for her accusations, but she only sighed, as if releasing pent hope, or fear.

"I hoped I'd find you here . . ." Grunting, she eased down beside him, unslung and handed him an earthenware pot with a narrow spout. "Better drink this before it gets cold."

He nodded, took a long swallow of fragrant herb tea laced with wine, then another, and set the pot down.

Gilla pulled her shawl around her, stretched out her legs and settled back against the wall. Two gulls swooped overhead, squabbling over a piece of flesh. A heavy swell set wavelets lapping against the pilings below them, then there was silence again.

In the shared stillness, warmed by the tea and by Gilla's body, something that had been wound tight within Lalo began to ease.

"Gilla . . ." he said at last, "what am I going to do?"

"The other two models failed?"

"They were worse than Zorra. Then I started the portrait of the Portmaster's wife . . . Fortunately I got the sketch away before she could see it. She looked like her lapdog!" He drank again.

"Poor Lalo," Gilla shook her head. "It's not your fault that all your unicorns turned out to be rhinoceroses!"

He remembered the old fable about the rhinoceros who looked into a magic mirror and saw there a unicorn, but it did not comfort him. "Is everything beautiful only a mask for rottenness, or is it only that way in Sanctuary?" He burst out then, "Oh Gilla, I've failed you and the children. We're ruined, don't you understand? I cannot even hope any more!"

She turned a little, but did not touch him, as if she understood that any attempt at comfort would be more than he could bear.

"Lalo . . ." she cleared her throat and started again. "It's all right—we'll get by some way. And

you haven't failed . . . you haven't failed our
dream! You made the right choice—don't I know
that it was me and the children in the first place
that kept you from what you were meant to do?

"Anyhow—" she tried to turn her emotion to
laughter, "if worst comes to worst *I* can model for
you—just for you to get the basic lines of the
figures, of course." she added apologetically.
"After all these years I doubt I have any flaws
that you don't already know . . ."

Lalo set down the teapot, turned and looked at
her. In the light of the setting sun Gilla's face,
into which the years had carved so many lines,
was like a weathered image which some worshipper had gilded in an attempt to disguise its
age. This bitter line for poverty endured, that, for
the death of a child . . . Could all the sorrows of
a world have marked a goddess more?

He laid his hand on her arm, seeing the size of
her body, but feeling the strength in it, and the
flow of energy between them which had bound
him to her, even more than her beauty, so many
years ago. She sat still, accepting his touch, although he thought she would have been well-
justified in turning away.

Do I know you?

Gilla's eyes were closed, her head tipped back
to rest against the wall in a rare moment of peace.
The deepening light upon her face seemed now
to come from within. Lalo's eyes blurred. *I have
been blind*, he thought, *blind, and a fool* . . .

"Yes . . ." he fought to steady his voice,
knowing how he would paint her, where he
would look for others to be his models now. His
breath caught, and he reached out to her. She

looked at him then, smiling questioningly, and received him into her embrace.

A hundred candles blazed in Molin Torchholder's Hall, set in silver candelabra wrought in the shape of torches upraised in clenched fists. Light shimmered in the gauzy silks of the ladies of Sanctuary, gleamed from the heavy brocades worn by their lords, flashed from each golden link of chain or faceted jewel as they moved across the floor, nearly eclipsing the splendor of the room.

Lalo observed the scene from a vantage point of relative quiet beside a pillar, tolerated for his role in creating the murals whose completion the party was intended to celebrate. Everyone of wealth or status who craved the favor of the Empire was there, which these days amounted to most of the upper crust of Sanctuary, everyone wearing the same mask of complacent gaiety. But Lalo could not help wondering how, if he had painted this scene, those faces would have appeared.

Several merchants for whom Lalo had worked in the past had wangled invitations, although most of his former clients would have felt as out of place in this gathering as he did. He recognized a few friends, among them Cappen Varra, who having just finished a song, was now warily watching Lady Danlis, who was far too busy being charming to a banker from Ranke to notice him.

Several other acquaintances from the Vulgar Unicorn had somehow managed to get hired as extra waiters and footmen. Lalo suspected that

not all of the jewels that winked so brightly tonight would leave the house in the hands of
those who had brought them, but he did not feel
compelled to point this out to anyone. He braced
himself as he recognized Jordis the stonemason
shouldering his way towards him through the
glittering crowd.

"Well, Master Limner, now that you've
finished serving the gods, you'll have a bit more
time for men, eh?" Jordis smiled broadly. "The
space on my wall that's waiting for my picture is
still bare . . ."

Lalo coughed deprecatingly. "I'm afraid that
in my concentration on heavenly things I've lost
my touch for earthly excellence . . ." The
stonemason's expression told him how pomp-
ous that sounded, but it would be far better for
everyone to think his head had been turned by
his new prosperity than for them to guess the
truth. The solution to his dilemma that had en-
abled him to complete the job for Lord Molin had
forever barred him from Society portraiture.

"Heavenly things . . . ah, yes . . ." Jordis'
eyes had moved to one of the nymphs painted on
the wall, whose limbs were supple and rounded,
whose eyes shone with youth and merriment. "If
I could make a living gazing at such lovelies, I
suppose I'd refuse to paint old men too!" He
laughed suggestively. "Where do you find them
in this town, eh?"

*Selling their bodies on the docks . . . or their
souls in the Bazaar . . . slaving in your kitchen
or scrubbing your floors . . .* thought Lalo bitterly. This was not the first time this evening that

he had been asked who his models were. The nymph at whom Jordis was now leering so eagerly was a crippled beggar girl whom he had probably passed in the street a dozen times. On another wall the whore Valira proudly presented a sheaf of grain to the Goddess, while her child tumbled like a cherub about her feet. And the Goddess they worshipped, who dominated all of the facile splendor in this room, was his Gilla, the rhinoceros who had been revealed as something greater than any unicorn.

You have hearts but you do not feel . . . Lalo's eyes moved over the dazzle of apparel and ornament in which Lord Molin's guests had disguised themselves. *You have eyes, but you do not see.* He murmured something about an artist's perspective.

"If you want a room decorated, I'll be happy to serve you, but I do not think that I will be doing portraits any more." Ever since he had learned to see Gilla, his sight had been changing. Now, when he was not painting, he could often see the truth behind the faces men showed the world. He added politely, "I trust that your work is going well?"

"Eh? My work—oh yes, but there's not much left for a stonemason now! What remains will require a different sort of craft . . ." His chuckle held a hint of complicity.

Lalo felt himself flushing, realizing that Jordis assumed he had been fishing for information about the new temple—the greatest decoration job that Sanctuary had ever known. *Wasn't I?* he wondered. *Is it unworthy to want my goddess to adorn something more worthy than this jumped-up engineer's feasting hall?*

His mouth dried as he saw Molin Torchholder himself approaching him. Jordis bowed, smirked, and melted back into the crowd. Lalo forced himself to stand up and meet his patron's eye, for Lord Molin's excess flesh covered a powerful frame, and there was something uncomfortably piercing about his gaze.

"I have to thank you." said Lord Molin. "Your work appears to be a success." His eyes roved ceaselessly from the crowd to Lalo's face and back again. "Perhaps *too* successful." he went on. "Next to your goddess, my guests appear to be the decorations here!"

Lalo found himself trying to apologize and froze, terrified that he would blurt out the truth.

Molin Torchholder laughed. "I am trying to compliment you, my good man—I would like to commission you to do the paintings on my new temple's walls . . ."

"Master Limner, you appear to be in good spirits today!"

Lalo, who had just turned from the Path of Money into the Avenue of Temples, on his way to make an inital survey of the spaces he was to decorate in the new temple to the Rankan gods, missed a step as the soft voice spoke in his ear. He heard a dry chuckle, felt the hairs rise on his neck and bent to peer more closely at the other man. All he could see beneath the hooded caravaneer's cloak was the gleam of crimson eyes.

"Enas Yorl!"

"More or less . . ." his companion agreed. "And you? Are you the same? You have been in my thoughts a great deal. Would you like me to change the gift I gave to you?"

Lalo shivered, remembering those moments when he would have given his soul to lose the power the sorcerer had bestowed upon him. But instead, his soul had been given back to him.

"No. I don't think so." he answered quietly, and sensed the sorcerer's surprise. "The debt is mine. Shall I paint you another picture to repay it?" He added, "Shall I paint a portrait of you, Enas Yorl?"

The sorcerer halted then, and for a moment the painter met fully the red gaze of those unearthly eyes, and he trembled at the immortal weariness he saw there.

Yet it was not Lalo, but Enas Yorl, who was the first to close his eyes and look away.

THEN AZYUNA DANCED

Lynn Abbey

He was a handsome man, somewhat less than
middle-aged, with a physique that bespoke a
soldier, not a priest. He entered the bazaar-stall
of Kul the Silkseller with an authority that sent
the other patrons back into the dusty afternoon
and brought bright-eyed Kul out from behind his
bolts of cloth.

"Your grace?" he fawned.

"I shall require a double length of your finest
silk. The color is not important—the texture is.
The silk must flow like water and a candleflame
must be bright through four thicknesses."

Kul thought for a moment, then rummaged up
an armload of samples. He would have displayed
each, slowly, in its turn, but his customer's eyes

fell on a sea-green bolt and Kul realized it would
be folly to test the priest's patience.

"Your grace has a fine eye," he said instead,
unrolling a half-length and letting the priest
examine the hand and transparency of the cloth.

"How much?"

"Two gold coronations for both lengths."

"One."

"But, your grace has only recently arrived
from the capital. Surely you recall the fetching-
price of such workmanship. See here, the right
border is shot with silver threads. It's certainly
worth one-and-seven."

"And this is certainly not the capital. Nine
Rankan soldats," the priest growled, reducing
his offer further.

Kul whisked the cloth out of the priest's hand,
spinning it expertly around the bolt. "Nine soldats . . . the silver in the cloth is worth more
than that! Very well. I've no choice, really. How
is a bazaar-merchant to argue with Molin Torchholder, High Priest of Vashanka? Very well, very
well—nine soldats it is."

The priest snapped his fingers and an adoles-
cent temple-mute scurried forward with the
priest's purse. The youth selected nine coins,
showed them to his master, then handed them to
Kul who checked both sides to be certain they
weren't shaved—as so much of Sanctuary's currency was. (It was not fitting that a priest handle
his own money.) When Kul slipped the small
handful of coins into his waist-pouch, Torchholder snapped his fingers a second time and
a massively built plainsman ducked under the
stall's lintel, holding the door-cloth until the

priest departed, then taking the bolt from the silent youth.

Molin Torchholder strode purposefully through the crowded bazaar, confident the slaves would keep pace with him somehow. The silk was almost as good as the merchant claimed, and in the capital, where better money flowed more freely, would have brought twice what the merchant had asked. The priest had not risen so high in the Rankan bureaucracy that he failed to savor a well-finessed haggling.

His sedan-chair awaited him at the bazaar-gate. A second plainsman was there to hold his heavy robes while he stepped over the carved-wood sides. The first had already placed the silk on the seat and stood beside the rearmost poles. The mute pulled a leather-wrapped forked stick from his belt, slapped it once against his thigh and the entourage headed back to the palace.

The plainsmen went to wherever it was that they abided when Molin didn't need their services; the youth carried the cloth to the family's quarters with the strictest instructions that the esteemable Lady Rosanda, Molin's wife, was not to see it. Molin himself wandered through the palace until he came to those rooms now allotted to Vashanka's servants and slaves.

It was the latter who interested him, specifically the lithe Northern slave they called Seylalha who practiced the arduous Dance of the Consort at this time each day. The dance was a mortal recreation of the divine dance Azyuna had performed before her brother, Vashanka, pursuading him to make her his concubine rather than relegate her to the traitorous ranks of their ten brothers. Seylalha would perform that dance in less than a week at the annual commemoration of the Ten-Slaying.

She had reached the climax of the music when he arrived, beginning the dervish swirls that brought her calf-length honey-colored hair out into a complete, dazzling circle. The tattered practice rags had long-since been discarded, but she was not yet twirling so fast that the priest could not appreciate the firmness of her thighs, the small, upturned breasts. (Azyuna's dance must be danced by a Northern slave or the movements became grotesque.) The slave's face, Molin knew, was as beautiful as her body though it was now hidden by the swinging hair.

He watched until the music exploded in a final crescendo, then slid the spy-hole shut with an audible click. Seylalha would see no virile man until the feast-night when she danced for the god himself.

2

The slave had been escorted to her quarters—more properly: returned to her cell. The beefy eunuch turned the key that slid a heavy bolt into place; he needn't have bothered. After ten years of captivity and especially now that she was in Sanctuary, Seylalha was not likely to risk her life in escape-attempts.

He had been there watching again; she knew that and more. They thought her mind was as blank as the surface of a pond on a windless day—but they were wrong. They thought she could remember nothing of her life before they had found her in a squalid slave-pen; she'd merely been too smart to reveal her memories. Neither had she ever revealed that she could understand their Rankan language—had always understood it. True, the women who taught her the dance were all mutes and could reveal nothing, but there were others who had tongues. That was how she came to learn of Sanctuary, of Azyuna and of the Feast of the Ten-Slaying.

Here in Sanctuary she was the only one who knew the whole dance but had not yet performed it for the god. Seylalha guessed that this year would be her year—the one fateful night in her constricted life. They thought she didn't know what the dance was. They thought she performed it out of fear for the bitter-faced women with their leather-bound clatter-sticks. But in her tribe nine-year-olds were considered of marriageable age, and a seduction was a seduction regardless of the language.

Seylalha had reasoned, as well, that if she did not want to become one of those mutilated women who had trained and taught her she'd best get a child from her bedding with the god. Legend said Vashanka's unfulfilled desire was to have a child by his sister; Seylalha would oblige the god in exchange for her freedom. The Ten-Slaying was a new-moon feast; she bled at the full-moon. If the god were man-like after the fashion of her clan-brothers, she would conceive.

She knelt on the soft bed-cushions they provided her, rocking back and forth until tears

flowed down her face; silent tears lest her guardians hear and force a drugged potion down her
throat. Calling on the sungod, the moongod, the
god who tended the herds in the night and every
other shadowy demon she could remember from
the days before the slave-pens, Seylalha repeated
her prayers: "Let me conceive. Let me bear the
god's child. Let me live! Keep me from becoming
one of *them!*"

In the distance, beyond walls and locked door,
she could hear her less-fortunate sisters speaking to each other on their tambours, lyres, pipes
and clatter-sticks. They'd danced their dance
and lost their tongues; their wombs were filled
with bile. Their music was a mournful, bitter
dirge—it told her fate if she did not bear a child.

As the tears dried she arched her back until her
forehead rested on the soft mass of her hair beneath her. Then, in rhythm to the distant conversation, she began her dance again.

3

Molin paced around the marble-topped table
he had brought with him from the capital. The
mute who always attended him hid in the far
corners of the room. Molin's wrath had touched
him three times and it was not yet high-noon.

The injustice, the indignity of being the supreme priest of Vashanka in a sink-hole like
Sanctuary. Construction lagged on the temple:
inept crews, unforeseen accidents, horrendous
omens. The old Ilsig hierarchy gloated and col-

lected the citizenry's irregular tithes. The Imperial entourage was cramped into inadequate quarters that shoved his household together. He was actually sharing rooms with his wife—a situation neither of them had ever desired and could no longer tolerate. The Prince was an idealist, an unmarried idealist, whose belief in the bliss of that inconvenient state was exceeded only by his naivete with regard to statecraft. It was difficult not to enjoy the Prince's company, however, despite his manifold shortcomings. He had the proper breeding for a useless younger son, and only the worst of fates had brought him so perilously close to the throne that he must be sent so depressingly far from it.

In Ranke, Molin had a fine house—as well as rooms within the temple. Rare flowers bloomed in his heated gardens; a waterfall coursed down one interior wall of the temple drowning out the street-noises and casting rainbows across this very table when it had resided in his audience chambers. Where had he gone wrong? Now he had a tiny room with one window looking out to an air shaft that must have sunk in the cesspools of hell itself and another one, the larger of the two, overlooking the gallows. Moreover, the Hounds were elsewhere this morning and yesterday's corpses still creaked in the breeze.

Injustice! Indignity! And so, of course, he must clothe himself in the majesty of his position as Vashanka's loyal and duly-initiated priest. Kadakithus must find his way to these forsaken quarters and endure them as the priests did if Molin was to acquire better lodgings. The Prince was late—no doubt he'd gotten lost.

●   ●   ●

"My Lord Molin?" a cheerful voice called
from the ante-chamber. "My Lord Molin? Are
you here?"

"I am, my Prince."

Molin gestured to the mute who poured two
goblets of fruit tea as the Prince entered the
room.

"My Lord Molin, your messenger said you
wished to see me urgently on matters concerning
Vashanka? This must be true, isn't it, or you
wouldn't have called me all the way out here.
Where are we? No matter. Are there problems
with the temple again? I've told Zalbar to see
to it that the conscripts perform their duties . . ."

"No, my Prince, there are no new problems
with the temple, and I have turned all those
matters over to the Hounds, as you suggested.
We are, by the way, in the outer wall of your
palace—just upwind of the gallows. You can see
them through the window—if you'd like."

The Prince preferred to sip his tea.

"My purpose in summoning you, my Prince,
has to do with the upcoming commemoration of
the Ten Slaying to take place at the new-moon. I
wished certain privacy and discretion which,
frankly, is not available in your own quarters."

If the Prince was offended by Molin's insinua-
tions he did not reveal it. "Do I have special
duties then?" he asked eagerly.

Molin, sensing the lad's excitement, pressed
his case all the harder. "Extremely special ones,
my Prince; ones not even your distinguished late
Father, the Emperor, was honored to perform.
As you are no doubt aware, Vashanka—

mayHisnamebepraised—has concerned Himself rather personally in the affairs of this city of late. My augurists report that on no less than three separate occasions since your arrival in this accursed place His power has been successfully invoked by one not of the temple hierarchy."

The Prince set down his goblet. "You know of these things?" he asked with open-faced incredulity. "You can tell when the god's used His power?"

"Yes, my Prince," Molin answered calmly. "That is the general purpose of our hierarchy. Working through the mandated rituals and in partnership with our God we incline Vashanka's blessings toward the loyal, righteous upholders of tradition, and direct His wrath toward those who would deny or harm the Empire."

"I know of no traitors . . ."

" . . . And neither do I, my Prince," Molin said, though he had his suspicions, "but I do know that our God, Vashanka—mayHisnamebepraised—is showing His face with increasing frequency and devastating effect in this town."

"Isn't that what he's supposed to do?"

It was difficult to believe that the vigorous Imperial household had produced so dense an heir; at such times as this Molin almost believed the rumors that circulated around the Prince. Some said that he was at least as clever and ambitious as his brother's advisers feared; Kadakithus was deliberately botching this gubernatorial appointment so he would have to be returned to the capital before the Empire faced rebellion. Unfortunately, Sanctuary was more than equal to the most artfully contrived incompetence.

"My Prince," Molin began again, snapping his fingers to the mute who immediately pushed a great-chair foward for the Prince to sit in. This was going to take longer than anticipated. "My Prince—a god, shall we say any god but most especially our own god Vashanka—may-Hisnamebepraised—is an awesomely powerful being who, even though He may beget mortal children on willing or unwilling women, is quite unlike a mortal man.

"A mere man who runs rampant in the streets with his sword drawn and shouting sedition would be an easy matter for the Hounds to control—assuming, of course, they even noticed him in this town . . ."

"Are you saying, my Lord Molin, that such a vagrant is plowing through my city? Is that why you've called me here, really? Does my suite harbor a viperous traitor?"

It must be an act, Molin decided. No one could attain physical maturity with only Kadakithus' apparent intelligence to guide him. He *had* attained maturity, hadn't he? Molin's plans demanded it. He was known to have concubines, but perhaps he merely talked them to sleep? It was time for a change of tactics.

"My Dear Prince, as hierarchical superior here in Sanctuary I can flatly state that the repeated incidents of divine intervention, unguided as they are by the rituals performed according to tradition by myself and my accolytes, constitute a severe threat to the well-being of your people and your mission to Sanctuary. They must be stopped by whatever means are necessary!"

"Oh . . . oh!" the Prince's face brightened. "I believe I understand. I'm to do something at next week's festival that will help you get control again. Do I get to bed Azyuna?"

The light in the young man's eyes reassured Molin that the Prince did understand the purpose of a concubine. "Indeed, my Prince! But that is only a small part of what we shall do next week. The Dance of Azyuna and the Divine Seduction are performed at the festival each year. Many children are born of such unions, many serve their ersatz-father with great dignity—I myself am a son of the Consort. But, under *extreme* circumstances the Dance of Azyuna will be preceeded by the most sacred recreation of the Ten-Slaying itself. Vashanka —mayHisnamebepraised—rediscovers His traitorous brothers plotting to overthrow the divine authority of Savankala, their father. He slays them on the spot and takes Azyuna, at her insistence, to bed at once as his consort. The child of such a union—if there were any—would be well-omened indeed.

"My Prince, the auguries indicate that such a child will be born here in Sanctuary—of all places—and our God's activity here would lend belief to this. It is imperative that such a child be born within the strictures of the temple; it would be fitting if the child's natural father were you . . ."

The Prince turned the color of the fruit tea, though his complexion quickly leveled off at a unique shade of green. "But Molin, that's general's work—killing surrendered officers of the enemy. Molin, you don't expect me to kill ten men, do you? Why, there aren't more than ten Vashankan priests in this whole city. I'd have to kill you. I couldn't do it, Molin—you mean too much to me."

"My Dear Prince," Molin poured another goblet of fruit tea and signaled the mute to bring a stronger libation for the next round. "My Dear Prince, while I would never hesitate to lay down my life for you or the Empire should, gods forfend, the need ever arise—nonetheless, I assure you, I am not about to make the supreme sacrifice at this time. There is nothing in the most sacred tomes of ritual dictating the nature or rank of the ten who must be slain—save that they must be undeformed and alive at the start."

At that moment there were shouts outside Molin's larger window and the all-too-familiar sound of the gallow's rope snapping another neck.

"Very simply, my Prince, cancel these daily executions and by the Ten-Slaying I'm sure we'll have our quota."

The Prince blanched at the thought of Sanctuary denizens whose activities so exceeded the norms of this none-too-civilized place that his judges would condemn them to death.

"They would be bound and drugged, of course," Molin consoled his Prince, "as is part of custom, if not tradition. Our hierarchy has suffered the discomfort of having the wrong man survive," Molin added quickly, without mentioning that they had also suffered the inconvenience of losing all eleven to their wounds before the ritual could be completed. The hierarchy had acquired an immense practicality over the generations when its own interests were concerned.

Kadakithus stared blankly into the corners of the room; he had stared briefly out the window but the busy gallows had not brought the peace of mind he sought Molin entertained hopes of getting new quarters in the near future. The mute offered them a fresh goblet of the local wine—a surprisingly potable beverage, given its origins. But then the priorities of the populace were such that the wine should be far better than their cheese or bread. Molin himself offered the strong drink to the Prince.

"Molin—I cannot. If it were just the Dance . . . well, no, not even then." The Prince squared his shoulders and simulated a stance of firm resolve. "Molin, you are wrong—it would not be fitting for a Prince of the blood. I mean no slurs, but I cannot be seen consorting with a temple slave at a public festival."

Molin considered the refusal; considered taking Vashanka's role himself—he'd seen the temple slave in question. But he had been honest with the Prince; it was of the utmost importance that the child be properly conceived.

"My Prince, I do not ask this lightly, any more lightly than I informed my brethen in Ranke of my decision in this matter. The slave is of the best Northern stock; the rite is held in strictest mystery.

"The Hand of Vashanka rests heavily on your

prefecture, my Prince. You cannot have failed to
notice His presence. The daily auguries show it
plainly. Your own Hell-Hounds, the very guardians of Imperial Order, are not immune to the
dangers of Vashanka's unbridled presence!"

The High Priest paused, staring hard into
Kadakithus' eyes, forcing the young governor to
acknowledge the rumors that flew freely and
were never disputed. Molin could trace his an-
cestry to the god in the time-honored way, but
what about Tempus? The Hell-Hound bore Vashanka's mark, but had been whelped far beyond
the ken of the priesthood.

"Who are we to channel the powers of the
gods?" the Prince responded, his gaze unfocused, his manner uncomfortably evasive.

Molin drew himself up to his full height, some
finger-widths taller than the Prince. His back
straightened as if the beaten gold headdress of
his office balanced on his brow. "My Prince, we
are the channels, the only true channels. Without the mediation of a duly consecrated hierarchy the bonds of tradition which make
Vashanka—mayHisnamebepraised—our God
and us His worshippers would be irreparably
sundered. The rituals of the temple, whose origins are one with the God Himself, are the balance between mortal and immortal. Anyone
who circumvents the rituals, for any reason
however well-intentioned . . ., anyone who
does not harken to the call of the hierarchy in its
needs subverts the proper relationship of god
and worshipper to the damning harm of both!"

Again the experienced Imperial Hierarch
stared down on the young, awestruck Prince.

Molin was only half-conscious of overstating the case for stringent observation of the rituals. Vashanka's displeasure when He was not properly appeased was extensively documented. The rituals were all intended to bind a capricious and hungry deity.

The crowd outside Molin's window raised its voice and shut down their conversation; the day's verdicts were being proclaimed. There would be two more hangings on the morrow. Kadakithus started when his name was used to justify the awful punishments the Empire meted out to its criminals. He shrank back from the window as a huge black crow landed on the sill, swiveling its head in a lopsided stare of dark curiosity. The Prince shooed it back to the gallows.

"I will do what I can, Molin. I will speak with my advisers."

"My Dear Prince, in matters regarding the spiritual well-being of the Imperial Presence in Sanctuary, I am your *only* trusted adviser."

Molin regretted his burst of temper at once; though the Prince gave him smooth verbal assurances, the Vashankan priest was now certain that the Hound, Tempus, would know by sundown.

Tempus: a plague, a thorn, a malignancy to the proper order of things. A son of Vashanka, a true-son no doubt, and utterly unfettered by the constraints of ritual and hierarchy. If even a fraction of the rumors about him were to be believed; if he had survived dissection on Kurd's tables . . . It could not be believed. Tempus could not be so far beyond the hierarchy's reach.

Well, Molin thought after a moment, I'm a
true-son too. Let the Prince run to him in sweating anxiety. Let him consult with Tempus; let
them conspire against me—I'll still succeed.

Generations of priests had bred generations of
true-sons to Vashanka. The god was not quite the
blood-drinker he once was. Vashanka could be
constrained and, after all, Molin's side of the
family was far bigger than Tempus'.

He watched the Prince leave without feeling
panic. The crow returned to the window-ledge
as was its daily custom. The bird cawed impatiently while Molin and the mute prepared its
feast: live mouse dipped in wine. The priest
watched the bird disappear back to the Maze
rooftops, staring after its flight long after his wife
had begun to shout his name.

4

Seylalha stood perfectly still while the dour-
faced women draped the sea-green froth around
her. The women would not hesitate to prick her
sharply with their bodkins and needles, though
they took the greatest of care with the silk. They
stepped back and signaled that she should spin
on her toes for them.

Deep folds of material billowed out into delicate clouds at her slightest movement. The texture of the cloth against her skin was so unlike
the heavy tatters of her usual attire that for once
she forgot to watch the intricate dance-language

of her instructors as they discussed their crea-
tion.

The time must be drawing near; they would
not dress her like this unless it was almost time
for her marriage to the god. The moon above her
cell was a thin crescent fading to blackness.

They got their instruments and began to play.
Without waiting for the sharp report of the
clatter-sticks, Seylalha began to dance, letting
the unhummed ends of the silk swirl out to accompany her as she moved through the hun-
dreds of poses—each painfully inured in her
muscles. She flowed with the atonal music,
throwing her soul into each leap and turn,
keenly aware that this meaningless collection of
movements would become her only, exquisite
plea for freedom.

When she settled into the final frantic moments of the dance the sea-green silk was caught
in her flying hair and lifted away from her body
until it was restrained only by the brooches at her
neck and waist. As she fell into the prostrate
bow, the silk floated down, hiding the rhythmic
heaving of her exhausted lungs. The clatter-
sticks were silent, without nagging corrections.

Seylalha separated her hair and stood up in
one graceful movement. Her teachers were motionless as well as speechless. Never again
would she be the bullied student. Clapping her
own hands at the quiet women, Seylalha waited
until the nearest one crept forward to unpin the
twisted silk and accompany her to her bath.

5

It was inky night and even the light of two dozen torches was insufficient to guide the procession along the treacherous, rutted streets of Sanctuary in safety. Molin Torchholder and five other ranking members of the hierarchy had excused themselves from the procession and waited in the relative comfort of the stone-porch of the still incomplete Temple of Vashanka. Behind the priests a great circular tent had been erected. The mute women could be heard tuning and conversing with their instruments. As the bobbing torches rounded into the plaza the women were silenced and Molin, ever-careful with his elaborate headdress, mounted a small dias on the porch.

The girl, Seylalha, shrouded in a cloak of feathers and spun gold, clutched the side-rail of the open platform as six bearers recruited from the garrison struggled with the rough-hewn steps. She lurched violently to one side, spilling the luxuriant cloth almost to the ground, but her dancer's reflexes saved her from an ill-omened tumble. Ten felons from the city dungeons, drugged into a stupor, clambered past— oblivious to the past and present as well as the limited future. Their white robes were already soiled by numerous falls in the muddy streets but none had seriously injured himself.

At the rear of the procession, wearing another mask of hammered gold and obsidian, Prince Kadakithus groped his way to the tent. He glanced at Molin as he passed though their masks made subtle communication impossible. It was enough, for Molin's purposes, that the Prince himself was entering the tent. He tied the cloth-door of the tent closed and braced three crossed spears against the lintel.

The Hell-Hounds formed an outer perimeter—the Hell-Hounds save for Tempus whom Molin, with self-congratulations, had had assigned to other duties in the palace; the man might not do as he was told, but he wouldn't be near this ritual. The Hounds held their drawn swords before them; they would administer the coup-de-grace should anyone leave or enter the tent before sunrise. Molin reminded them of their obligations in a voice that carried well beyond the unfinished walls.

"Those Ten whom Vashanka destroyed have been disgraced and remain unworshipped to this day; their very names have been unlearned. But the wraith of a god is far stronger than the spirit of a mortal man. They will feel their deaths again and converge upon this site seeking an unwitting or feeble mortal whom they can usurp and use against their brother. It is your duty to see that this does not occur!"

Zalbar, captain of the Hell-Hounds bellowed his comprehension of Molin's order.

6

The women, and they were all dressed as women though Seylalha knew some of them

were the eunuchs who routinely guarded her,
crept forward to remove the heavy cloak from her
shoulders. She shook the cramped silk and knotted her fingers in anticipation. A partition of fine
netting separated the musicians from the other
participants in this drama, but their sounds were
familiar and oddly soothing. The carpet on
which she had always danced lay slightly to one
side of the center of the tent and behind the
carpet was a mound of pillows to which the
burly "women" directed her.

The white-robed men were invited to partake
of a banquet laid out on a low table and fell over
each other rushing to the sumptuous food. The
masked figure who stood apart from the rest and
seemed distinctly uncomfortable under his
splendid robe was led to a separate table where
only stale bread and water had been laid and an
ugly, heavy short-sword awaited him.

So, that was the god, Seylalha thought, as the
mask was lifted from his face. He was weak-
chinned—but what civilized man did not show
the stains of his rich foods and soft bed? He was,
at least, a whole man.

The man-god would not look at her, preferring
to watch the darkest, least penetrable recesses of
the tent. Seylalha knew fear for his curiously
absent passions. Sliding off the cushions she
struck the first position of her dance, expecting
the musicians to lift their instruments.

But the musicians reached for their clatter-
sticks and the eunuchs guided her rudely back to
the cushions. She shook their hands away, aware
that they dared not hurt her, but then her attention, and the attention of everyone in the tent,

was riveted to a newcomer, a more appropriate man-god who had eased out of the darkness and held an unsheathed dagger in his left hand.

He was tall, massive, etched with the harsh lines of a rough and feral man. The one whom she had mistaken for the man-god embraced the newcomer with hearty familiarity.

"I was afraid you wouldn't show up, Tempus."

"Both you and He had my word. Torchholder is a canny man; he distrusts me already—I could not walk in right behind you, my Prince."

"She is beautiful . . ." the prince mused, glancing to Seylalha for the first time.

"You've reconsidered? It would be for the best if you did . . . even now. Her beauty means nothing to me. None of this means anything to me except that it must be done and I must do it."

"Yes, you're the one to do it . . . though she is more tempting than I would have thought possible."

The chiefmost of the gowned eunuchs moved to separate the men, giving the interloper a stiff punch on the shoulder. Seylalha, who could read the language of movement, froze in terror as the feral stranger turned, hesitated and plunged the dagger deep into the eunuch's chest all within the space of a few heartbeats. The other "women" who saw little more than a blur of movement, wailed and groaned in terror as the dead eunuch collapsed to the rough ground. Even the white-robed feasters ceased their eating and became a frightened knot of sheep-like men.

"It will be as I warned you, my Prince—not merely the Ten but all the others. If you've no taste for bloodshed it would be best if you depart now. My men await you. I will do my father's work."

"What of Zalbar? I knew nothing about that until Molin addressed them."

"They did not see me; it is unlikely they will see you."

The one who had been called the Prince slunk into the darkness. The other retrieved his dagger from the corpse.

"Our Imperial Prince is not one for rituals of bloodshed and violence," he said to everyone in the tent. "He has asked me to take the role of my father in his stead. Would any here gainsay my right to act for Vashanka and my Prince?"

The question was purest rhetoric. The bloody corpse was testimony to the price of gainsaying this intruder. Seylalha wrenched a heavy tassel from one of the pillows and shredded it behind her. She clung to the belief that her life had been an arrow directed to this night, her dance would be her salvation; but that belief was shaken as the eunuchs who had ruled her for so many years cowered in fear and the feasting men made a doomed attempt to find hiding places.

With an unpleasant smile the man-god strode to the table where he ripped a mouthful of bread from the loaf, drained the beaker of salted water and lifted the crude sword. He shifted it once or twice in his hand, his fingers adjusting to its awkward balance. With the same smile still on his lips he advanced toward the terrified men in white.

Screaming, despite the drugs, they raced through the tent as he winnowed through their

numbers. The wisest, least drugged, plunged
through the netting into the company of musicians. The man-god stalked his ersatz-brethren
if the darkness did not exist and with a vicious
determination that bespoke his acceptance of the
role. He shoved the shrieking women aside with
his free hand and delivered the final strokes with
the bloody sword. The killing completed, he set
about gathering the heads of his enemies and
placing them in a gory heap on the banquet
table—a task made no easier to do or watch by
the edgeless sword he wielded.

Still kneeling among the pillows, Seylalha
drew the sheer silk tightly around herself, twisting the loose ends about her arms until she had
became a sea-green statue, for the cloth did nothing to conceal her beauty and little to conceal her pale, quivering fear. When the blood-
smeared stranger who was more god than man
had placed the last trophy upon the table he
vented his divine violence on the woman-garbed
eunuchs. Seylalha pulled the pins from her hair;
the honey-brown cascade covered her eyes and
hid her from the sight of the guardians lying
butchered on the ground. She took fistfuls of hair
and pressed them against her ears, but that was
not enough to block the knowledge of how the
half-men had died. As she had done so many
times as a child and as a woman, she began to
rock back and forth, keening softly to gods
whose names she had long since forgotten.

"It is time, Azyuna."

His voice broke into her prayers. His hand
clamped over her wrist and drew her inexorably
to her feet. Her legs shook and she could not

remain upright except through his hold on her.
When he shook her slightly she only closed her
eyes tighter and swayed limply in his grasp.

"Open your eyes, girl. It is time!"

Obedient to the outside will Seylalha opened
her eyes and shook back her hair. The hand that
gripped her was clean. The voice that commanded her had something of that forgotten
wild land of her birth in it. His hair was the same
color as her own, but he was not a man come to
claim his bride. She hung from his grip as mute
and fearful as the quiet women behind the torn
netting.

"You are obviously the one to make Azyuna's
pleas—however little you resemble her. Do not
force me to hurt you more than I must already!"
he whispered urgently, leaning close to her ear,
his breath as warm and thick as blood. "Or have
they not told you the whole legend? I am myself,
I am Vashanka—we both grow impatient, girl.
Dance because your life depends on it."

He flicked her wrist and sent her sprawling to
the blood-dampened carpet. She brushed her
hair away with a forearm made red from his grip.
The man-god had shed the somber clothing he
had worn for the killing and stood near the pillows in a clean gold-worked tunic, but the crude
sword still hung by his thigh—a rusty blush on
the white tunic to mark where its cleaning had
not been complete. She read the tension in his
legs, the minute extension of his left hand toward the sword-hilt, the slight lowering of one
eyebrow and remembered that the dance was
her freedom.

Seylalha brought one hand through the tan-

gled mane of her hair, pointed two fingers to her
musicians. They struck a ragged, jarring chord to
mark their own apprehensions but the tam-
bourist found her throbbing drone and the dance
began.

At first she felt the uneven ground beneath the
rug and the damp spots upon it, just as she saw
those icy eyes and the outstretched fingers. Then
there were only the years of practice, the music
and the desperation of the dance itself. Three
times she felt herself collapse on a misplaced
foot; three times the music saved her and, writhing, twisting, she caught herself with will-
driven muscles that dared not feel their torture.

Her lungs were on fire, her heartbeat louder
than the droning tambour and she danced. She
heard only the pounding rhythms of the music
and her heart; she saw Azyuna, dark and volup-
tuous, as she had first performed it before her
long-toothed, blood-stained brother.

The god Vashanka smiled and Seylalha,
honey-hair and sea-green silk twined together,
began the dervish finale of the dance. There was
a salt-metal taste in her mouth when she doubled
into a barely controlled collapse on the carpet,
limbs trembling and glimmering with sweat in
the torchlight.

Darkness hovered at the end of her thoughts,
the total darkness of exhaustion and death; a
freedom she had not anticipated, but in the
still-bright center of her thoughts she saw first
the bloody god then the white-and-honey
stranger, both smiling, both walking slowly toward her. The sword was gone.

Strong arms parted the hair from her shoul-

ders, lifted her effortlessly from the carpet and
held her close against cool, dry skin. A leaden
arm shook off its tiredness and found his shoulder to rest on. Had Azyuna loved her brother so
deeply?

"Release her! I'm the proper sister for your
lusts." A voice which was not Seylalha's filled
the tent with images of fire and ice.

"Cime!" the white-and-honey man said while
Seylalha slid helplessly back to the carpet.

"She is a slave, a temple's pawn—their tool to
capture you and Vashanka both!"

"What brought you here?" the man's voice
was filled with wonder as well as anger and,
perhaps, a trace of fear. "You did not know . . ."

"The smells of sorcery, priests and the timely
knowledge of intrigue. I owe you this much.
They mean to bind the God."

"They meant to fill the lily-Prince with Vashanka and gain a Prince if not a child. Their
plans are sufficiently thwarted."

Seylalha twisted slowly, raising an arm
slightly to see past her hair to the tall, slender
woman with the steel-streaked hair. Her breath
came easier now; the dance had not killed her—
only the god could give her freedom now.

"Mortal flesh is no bond—as you well know.
Vashanka's children bear a special curse . . ."
the man-god said, taking a step toward the woman.

"Then we'll complete their sorry ritual and
damn the curse. They'll kill the slut when she
bleeds again and for us—who knows? A god's
freedom?"

The woman, Cime, jerked the knot loose from

her vest, revealing a body that belied the steel in
her hair. Seylalha felt the man step further away
from her. Cime's words echoed mockingly in her
ears. She had envisioned Vashanka falling upon
his dark sister, this man-god would do no less.
And she, Seylalha, would lie unbroken until the
full moon. While brother and sister advanced
slowly toward each other Seylalha's toes closed
over the hilt of the discarded sword and dragged
it into her reach. With serpentine swiftness and
silence she shot between the pair, facing the
woman, breaking the spell that drew them together.

"He is mine!" she screamed in a voice so seldom used that it might have belonged to Azyuna
herself. "He is mine to bring my child, my freedom!" She held the sword to the other woman's
breast.

The sister stepped back, anger, thwarted desire and more burned in her eyes, but Seylalha
saw the fear in her movements and knew she had
won. The man's fingers wove through her honey
hair, closing on the neck brooch that held the
cloth at her shoulder, ripping it from the soft silk.

"She's right, Cime. You can't lure me with His
freedom; I've felt it for too long already. We'll
play Torchholder's little game to the end and let
the Face of Chaos laugh at us all. The girl's won
her child, so leave—or I'll let her use the tent-peg
on you."

Cime's face was fury unbounded, but Seylalha
no longer cared. The sword dropped from her
fingers as soon as his arms lifted her a second
time and carried her, without interruption, to the
pillows. She grasped his tunic and tore it back

from his shoulders with a determination equal to his own. The mute women gathered their instruments and found a compelling harmony with which to fill the tent.

Seylalha lost herself with him until there was nothing beyond the pillows and the memory of the music. The torches were long since exhausted and in the darkness her god-lover was neither awesome nor cruel. He might have intended rape and pain, but her passion for a child and freedom consumed him and he lay asleep across her breast. Her body curved against his and though she had not meant it to happen, she fell asleep as well.

He grunted and jerked upright, leaving her puzzled and cold on the pillows. Wariness tightened the muscles of his leg. She raised herself up on one elbow without learning the source of his sudden concern.

"Cover yourself," he instructed, thrusting his torn tunic at her.

"Why?"

"There'll be a fire here," he spoke as if repeating words that swam in his head already. "By Wrigglies, Cime or what . . . we're betrayed."

He gripped her arm and hauled her to her feet as the tent burst into flames around them. Clutching the tunic to her breast, Seylalha molded herself against him. He was motionless for less than a second; the fire swept through the roof-cloth and raced toward the carpet and pillows where they stood. Sparks jumped toward her long hair; she screamed and flailed at the flames until he put them out with his hands and hoisted her rudely in his arms.

The firelight leeched all gentleness from his face, replacing it with pain and a glint of vengeance. One of the beams that supported the tent cracked down before them, sending a blaze of fire up past his knees. He cursed names that meant nothing to her as he walked through the inferno.

They broke through the ring of flames into the predawn moistness of the port-city air. She coughed, realizing she had scarcely breathed since he had lifted her. With the gasps of cool air she caught the bitter scents of singed hair and charred flesh.

"Your legs?" she whispered.

"They'll mend; they always do."

"But you're hurt now," she protested. "I can walk—there's no need to carry me."

She twisted to be free of him but his grip grew tighter and unfriendly. She began to fear him again as if their moments together in the tent had been a dream. The pinching fingers holding her arms and thighs could never have been gentle.

"I have not hurt you," he snarled. "Of more women than I care to remember you alone had demands that would sate me. You've gotten your freedom and I've gotten rest in a woman's arms. When it is safe I'll put you down, but not before."

He carried her past the scattered stones of the unfinished temple and out into the open land beyond the limits of Ranken Sanctuary toward the houses left to ruins since Ilsig abandoned the town. She shivered and shed quiet tears, but clung tightly as he assaulted the uneven, over-

grown fields in the gray predawn light. He
stopped by a crumbling wall and set her down
upon it.

"The Hounds patrol here at dawn; they'll find
you and bring you safely to the Prince and
Torchholder."

She didn't ask to go with him, holding the
request firmly within herself. The one for whom
she had danced was gone, probably forever, and
the one who remained was not the sort a dancer-
slave would be wise to follow. And there was the
child to consider . . . Still, she could not turn
away from him as he glared at her. His face sof-
tened slightly, as if her lover might live somewhere behind that grim visage.

"Tell me your name," he demanded in a voice
half-gentle, half-mocking.

"Seylalha."

"A Northern name, isn't it? A pretty name to
remember."

And he was gone, striding back across the
fallow gardens to the town. She wrapped the
torn, scorched tunic around her bare shoulders
and waited.

7

Molin Torchholder hurried down the polished
stone corridors of the palace; his new sandals
slapped the soles of his feet and echoed in the
empty hallways. The sound reminded him of his
slaves' leather-wrapped sticks and that re-

minded him of how few slaves were left in the
temple since the mysterious fire had taken so
many lives the night of the Ten-Slaying two
weeks before.

He had sent a messenger to the capital the next
day with a full report of the events as he understood them. He'd written and sealed it himself.
The Prince could not have sent word faster; no
post could have returned in that time. There was
no reason to think that Kadakithus or the Emperor himself would be thinking about Vashanka
today. But the Prince's summons had been
preemptive, so Molin hiked the long, empty corridors with a worried look on his face.

The Ten-Slaying had convinced him to take
his prince more seriously. When the charred tatters of cloth and wood had cooled enough to let
the Hounds investigate the blaze, they had found
a heap of blackened skulls in one place and the
bodies of the ten felons scattered throughout the
burned wreckage. For one who had expressed a
distaste for bloodshed, Kadakithus had recreated
Vashanka's vengeance to the final letter of the
legends—a precision not required and which
Molin could not even remember describing to
the Prince.

Tempus stood beside the Prince's throne, back
in town after another unexplained absence. The
massive, cruel Hell-Hound did not look
happy—perhaps the strains of the Sacred
Brotherhoods' loyalty were beginning to show.
Molin wished, for the last time, that he knew
why he had been summoned, then nodded to the
herald and heard himself announced.

"Ah, Molin, there you are. We'd been wondering what was keeping you," the Prince said with his usual charm.

"My new quarters, while much appreciated, seem to be several leagues from here. I'd never thought there could be so much corridor in a small palace."

"The rooms are adequate? The Lady Rosanda . . ."

"The girl who danced Azyuna's Dance—what has become of her?" Tempus interrupted and Molin turned his attention at once from the Prince to the Hell-Hound.

"A few burns," he responded cautiously, seeing displeasure in Tempus' eyes. The Hound had called this interview; Molin no longer doubted it. "Minor ones," he added. "What little discomfort she may have experienced seems to have passed completely."

"You've freed her, haven't you, Molin?" the Prince chimed in nervously.

"As a matter of course, though it's too soon to tell if she'll bear a child. I thought it best to take her survival as a sign of the god's favor—in the absence of any other information. You haven't remembered anything yourself, my Prince?" Molin faced the Prince but glanced at Tempus. There was something in the Hound's face whenever the Ten-Slaying was discussed, but Molin doubted he'd ever get to the bottom of it. Kadakithus claimed the god had so completely possessed him that he remembered nothing from the moment the tent was sealed until sunrise when he found himself in his own bed.

"If she is with child?" Tempus continued.

"Then she will live out her days at the temple with the full honors of a freedwoman and the living consort of our god—as you know. Her power could become considerable—though only time will tell. It depends on her, and the child— if there is a child."

"And if there is no child?"

Molin shrugged. "In many respects it will be no different. It is not in the temple's power to remove the honors we have bestowed. Vashanka saw fit to remove her from the inferno." It was easier to imagine Vashanka possessing Tempus than the Prince, but Molin had not become High Priest by speaking his mind. "We acknowledge her as First Consort of Sanctuary. It would be best if she had conceived."

Tempus nodded and looked away. It was the signal the Prince had been waiting for. He had been even more uncomfortable at this interview than Molin; Molin was used to hiding secrets. The Prince left the chamber without ritual, leaving the High Priest and the Hell-Hound together for a moment.

"I've talked with her often these past few days. Remarkable, isn't it, to discover that a slave has a mind?" Molin said aloud to himself but for Tempus' benefit. If the Hound had an interest in Seylalha the Priesthood wished to use it. "She is convinced she slept with the god—in all other respects she is intelligent and not given to false beliefs, but her faith in her lover will not be shaken. She dances for him still, in silence. I've replaced the silks, but women and eunuchs must come from the capital and that will take time.

"I watch her each evening at sunset; she

doesn't seem to mind. She is very beautiful, but sad and lonely as well—the dance has changed since the Ten-Slaying. You must come and watch for yourself sometime."

A MAN AND HIS GOD

Janet Morris

Solstice storms and heat lightning beat upon Sanctuary, washing the dust from the gutters and from the faces of the mercenaries drifting through town on their way north where (seers proclaimed and rumor corroborated) the Rankan Empire would soon be hiring multitudes, readying for war.

The storms doused cookfires west of town, where the camp followers and artificers that Sanctuary's ramshackle facilities could not hold had overflowed. There squatted, under stinking ill-tanned hide pavilions, custom weaponers catering to mercenaries whose eyes were keener than the most carefully wax-forged iron and whose panoplies must bespeak their where-abouts in battle to their comrades; their deadly

efficacy to strangers and combatants; the dear
cost of their hire to prospective employers. Fine
corselets, cuirasses ancient and modern, custom's best axes and swords, and helmetry with
crests dyed to order could be had in Sanctuary
that summer; but the downwind breeze had
never smelled fouler than after wending through
their press.

Here and there among the steaming firepots
siegecrafters and commanders of fortifications
drilled their engineers, lest from idleness picked
men be suborned by rival leaders seeking to up-
grade their corps. To keep order here, the Emperor's halfbrother Kadakithis had only a handful of Rankan Hell-Hounds in his personal
guard, and a local garrison staffed by indigenous
Ilsigs, conquered but not assimilated. The Rankans called the Ilsigs "Wrigglies," and the
Wrigglies called the Rankans naked barbarians
and their women worse, and not even the rain
could cool the fires of that age-old rivalry.

On the landspit north of the lighthouse, rain
had stopped work on Prince Kadakithis's new
palace. Only a man and horse, both bronze, both
of heroic proportions, rode the beach. Doom
criers of Sanctuary, who once had proclaimed
their town "just left of heaven," had changed
their tune: they had dubbed Sanctuary Death's
Gate and the one man, called Tempus, Death
Himself.

He was not. He was a mercenary, envoy of a
Rankan faction desirous of making a change in
emperors; he was a Hell-Hound, by Kadakithis's
good offices; and marshal of palace security, because the prince, not meant to triumph in his

governorship/exile, was understaffed. Of late
Tempus had become a royal architect, for which
he was as qualified as any man about, having
fortified more towns than Kadakithis had years.
The prince had proposed the site; the soldier
examined it and found it good. Not satisfied, he
had made it better, dredging deep with oxen
along the shore while his imported fortifications
crews raised double walls of baked brick filled
with rubble and faced with stone. When complete, these would be deeply crenelated for archers, studded with gatehouses, double-gated
and sheer. Even incomplete, the walls which
barred the folk from spit and lighthouse grinned
with a death's head smirk toward the town, en-
closing granaries and stables and newly whited
barracks and a spring for fresh water: if War came
hither, Tempus proposed to make Him welcome
for a long and arduous siege.

The fey, god's breath weather might have
stopped work on the construction, but Tempus
worked without respite, always: it eased the soul
of the man who could not sleep and who had
turned his back upon his god. This day, he
awaited the arrival of Kadakithis and that of his
own anonymous Rankan contact, to introduce
emissary to possible figurehead, to put the two
together and see what might be seen.

When he had arranged the meeting, he had yet
walked in the shelter of the god Vashanka's arm.
Now, things had changed for him and he no
longer cared to serve Vashanka, the Storm God,
who regulated kingship. If he could, he was
going to contrive to be relieved of his various
commissions and of his honor bond to

Kadakithis, freed to go among the mercenaries to whom his soul belonged (since he had it back) and put together a cohort to take north and lease to the highest bidder. He wanted to wade thigh-deep in gore and guts and see if, just by chance, he might manage to find his way back through the shimmering dimensional gate beyond which the god had long ago thrust him, back into the world and into the age to which he was born.

Since he knew the chances of that were less than Kadakithis becoming Emperor of Upper and Lower Ranke, and since the god's gloss of rationality was gone from him, leaving him in the embrace of the curse, yet lingering, which he had originally become the god's suppliant to thwart, he would settle for a small mercenary corps of his own choosing, from which to begin building an army that would not be a puerile jest, as Kadakithis's forces were at present. For this he had been contacted, to this he had agreed. It remained only to see to it that Kadakithis agreed.

The mercenary who was a Hell-Hound scolded the horse, who did not like its new weighted shoes or the water surging around its knees, white as its stockings. Like the horse, Kadakithis was only potential in quest of actualization; like the horse, Kadakithis feared the wrong things, and placed his trust in himself only, an untenable arrogance in horse or man, when the horse must go to battle and the man also. Tempus collected the horse up under him, shifting his weight, pulling the red-bronze beast's head in against its chest, until the combination of his guidance and the toe-weights on its hooves and the waves' kiss showed the horse what he wanted. Tempus could feel it in the stallion's gaits; he did not need to see the result: like a dancer, the sorrel lifted each leg high. Then it gave a quizzical snort as it sensed the power to be gained from such a stride: school was in session. Perhaps, despite the four white socks, the horse would suit. He lifted it with a touch and a squeeze of his knees into a canter no faster than another horse might walk. "Good, good," he told it, and from the beach came the *pat-pat* of applause.

Clouds split; sunrays danced over the wrack-strewn shore and over the bronze stallion and its rider, stripped down to plated loinguard, making a rainbow about them. Tempus looked up, landward to where a lone eunuch clapped pink palms together from one of Prince Kadakithis's chariots. The rainbow disappeared, the clouds suppressed the sun, and in a wrap of shadow the enigmatic Hell-Hound (whom the eunuch knew from his own experience to be capable of regenerating a severed limb and thus veritably eternal; and who was indubitably deadlier than all the mercenaries descended on Sanctuary like flies upon a day-old carcass) trotted the horse up the beach to where the eunuch in the chariot was waiting on solid ground.

"What are you doing here, Sissy? Where is your lord, Kadakithis?" Tempus stopped his horse well back from the irascible pair of blacks in their traces. This eunuch was near their color: a Wriggly. Cut young and deftly, his answer came in a sweet alto:

"Lord Marshal, most daunting of Hell-Hounds, I bring you His Majesty's apologies, and true word, if you will heed it."

The eunuch, no more than seventeen, gazed at him longingly. Kadakithis had accepted this fancy toy from Jubal, the slaver, despite the slavemaster's own brand on its high rump, and the deeper dangers implied by the identity of its fashioner. Tempus had marked it, when first he heard its lilting voice in the palace, for he had heard that voice before. Foolish, haughty, or merely pressed beyond a bedwarmer's ability to cope: no matter; this creature of Jubal's, he had long wanted. Jubal and Tempus had been making private war, the more fierce for being undeclared, since Tempus had first come to Sanctuary and seen the swaggering, masked killers Jubal kept on staff terrorizing whom they chose on the town's west side. Tempus had made those masked murderers his private game stock, the west end of Sanctuary his personal preserve, and the campaign was on. Time and again, he had dispatched them. But tactics change, and Jubal's had become too treacherous for Tempus to endure, especially now with the northern insurrection half out of its egg of rumor. He said to the parted lips awaiting his permission to speak and to the deer-soft eyes doting on his every move that the eunuch might dismount the car, prostrate itself before him, and from there deliver its message.

It did all of those, quivering with delight like a dog enraptured by the smallest attention, and said with its forehead to the sand: "My lord, the

Prince bids me say he has been detained by Certain Persons, and will be late, but means to attend you. If you were to ask me why that was, then I would have no choice but to admit to you that the three most mighty magicians, those whose names cannot be spoken, came down upon the summer palace in billows of blackest smoke and foul odors, and that the fountains ran red and the sculptures wept and cried, and frogs jumped upon my lord in his bath, all because the Hazards are afraid that you might move to free the slayer-of-sorcerers called Cime before she comes to trial. Although my master assured them that you would not, that you had said nothing to him about this woman, when I left they still were not satisfied, but were shaking walls and raising shades and doing all manner of wizardly things to demonstrate their concern."

The eunuch fell quiet, awaiting leave to rise. For an instant there was total silence, then the sound of Tempus's slithering dismount. Then he said: "Let us see your brand, pretty one," and with a wiggling of its upthrust rump the eunuch hastened to obey.

It took Tempus longer than he had estimated to wrest a confession from the Wriggly, from the Ilsig who was the last of his line and at the end of his line. It did not make cries of pleasure or betrayal or agony, but accepted its destiny as good Wrigglies always did, writhing soundlessly.

When he let it go, though the blood was running down its legs and it saw the intestine like wet parchment caught in his fingernails, it wept with relief, promising to deliver his exhortation posthaste to Kadakithis. It kissed his hand, pressing his palm against its beardless cheek, never realizing that it was, itself, his message, or that it would be dead before the sun set.

2

Kneeling to wash his arm in the surf, he found himself singing a best-forgotten funerary dirge in the ancient argot all mercenaries learn. But his voice was gravelly and his memories were treacherous thickets full of barbs, and he stopped as soon as he realized that he sang. The eunuch would die because he remembered its voice from the workshop of despicable Kurd, the frail and filthy vivisectionist, while he had been an experimental animal therein. He remembered other things, too: he remembered the sear of the branding iron and the smell of flesh burning and the voices of two fellow guardsmen, the Hell Hounds Zalbar and Razkuli, piercing the drug-mist through holes the pain poked in his stupor. And he recalled a protracted and hurtful healing, shut away from any who might be overawed to see a man regrow a limb. Mending, he had brooded, seeking certainty, some redress fit to his grievance. But he had not been sure enough to act. Now, after hearing the eunuch's tale, he was certain. When Tempus was certain, Destiny got out its ledger.

But what to write therein? His instinct told him it was Black Jubal he wanted, not the two

Hell-Hounds; that Razkuli was a nonentity and Zalbar, like a raw horse, was merely in need of schooling. Those two had single-handedly arranged for Tempus's snuff to be drugged, for him to be branded, his tongue cut out, then sold off to wicked little Kurd, there to languish interminably under the knife? He could not credit it. Yet the eunuch had said—and in such straits no one lies—that though Jubal had gone to Zalbar for help in dealing with Tempus, the slave trader had known nothing of what fate the Hell Hounds had in mind for their colleague. Never mind it; Jubal's crimes were voluminous. Tempus would take him for espionage—that punishment could only be administered once. Then personal grudges must be put aside: it is unseemly to hold feuds with the dead.

But if not Jubal, then who had written Tempus's itinerary for Hell? It sounded, suspiciously, like the god's work. Since he had turned his back upon the god, things had gone from bad to worse. And if Vashanka had not turned His face away from Tempus even while he lay helpless, the god had not stirred to rescue him (though any limb lopped off him still grew back, any wound he took healed relatively quickly, as men judge such things). No, Vashanka, his tutelary, had not hastened to aid him. The speed of Tempus's healing was always in direct proportion to the pleasure the god was taking in His servant. Vashanka's terrible rebuke had made the man wax terrible, also. Curses and unholy insults rang down from the mind of the god and up from the mind of the man who then had no tongue left with which to scream. It had taken

Hanse the thief, young Shadowspawn, chance-
met and hardly known, to extricate him from
interminable torture. Now he owed more debt
than he liked to Shadowspawn, and Shadowspawn knew more about Tempus than even
that backstreeter could want to know, so that the
thief's eyes slid away, sick and mistrust-
ful, when Tempus would chance upon him in
the Maze.

But even then, Tempus's break with divinity
was not complete. Hopefully, he stood as Vashanka in the recreation of the Ten-Slaying and
Seduction of Azyuna, thinking to propitiate the
god while saving face—to no avail. Soon after,
hearing that his sister, Cime, had been appre-
hended slaying sorcerors wantonly in their beds,
he had thrown the amulet of Vashanka, which he
had worn since former times, out to sea from this
very shore—he had had no choice. Only so much
can be borne from men, so much from gods.
Zalbar, had he the wit, would have revelled in
Tempus's barely-hidden reaction to his news
that the fearsome mage-killer was now in cus-
tody, her diamond rods locked away in the Hall
of Judgement awaiting her disposition.

He growled to him, thinking about her, her
black hair winged with gray, in Sanctuary's un-
segregated dungeons where any syphilitic rapist
could have her at will, while he must not touch
her at all, or raise hand to help her lest he start
forces in motion he could not control. His break
with the god stemmed from her presence in
Sanctuary, at his endless wandering as Vashanka's minion had stemmed from an altercation he
had over her with a mage. If he went down into

the pits and took her, the god would be placated; he had no desire to reopen relations with Vashanka, who had turned His face away from His servant. If Tempus brought her out under his own aegis, he would have the entire Mageguild at his throat; he wanted no quarrel with the Adepts. He had told her not to slay them here, where he must maintain order and the letter of the law.

By the time Kadakithis arrived in that very same chariot, its braces sticky with Wriggly blood, Tempus was in a humor darker than the drying clots, fully as dark as the odd, round cloud coming fast from the northeast.

Kadakithis's noble Rankan visage was suffused with rage, so that his skin was darker than his pale hair: "But *why*? In the name of all the gods, what did the poor little creature ever do to you? You owe me a eunuch, and an explanation." He tapped his lacquered nails on the chariot's bronze rim.

"I have a perfect replacement in mind," smiled Tempus smoothly, "my lord. As for why . . . all eunuchs are duplicitous. This one was an information conduit to Jubal. Unless you would like to invite the slaver to policy sessions and let him stand behind those ivory screens where your favorites eavesdrop as they choose, I have acted well within my prerogatives as marshal. If my name is attached to your palace security, then your palace *will be* secure."

"Bastard! How dare you even imply that *I* should apologize to *you*? When will you treat me with the proper amount of respect? You tell me all eunuchs are treacherous, the very breath after offering me another one!"

"I am giving you respect. Reverence I reserve
for better men than I. When you have attained
that dignity, we shall both know it: you will not
have to ask. Until then, either trust or discharge
me." He waited, to see if the prince would speak.
Then he continued: "As to the eunuch I offer as
replacement, I want you to arrange for his training. You like Jubal's work; send to him saying
yours has met with an accident and you wish to
tender another into his care to be similarly instructed. Tell him you paid a lot of money for it,
and you have high hopes."

"You have such a eunuch?"

"I will have it."

"And you expect me to conscion your sending
of an agent in there—aye, to aid you— without
knowing your plan, or even the specifics of the
Wriggly's confession?"

"Should you know, my lord, you would have
to approve, or disapprove. As it lies, you are free
of onus."

The two men regarded each other, checked
hostility jumping between them like Vashanka's
own lightning in the long, dangerous pause.

Kadakithis flicked his purple mantle over his
shoulder. He squinted past Tempus, into the
waning day. "What kind of cloud is that?"

Tempus swung around in his saddle, then
back. "That should be our friend from Ranke."

The prince nodded. "Before he arrives, then,
let us discuss the matter of the female prisoner
Cime."

Tempus's horse snorted and threw its head,
dancing in place. "There is nothing to discuss."

"But . . .? Why did you not come to me about it? I could have done something, previously. Now, I cannot . . ."

"I did not ask you. I am not asking you." His voice was a blade on whetstone, so that Kadakithis pulled himself up straight. "It is not for me to take a hand."

"Your own sister? You will not intervene?"

"Believe what you will, prince. I will not sift through gossip with any man, be he prince or king."

The prince lost hold, then, having been "princed" too often back in Ranke, and berated the Hell-Hound.

The man sat quite still upon the horse the prince had given him, garbed only in his loin-guard though the day was fading, letting his gaze full of festering shadows rest in the prince's until Kadakithis trailed off, saying," . . . the trouble with you is that anything they say about you could be true, so a man knows not what to believe."

"Believe in accordance with your heart," the voice like grinding stone suggested, while the dark cloud came to hover over the beach.

It settled, seemingly, into the sand, and the horses shied back, necks outstretched, nostrils huge. Tempus had his sorrel up alongside the chariot team and was leaning down to take the lead-horse's bridle when an earsplitting clarion came from the cloud's transluscent center.

The Hell-Hound raised his head then, and Kadakithis saw him shiver, saw his brow arch, saw a flicker of deepset eyes within their caves of bone and lid. Then again Tempus spoke to the chariot horses, who swiveled their ears toward him and took his counsel, and he let loose the lead-horse's bridle and spurred his own between Kadakithis's chariot and what came out of the cinereous cloud which had been so long descending upon them in opposition to the prevailing wind:

The man on the horse who could be seen within the cloud waved: a flash of scarlet glove, a swirl of burgundy cloak. Behind his tasseled steed he led another, and it was this second gray horse who again challenged the other stallions on the beach, its eyes full of fire. Farther back within the cloud, stonework could be seen, masonry like none in Sanctuary, a sky more blue and hills more virile than any Kadakithis knew.

The first horse, reins flapping, was emerging, nose and neck casting shadows upon solid Sanctuary sand; then its hooves scattered grains, and the whole of the beast, and its rider, and the second horse he led on a long tether, stood corporeal and motionless before the Hell-Hound, while behind, the cloud whirled in upon itself and was gone with an audible "pop."

"Greetings, Riddler," said the rider in burgundy and scarlet, as he doffed his helmet with its blood-dark crest to Tempus.

"I did not expect you, Abarsis. What could be so urgent?"

"I heard about the Trôs horse's death, so I thought to bring you another, better auspiced, I hope. Since I was coming anyway, our friends suggested I bring what you require. I have long wanted to meet you." Spurring his mount forward, he held out his hand.

Red stallion and iron gray snaked arched necks, thrusting forth clacking teeth, wide-gaped jaws emitting squeals to go with flattened ears and rolling eyes. Above horse hostilities could be heard snatches of low wordplay, parry and riposte: ". . . disappointed that you could not build the temple." ". . . welcome to take my place here and try. The foundations of the temple grounds are defiled, the priest in charge more corrupt than even politics warrants. I wash my hands . . ." ". . . with the warring imminent, how can you . . . ?" "Theomachy is no longer my burden." "That cannot be so." ". . . hear about the insurrection, or take my leave!" ". . . His name is unpronounceable, and that of his empire, but I think we all shall learn it so well we will mumble it in our sleep . . ." "I don't sleep. It is a matter of the right field officers, and men young enough not to have fought upcountry the last time." "I am meeting some Sacred Band members here, my old team. Can you provision us?" "Here? Well enough to get to the capital and do it better. Let me be the first to . . ."

Kadakithis, forgotten, cleared his throat.

Both men stared at the prince severely, as if a child had interrupted adults. Tempus bowed low in his saddle, arm outswept. The rider in reds with the burnished cuirass tucked his helmet under his arm and approached the chariot, handing the second horse's tether to Tempus as he passed by.

"Abarsis, presently of Ranke," said the dark,

cultured voice of the armored man, whose hair
swung black and glossy on a young bull's neck.
His line was old, one of court graces and bas-
relief faces and upswept, regal eyes that were
disconcertingly wise and as gray-blue as the
huge horse Tempus held with some difficulty.
Ignoring the squeals of just-met stallions, the
man continued: "Lord Prince, may all be well
with you, with your endeavors and your hold-
ings, eternally. I bear reaffirmation of our bond to
you." He held out a purse, fat with coin.

Tempus winced, imperceptibly, and took
wraps of the gray horse's tether, drawing its head
close with great care, until he could bring his fist
down hard between its ears to quiet it.

"What is this? There is enough money here to
raise an army!" scowled Kadakithis, tossing the
pouch lightly in his palm.

A polite and perfect smile lit the northern face,
so warmly handsome, of the Rankan emissary.
"Have you not told him, then, O Riddler?"

"No, I thought to, but got no opportunity.
Also, I am not sure whether we *will* raise it, or
whether that is my severance pay." He threw a
leg over the sorrel's neck and slid down it, butt to
horse, dropped its reins and walked away down
the beach with his new Trôs horse in hand.

The Rankan hooked his helmet carefully on
one of the saddle's silver rosettes. "You two are
not getting on, I take it. Prince Kadakithis, you
must be easy with him. Treat him as he does his
horses; he needs a gentle hand."

"He needs his comeuppance. He has become
insufferable! What is this money? Has he told
you I am for sale? I am not!"

"He has turned his back on his god and the god is letting him run. When he is exhausted, the god will take him back. You found him pleasant enough, previously, I would wager. He has been set upon by your own staff, men to whom he was sworn and who gave oaths to him. What do you expect? He will not rest easy until he has made that matter right."

"What is this? My men? You mean that long unexplained absence of his? I admit he is changed. But how do you know what he would not tell me?"

A smile like sunrise lit the elegant face of the armored man. "The god tells me what I need to know. How would it be, for him to come running to you with tales of feuding among your ranks like a child to his father? His honor precludes it. As for the . . . funds . . . you hold, when we sent him here, it was with the understanding that should he feel you would make a king, he would so inform us. This, I was told you knew."

"In principle. But I cannot take a gift so large."

"Take a loan, as others before you have had to do. There is no time now for courtship. To be capable of becoming a king insures no seat of kingship, these days. A king must be more than a man, he must be a hero. It takes many men to make a hero, and special times. Opportunities approach, with the upcountry insurrection and a new empire rising beyond the northern range. Were you to distinguish yourself in combat, or field an army that did, we who seek a change could rally around you publicly. You cannot do it with what you have, the emperor has seen to that."

"At what rate am I expected to pay back this loan?"

"Equal value, nothing more. If the prince, my lord, will have patience, I will explain all to Your Majesty's satisfaction. That, truly, is why I am come."

"Explain away, then."

"First, one small digression, which touches a deeper truth. You must have some idea who and what the man you call Tempus is, I am sure you have heard it from your wizards and from his enemies among the officials of the Mageguild. Let me add to that this: Where he goes, the god scatters His blessings. By the cosmological rules of state cult and kingship, He has invested this endeavor with divine sanction by his presence. Though he and the god have their differences, without him, no chance remains that you might triumph. My father found that out. Even sick with his curse, he is too valuable to waste, unappreciated. If you would rather remain a princeling forever, and let the empire slide into ruin apace, just tell me and I will take word home. We will forget this matter of the kingship and this corollary matter of a small standing army, and I will release Tempus. He would as soon it, I assure you."

"Your *father*? Who in the God's Eye *are* you?"

"Ah, my arrogance is unforgivable; I thought you would know me. We are all so full of ourselves, these days, it is no wonder events have come to such a pass. I am Man of the God in Upper Ranke, Sole Friend to the Mercenaries, the hero, Son of the Defender, and so forth."

"High Priest of Vashanka."

"In the Upper Land."

"My family and yours thinned each others
line," stated Kadakithis baldly, no apology, no
regret in his words. Yet he looked differently
upon the other, thinking they were of an age,
both wielding wooden swords in shady courts
while the slaughter raged, far off at the fronts.

"Unto eradication," remarked the dark young
man. "But we did not contest, and now there is a
different enemy, a common threat. It is enough."

"And you and Tempus have never met?"

"He knew my father. And when I was ten, and
my father died and our armies were disbanded,
he found a home for me. Later, when I came to
the god and the mercenaries' guild, I tried to see
him. He would not meet with me." He shrugged,
looking over his shoulder at the man walking the
blue-gray horse into blue-gray shadows falling
over the blue-black sea. "Everyone has his hero,
you know. A god is not enough for a whole man;
he craves a fleshly model. When he sent to me for
a horse, and the god approved it, I was elated.
Now, perhaps, I can do more. The horse may not
have died in vain, after all."

"I do not understand you, Priest."

"My Lord, do not make me too holy. I am
Vashanka's priest: I know many requiems and
oaths, and thirty-three ways to fire a warrior's
bier. They call me Stepson, in the mercenaries'
guild. I would be pleased if you would call me
that, and let me talk to you at greater length about
a future in which your destiny and the wishes of
the Storm God, our Lord, could come to be the
same."

"I am not sure I can find room in my heart for

such a god; it is difficult enough to pretend to piety," grated Kadakithis, squinting after Tempus in the dusk.

"You will, you will," promised the priest, and dismounted his horse to approach Tempus's ground-tied sorrel. Abarsis reached down, running his hand along the beast's white-stocking'd leg. "Look, Prince," he said, craning his neck up to see Kadakithis's face as his fingers tugged at the gold chain wedged in the weight-cleat on the horse's shoe. At the end of the chain, sandy but shining gold, was an amulet. "The god wants him back."

3

The mercenaries drifted into Sanctuary dusty from their westward trek or blue-lipped from their rough sea passage and wherever they went they made hellish what before had been merely dissolute. The Maze was no longer safe for pickpocket or pander; usurer and sorcerer scuttled in haste from street to doorway, where before they had swaggered virtually unchallenged, crime lords in fear of nothing.

Now the whores walked bowlegged, dreamy-eyed, parading their new finery in the early hours of the morning while most mercenaries slept; the taverns changed shifts but feared to close their doors, lest a mercenary find that an excuse to take offense. Even so early in the day, the inns were full of brawls and the gutters full of casualties. The garrison soldiers and the Hell-

Hounds could not be omnipresent: wherever they were not, mercenaries took sport, and they were not in the Maze this morning.

Though Sanctuary had never been so prosperous, every guild and union and citizen's group had sent representatives to the palace at sunrise to complain.

Lastel, a/k/a One-Thumb, could not understand why the Sanctuarites were so unhappy. Lastel was very happy: he was alive and back at the Vulgar Unicorn tending bar, and the Unicorn was making money, and money made Lastel happy, always. Being alive was something Lastel had not fully appreciated until recently, when he had spent aeons dying a subjective death in thrall to a spell he had paid to have laid upon his own person, a spell turned against him by the sons of its deceased creator, Mizraith of the Hazard class, and dispelled by he-knew-not-whom. Though every night he expected his mysterious benefactor to sidle up to the bar and demand payment, no one ever came and said: "Lastel, I saved you. I am the one. Now show your gratitude." But he knew very well that someday soon, someone would. He did not let this irritation besmirch his happiness. He had gotten a new shipment of Caronne krrf (black, pure drug, foil stamped, a full weight of it, enough to set every mercenary in Sanctuary at the kill) and it was so good that he considered refraining from offering it on the market. Having considered, he decided to keep it all for himself, and so was very happy indeed, no matter how many fistfights broke out in the bar, or how high the sun was, these days, before he got to bed . . .

Tempus, too, was happy that morning, with
the magnificent Trôs horse under him and signs
of war all around him. Despite the hour, he saw
enough rough hoplites and dour artillery fighters with their crank-bows (whose springs were
plaited from women's hair) and their quarrels
(barbed and poisoned) to let him know he was
not dreaming: these did not bestir themselves
from daydreams! The war was real to them. And
any one of them could be his. He felt his troop-
levy money cuddled tight against his groin, and
he whistled tunelessly as the Trôs horse
threaded his way toward the Vulgar Unicorn.

One-Thumb was not going to be happy much
longer.

Tempus left the Trôs horse on its own recogni-
zance, dropping the reins and telling it, "Stay."
Anyone who thought it merely ripe for stealing
would learn a lesson about the strain which is
bred only in Syr from the original line of Trôs's.

There were a few locals in the Unicorn, most
snoring over tables along with other, bagged
trash ready to be dragged out into the street.

One-Thumb was behind his bar, big shoulders
slumped, washing mugs while watching everything through the bronze mirror he had had in-
stalled over his stock.

Tempus let his heels crack against the board
and his armor clatter: he had dressed for this,
from a box he had thought he might never again
open. The wrestler's body which Lastel had built
came alert, pirouetted smoothly to face him, staring unabashedly at the nearly god-sized apparition in leopard-skin mantle and helmet set with

boar's tusks, wearing an antique enameled breastplate and bearing a bow of ibex-horn morticed with a golden grip.

"*What* in Azyuna's twat are *you*?" bellowed One-Thumb, as every waking customer he had hastened to depart.

"I," said Tempus, reaching the bar and removing his helmet so that his yarrow-honey hair spilled forth, "am Tempus. We have not chanced to meet." He held out a hand whose wrist bore a golden bracer.

"Marshal," acknowledged One-Thumb, carefully, his pate creasing with his frown. "It is good to know you are on our side. But you cannot come in here . . . My—"

"I am here, *Lastel*. While you were so inexplicably absent, I was often here, and received the courtesy of service without charge. But now I am not here to eat or drink with those who recognize me for one who is fully as corrupt as are they themselves. There are those who know where you were, *Lastel*, and why—and *one* who broke the curse that bound you. Truly, if you had cared, you could have found out." Twice, Tempus called One-Thumb by his true name, which no palace personage or Mazedweller should have known enough to do.

"Marshal, let us go to my office." Lastel fairly ramped behind his bar.

"No time, krrf-dealer. Mizraith's sons, Stefab and Marype; Markmor: those three and more were slain by the woman Cime who is in the pits awaiting sentence. I thought that you should know."

"What are you saying? You want me to break her out? Do it yourself."

"No one," said the Hell-Hound, "can break anyone out of the palace. *I* am in charge of security there. If she were to escape, I would be very busy explaining to Kadakithis what went wrong. And tonight I am having a reunion here with fifty of my old friends from the mercenaries' guild. I would not want anything to spoil it. And, too, I ask no man to take me on faith, or go where I have not been." He grinned like the Destroyer, gesturing around. "You had better order in extra. And half a piece of krrf, your courtesy to me, of course. Once you have seen my men when well in hand, you will be better able to conjecture what might happen should they get out of hand, and weigh your alternatives. Most men I solicit find it to their benefit to work in accord with me. Should you deem it so for you, we will fix a time, and discuss it."

Not the cipher's meaning, nor the plan it shrouded, nor the threat that gave it teeth were lost on the man who did not like to be called "Lastel" in the Maze. He bellowed: "You are addled. You cannot do this. I cannot do that! As for krrf, I know nothing about. . .any. . .krrf."

But the man was gone, and Lastel was trembling with rage, thinking he had been in purgatory too long; it had eroded his nerves!

4

When the dusk cooled the Maze, Shadow-spawn ducked into the Unicorn. One-Thumb was not in evidence; Two-Thumbs was behind the bar.

He sat with the wall supporting him, where the story-teller liked to sit, and watched the door, waiting for the crowd to thicken, tongues to loosen, some caravan driver to boast of his wares. The mercenaries were no boon to a thief, but dangerous playmates, like Kadakithis's palace women. He did not want to be intrigued; he was being distracted moment by moment. As a consequence, he was very careful to keep his mind on business, so that he would not come up hungry next Ilsday, when his funds, if not increased, would run out.

Shadowspawn was dark as iron and sharp like a hawk; a cranked crossbow, loaded with cold bronze and quarrels to spare. He wore knives where a professional wears them, and sapphire and gold and crimson to draw the eye from his treasured blades.

Sanctuary had spawned him: he was hers, and he had thought nothing she did could surprise him. But when the mercenaries arrived as do clients to a strumpet's house, he had been hurt like a whore's bastard when first he learns how his mother feeds him.

It was better, now; he understood the new rules.

One rule was: get up and give them your seat.
Hanse gave no one his seat. He might recall
pressing business elsewhere, or see someone he
just had to hasten over to greet. Tonight, he remembered nothing earlier forgotten; he saw no
one he cared to bestir himself to meet. He prepared to defend his place as seven mercenaries
filled the doorway with plumes and pelts and
hilts and mail, and looked his way. But they
went in a group to the bar, though one, in a black
mantle, with iron at chest and head and wrists,
pointed directly to him like a man sighting his
arrow along an outstretched arm.

The man talked to Two-Thumbs awhile, took
off his helmet with its horsehair crests that
seemed blood-red, and approached Hanse's
table alone. A shiver coursed the thief's flesh,
from the top of his black thatch to his toetips.

The mercenary reached him in a dozen swinging strides, drawing a stabbing sword as he came
on. If not for the fact that the other hand held a
mug, Shadowspawn would have aired iron by
the time the man (or youth from his smooth,
heartshaped face) spoke: "Shadowspawn, called
Hanse? I am Stepson, called Abarsis. I have been
hoping to find you." With a grin full of dazzling
teeth, the mercenary put the ivory-hilted sword
flat in the wet-rings on the table, and sat, both
hands well in evidence, clasped under his chin.

Hanse gripped his beltknife tightly. Then the
panic-flash receded, and time passed, instead of
piling all its instants terrifyingly on top of one
another. Hanse knew that he was no coward, that
he was plagued by flashbacks from the two times
he had been tapped with the fearstick of Va-

shanka, but his chest was heaving, and the mercenary might see. He slumped back, for camouflage. The mercenary with the expensive taste in accouterments could be no older than he. And yet, only a king's son could afford such a blade as that before him. He reached out hesitantly to touch its silvered guard, its garnet pommel, his gaze locked in the sellsword's soulless pale one, his hand slipping closer and closer to the elegant sword of its own accord.

"Ah, you do like it then," said Stepson. "I was not sure. You will take it, I hope. It is customary in my country, when meeting a man who has performed heroically to the benefit of one's house, to give a small token." He withdrew a silver scabbard from his belt, laid it with the sword, which Hanse put down as if burned.

"What did I ever do for you?"

"Did you not rescue the Riddler from great peril?"

"Who?"

The tanned face grinned ingenuously. "A truly brave man does not boast. I understand. Or is it a deeper thing? That—"He leaned forward; he smelled sweet like new-mown hay"—is truly what I need to know. Do you comprehend me?"

Hanse gave him an eagle's look, and shook his head slowly, his fingers flat on the table, near the magnificent sword that the mercenary Stepson had offered to give him. *The Riddler?* He knew no one of that name.

"Are you protecting him? There is no need, not from me. Tell me, Shadowspawn, are you and Tempus lovers?"

"Mother—!" His favorite knife leapt into his

palm, unbidden. He looked at it in his own grasp
in consternation, and dropped his other hand
over it, and began paring his nails. *Tempus! The
Riddler?* Hanse's eyes caressed the covetable
blade. "I helped him out, once or twice, that's
all."

"That is good," the youth across from him
approved. "Then we will not have to fight over
him. And, too, we could work a certain bargain,
service for service, that would make me happy
and you, I modestly estimate, a gentleman of
ease for at least six months."

"I'm listening," said Shadowspawn, taking a
chance, commending his knife to its sheath. The
short sword too, he handled, fitting it in the
scabbard and drawing it out, fascinated by the
alert scrutiny of Abarsis the Stepson's six companions.

When he began hearing the words "diamond
rods" and "Hall of Judgment" he waxed uneasy.
But by then, he could not see any way that he
could allow himself to appear less than heroic in
the pale, blue-gray eyes of the Stepson. Not
when the amount of money Stepson had offered
hung in the balance, not when the nobly
fashioned sword he had been given as if it were
merely serviceable proclaimed the flashy
mercenary's ability to pay that amount. But too,
if he would pay that, he would pay more. Hanse
was not so enthralled by the mercenaries' mys-
tique to hasten into one's pay without some good
Sanctuary barter. Watching Stepson's six for-
midable companions, waiting like purebred
hunting dogs curried for show, he spied a certain

litheness about them, an uncanny cleanliness of limb and nearness of girded hips. Close friends, these. Very close.

Abarsis's sonorous voice had ceased, waiting for Hanse's response. The disconcertingly pale eyes followed Hanse's stare, frank now, to his companions.

"Will you say yea, then, friend of the Riddler? And become my friend, also? These other friends of mine await only your willingness to embrace you as a brother."

"I own," Hanse muttered.

Abarsis raised one winged brow. "So? They are members of a Sacred Band, my old one; most prized officers; heroes, every pair." He judged Hanse's face. "Can it be you do not have the custom, in the south? From your mien I must believe it." His voice was liquid, like deep running water. "These men, to me and to their chosen partners, have sworn to forsake life before honor, to stand and never retreat, to fall where they fight if need be, shoulder to shoulder. There is no more hallowed tryst than theirs. Had I a thousand such, I would rule the earth."

"Which one is yours?" Hanse tried not to sneer, to be conversational, unshaken, but his eyes could find no comfortable place to rest, so that at last he took up the gift-sword and examined the hieratic writing on its blade.

"None. I left them, long ago, when my partner went up to heaven. Now I have hired them back, to serve a need. It is strictly a love of spirit, Hanse, that is required. And only in Sacred Bands is a mercenary asked so much."

"Still, it's not my style."

"You sound disappointed."

"I am. In your offer. Pay me twice that, and I will get the items you desire. As for your friends, I don't care if you bugger them each twice daily. Just as long as it's not part of my job and no one thinks I am joining any organizations."

A swift, appreciative smile touched Abarsis. "Twice, then. I am at your mercy."

"I stole those diamond rods once before, for Tem—, for the Riddler. He'll just give them back to her, after she does whatever it is she does for him. I had her once, and she did nothing for me that any other whore would not do."

"You *what*? Ah, you do not know about them, then? Their legend, their curse?"

"Legend? Curse? I *knew* she was a sorceress. Tell me about it! Am I in any danger? You can forget the whole idea, about the rods. I keep shut of sorcery."

"Hardly sorcery, no need to worry. They cannot transmit any of it. When he was young and she was a virgin, he was a prince and a fool of ideals. I heard it that the god is his true father, and thus she is *not* his sibling, but you know how legends are. As a princess, her sire looked for an advantageous marriage. An archmage of a power not seen anymore made an offer, at about the time the Riddler renounced his claim to the throne and retired to a philosopher's cave. She went to him begging aid, some way out of an unacceptable situation, and convinced him that should she be deflowered, the mage would not want her, and of all men the Riddler was the only one she trusted with the task; anyone else would despoil her. She seduced him easily, for he had loved her all his young life and that unacceptable attraction to flesh of his flesh was part of what drove him from his primogeniture. She loved nothing but herself; some things never change. He was wise enough to know he brought destruction upon himself, but men are prone to ruin from women. In passion, he could not think clearly; when it left him he went to Vashanka's altar and threw himself upon it, consigning his fate to the god. The god took him up, and when the archmage appeared with four eyes spitting fire and four mouths breathing fearful curses, the god's aegis partly shielded him. Yet, the curse holds. He wanders eternally bringing death to whomever loves him and being spurned by whomsoever he shall love. She must offer herself for pay to any comer, take no gift of kindness on pain of showing all her awful years, incapable of giving love as she has always been. So thus, the gods, too, are barred to her, and she is truly damned."

Hanse just stared at Stepson, whose voice had grown husky in the telling, when the mercenary left off.

"Now, will you help me? Please. He would want it to be you."

Hanse made a sign.

"*Would* want it to be me?" the thief frowned. "He does not *know* about this?" There came the sound of Shadowspawn's bench scraping back.

Abarsis reached out to touch the thief's shoulder, a move quick as lightning and soft as a butterfly's landing. "One must do for a friend what the friend cannot do for himself. With such a man, opportunities of this sort come seldom. If not for him, or for your price, or for whatever you hold sacred, do this thing for me, and I will be eternally in your debt."

A sibilant sound, part impatience, part exasperation, part irritation, came sliding down Shadowspawn's hawkish nose.

"Hanse?"

"You are going to *surprise* him with this deed, done? What if he has no taste for surprises? What if you are wrong, and he refrains from aiding her because he prefers her right where she is? And besides, I am staying away from him and his affairs."

"No surprise: I will tell him once I have arranged it. I will make you one more offer: Half again the doubled fee you suggested, to ease your doubts. But that is my final bid."

Shadowspawn squinted at the heartshaped face of Stepson. Then, without a word, he scooped up the short stabbing sword in its silver sheath, and found it a home in his belt. "Done," said Hanse.

"Good. Then, will you meet my companions?" The long-fingered, graceful hand of Stepson, called Abarsis, made a gesture that brought them, all smiles and manly welcomes, from their exile by the bar.

5

Kurd, the vivisectionist who had tried his skills on Tempus, was found a fair way from his adobe workshop, his gut stretched out for thirty feet before him: he had been dragged by the entrails; the hole cut in his belly to pull the intestines out was made by an expert: a mercenary had to be at fault. But there were so many mercenaries in Sanctuary, and so few friends of the vivisectionist, that the matter was not pursued.

The matter of the Hell-Hound Razkuli's head, however, was much more serious. Zalbar (who knew why both had died and at whose hands, and who feared for his own life) went to Kadakithis with his friend's staring eyes under one arm, sick and still tasting vomit, and told the prince how Tempus had come riding through the gates at dawn and called up to him where he was checking pass-bys in the gatehouse: "Zalbar, I've a message for you."

"Yo!" Zalbar had waved.

"Catch," Tempus laughed, and threw something up to him while the gray horse reared, uttered a shrill, demonic scream, and clattered off by the time Zalbar's hand had said *head: human;* and his eyes had said, *head: Razkuli's* and then begun to fill with tears.

Kadakithis listened to his story, looking beyond him out the window the entire time. When Zalbar had finished, the prince said,

"Well, I don't know what you expected, trying to take him down so clumsily."

"But he said it was a message for me," Zalbar entreated, caught his own pleading tone, scowled and straightened up.

"Then take it to heart, man. I can't allow you two to continue feuding. If it is anything other than simple feuding, I do not want to know about it. Stepson, called Abarsis, told me to expect something like this! I demand a stop to it!"

"*Stepson!*" Tall, lank Zalbar snarled like a man invoking a vengeful god in close fighting. "An ex-Sacred Bander looking for glory and death with honor, in no particular order! *Stepson* told you? The Slaughter Priest? My lord prince, you are keeping deadly company these days! Are all the gods of the armies in Sanctuary, then, along with their familiars, the mercenary hordes? I had wanted to discuss with you what could be done to curb them—"

"Zalbar," interrupted Kadakithis firmly. "In the matter of gods, I hold firm: I do not believe in them. In the matter of mercenaries, let them be. You broach subjects too sensitive for your station. In the matter of Tempus, I will talk to him. You change your attitude. Now, if that is *all* . . . ?"

It *was* all. It was nearly the end of Zalbar the Hell-Hound's entire career; he almost struck his commander-in-chief. But he refrained, though he could not utter even a civil goodbye. He went to his billet and he went into the town, and he worked wrath out of himself, as best he could. The dregs he washed away with drink, and after

that he went to visit Myrtis, the whoremistress of
Aphrodisia House who knew how to soothe him.
And she, seeing his heart breaking and his fists
shaking, asked him nothing about why he had
come, after staying away so long, but took him to
her breast and healed what she might of his
hurts, remembering that all the protection he
provided her and good he did for her, he did
because of a love spell she had bought and cast
on him long since, and thus she owed him at
least one night to match his dreams.

6

Tempus had gone among his own kind, after
he left the barracks. He had checked in at the
guild hostel north of the palace, once again in
leopard and bronze and iron, and he was welcome there.

Why he had kept himself from it for so long, he
could not have reasoned, unless it was that without these friends of former times the camaraderie
would not have been as sweet.

He went to the sideboard and got hot mulled
wine from a krater, sprinkling in goat's cheese
and grain, and took the posset to a corner, so the
men could come to him as they would.

The problem of the eunuch was still unsolved;
finding a suitable replacement was not going to
be easy: there were not many eunuchs in the
mercenaries' guild. The clubroom was red as
dying day and dark as backlit mountains, and he

felt better for having come. So, when Abarsis,
high priest of Upper Ranke, left his companions
and approached, but did not sit among, the mercenaries Tempus had collected, he said to the
nine that he would see them at the appointed
time, and to the iron-clad one:

"Life to you, Stepson. Please join me."

"Life to you, Riddler, and everlasting glory."
Cup in hand, he sipped pure water, eyes hardly
darker never leaving Tempus's face. "Is it
Sanctuary that has driven you to drink?" He
indicated the posset.

"The dry soul is wisest? Not at the empire's
anus, where the water is chancy. Anyway, those
things I said long ago and far away: do not hold
me to any of that."

The smooth cheek of Stepson ticced. "I must,"
he murmured. "You are the man I have emu-
lated. All my life I have listened after word of you
and collected intelligence of you and studied
what you left us in legend and stone in the north.
Listen: 'War is sire of all and king of all, and some
He has made gods and some men, some bond and
some free'. Or: 'War is ours in common; strife is
justice; all things come into being and pass away
through strife'. You see, I know your work, even
those other names you have used. Do not make
me speak them. I would work with you, O Sleep-
less One. It will be the pinnacle of my career." He
flashed Tempus a bolt of naked entreaty, then his
gaze flickered away and he rushed on: "You
need me. Who else will suit? Who else here has a
brand and gelding's scars? And time in the arena
as a gladiator, like Jubal himself? Who could

intrigue him, much less seduce him among these? And though I—"

"No."

Abarsis dug in his belt and tossed a golden amulet onto the table. "The god will not give you up; this was caught in the sorrel's new shoe. That teacher of mine whom you remember . . .?"

"I know the man," Tempus said grimly.

"He thinks that Sanctuary is the endpoint of existence; that those who come here are damned beyond redemption; that Sanctuary is Hell."

"Then how is it, Stepson," said Tempus almost kindly, "that folk experience fleshly death here? So far as I know, I am the only soul in Sanctuary who suffers eternally, with the possible exception of my sister, who may not have a soul. Learn not to listen to what people say, priest. A man's own mistakes are load enough, without adding others'."

"Then let me be your choice! There is no time to find some other eunuch." He said it flatly, without bitterness, a man fielding logic. "I can also bring you a few fighters whom you might not know and who would not dare, on their own, to approach you. My Sacred Band yearns to serve you. You dispense your favor to provincials and foreigners who barely recognize their honor! Give it to me, who craves little else . . . ! The prince who would be king will not expose me, but pass me on to Jubal as an untrained boy. I am a little old for it, but in Sanctuary, those niceties seem not to matter. I have increased your lot here. You owe me this opportunity."

Tempus stirred his cooling posset with a

finger. "That prince . . ." Changing the subject, he sighed glumly, a sound like rattling bones. "He will never be a Great King, such as your father. Can you tell me why the god is taking such an interest?

"The god will tell you, when you make of the Trôs horse a sacrifice. Or some person. Then He will be mollified. You know the ritual. If it be a man you choose, I will gladly volunteer . . . Ah, you understand me, now? I do not want to frighten you . . ."

"Take no thought of it."

"Then . . . though I risk your displeasure, yet I say it: I love you. One night with you would be a surfeit, to work under you is my long-held dream. Let me do this, which none can do better, which no *whole* man can do for you at all!"

"I cede you the privilege, since you value it so; but there is no telling what Jubal's hired hawk-masks might do to the eunuch we send in there."

"With your blessing and the god's, I am fearless. And you will be close by, busy attacking Black Jubal's fortress. While you are arresting the slavemaster for his treasonous spying, whosoever will make good the woman's escape. I understand your thought; I have arranged for the retrieval of her weapons."

Tempus chuckled. "I hardly know what to say."

"Say you look kindly upon me, that I am more than a bad memory to you."

Shaking his head, Tempus took the amulet Abarsis held out to him. "Come then, Stepson, we will see what part of your glorious expectations we can fulfill."

7

It was said, ever after, that the Storm God took part in the sack of the slaver's estate. Lighting crawled along the gatehouses of its defensive wall and rolled in balls through the inner court and turned the oaken gates to ash. The ground rumbled and buckled and bucked and great crumbling cracks appeared in its inner sanctum, where the slaver dallied with the glossy-haired eunuch Kadakithis had just sent up for training. It was profligate waste to make a fancy boy out of such a slave: the arena had muscled him up and time had grown him up, and to squeeze the two or three remaining years of that sort of pleasure out of him seemed to the slaver a pity. If truth be known, blood like his came so rarely to the slavepens that gelding him was a sin against future generations: had Jubal gotten him early on—when the cuts had been made, at nine, or ten—he would have raised him with great pains and put him to stud. But his brand and tawny skin smacked of northern mountains and high wizards' keeps where the wars had raged so savagely that no man was proud to remember what had been done there, on either side.

Eventually, he left the eunuch chained by the neck to the foot of his bed and went to see what the yelling and the shouting and the blue flashes and the quivering floorboards could possibly mean.

What he saw from his threshhold he did not understand, but he came striding back, stripping off his robe as he passed by the bed, rushing to arm himself and do battle against the infernal forces of this enemy, and, it seemed, the whole of the night.

Naphtha fireballs came shooting over his walls into the courtyard; flaming arrows torqued from spring-wound bows; javelins and sword-play glittered nastily, singing as they slew in soft susurrusings Jubal had hoped never to hear there.

It was eerily quiet: no shouting, not from his hawk-masks, or the adversaries; the fire crackled and the horses snorted and groaned like the men where they fell.

Jubal recollected the sinking feeling he had had in his stomach when Zalbar had confided to him that the bellows of anguish emanating from the vivisectionist's workshop were the Hell-Hound Tempus's agonies, the forebodings he had endured when a group of his beleaguered sellswords went after the man who killed those who wore the mask of Jubal's service for sport, and failed to down him.

That night, it was too late for thinking. There was time enough only for wading into the thick of battle (if he could just find it: the attack was from every side, out of darkness); hollering orders; mustering point leaders (two); and appointing replacements for the dead (three). Then he heard whoops and abysmal screams and realized that someone had let the slaves out of their pens; those who had nothing to lose bore haphazard arms, but sought only death with vengeance. Jubal, seeing wide, white rimmed eyes and murderous mouths and the new

eunuch from Kadakithis's palace dancing ahead
of the pack of them, started to run. The key to its
collar had been in his robe; he remembered dis-
carding it, within the eunuch's reach.

He ran in a private wash of terror, in a bubble
through which other sounds hardly penetrated,
but where his breathing reverberated stentorian,
rasping, and his heart gonged loud in his ears.
He ran looking back over his shoulder, and he
saw some leopard-pelted apparition with a horn
bow in hand come sliding down the gatehouse
wall. He ran until he reached the stable, until he
stumbled over a dead hawk-mask, and then he
heard everything, cacophonously, that had been
so muted before: swords rasping; panoplies rattling; bodies thudding and greaved men running; quarrels whispering bright death as they
passed through the dark press; javelins ringing
as they struck helm or shield suddenly limned in
lurid fiery light.

Fire? Behind Jubal flame licked out the stable
windows and horses whistled their death
screams.

The heat was singeing. He drew his sword and
turned in a fluid motion, judging himself as he
was wont to do when the crowds had been about
him in applauding tiers and he must kill to live
to kill another day, and do so pleasingly.

He felt the trill of it, the immediacy of it, the joy
of the arena, and as the pack of freed slaves came
shouting, he picked out the prince's eunuch and
reached to wrest a spear from the dead hawk-
mask's grip. He hefted it, left-handed, to cast,
just as the man in leopard pelt and cuirass and a
dozen mercenaries came between him and the

slaves, cutting him off from his final refuge, the
stairs to the westward wall.

Behind him, the flames seemed hotter, so that
he was glad he had not stopped for armor. He
threw the spear, and it rammed home in the
eunuch's gut.

The leopard leader came forward, alone,
sword tip gesturing three times, leftward.

Was it Tempus, beneath that frightful armor?
Jubal raised his own blade to his brow in acceptance, and moved to where his antagonist indicated, but the leopard leader was talking over his
shoulder to his front-line mercenaries, three of
whom were clustered around the downed
eunuch. Then one archer came abreast of the
leader, touched his leopard pelt. And that bow-
man kept a nocked arrow on Jubal, while the
leader sheathed his sword and walked away, to
join the little knot around the eunuch.

Someone had broken off the haft; Jubal heard
the grunt and the snap of wood and saw the shaft
discarded. Then arrows whizzed in quick succession into both his knees and beyond the shat-
tering pain, he knew nothing more.

8

Tempus knelt over Abarsis, bleeding out his
life naked in the dirt. "Get me light," he rasped.
Tossing his helmet aside, he bent down until his
cheek touched Stepson's knotted, hairless belly.
The whole bronze head of the spear, barbs and
all, was deep in him. Under his lowest rib, the

shattered haft stuck out, quivering as he breathed. The torch was brought; the better light told Tempus there was no use in cutting the spearhead loose; one flange was up under the low rib; vital fluids oozed out with the youth's blood. Out of age-old custom, Tempus lay his mouth upon the wound and sucked the blood and swallowed it, then raised his head and shook it to those who waited with a hot blade and hopeful, silent faces. "Get him some water, no wine. And give him some air."

They moved back and as the Sacred Bander who had been holding Abarsis's head put it down, the wounded one murmured; he coughed, and his frame shuddered, one hand clutching spasmodically at the spear. "Rest now, Stepson. You have got your wish. You will be my sacrifice to the god." He covered the youth's nakedness with his mantle, taking the gory hand from the broken haft, letting it fasten on his own.

Then the blue-gray eyes of Abarsis opened in a face pale with pain, and something else: "I am not frightened, with you and the god beside me."

Tempus put an arm under his head and gathered him up, pulling him across his lap. "Hush, now."

"Soon, soon," said the paling lips. "I did well for you. Tell me so . . . that you are content. O Riddler, so well do I love you, I go to my god singing your praises. When I meet my father, I will tell him . . . I . . . fought beside you."

"Go with more than that, Stepson," whispered Tempus, and leaned forward, and kissed him gently on the mouth, and Abarsis breathed out his soul while their lips yet touched.

9

Now, Hanse had gotten the rods with no difficulty, as Stepson had promised he would be able to do, citing Tempus's control of palace personnel as surety. And afterward, the young mercenary's invitation to come and watch them fight up at Jubal's rang in his head until, to banish it, he went out to take a look.

He knew it was foolish to go, for it was foolish even to *know*, but he knew that he wanted to be able to say, "Yes, I saw. It was wonderful," the next time he saw the young mercenary, so he went very carefully and cautiously. If he were stopped, he would have all of Stepson's Sacred Band as witnesses that he had been at Jubal's, and nowhere near the palace and its Hall of Judgment.

He knew those excuses were flimsy, but he wanted to go, and he did not want to delve into why: the lure of mercenary life was heady in his nostrils; if he admitted how sweet it seemed, he might be lost. If he went, perchance he would see something not so sweet, or so intoxicating, something which would wash away all this talk of friendship and honor. So he went, and hid on the roof of a gatehouse abandoned in the confusion. Thus he saw all that transpired.

When he could in safety leave his roost, he followed the pair of gray horses bearing Tempus and the corpse ridgeward, stealing the first mount he came to that looked likely.

The sun was risen when Tempus reached the

ridgetop and called out behind: "Whoever you are, ride up," and set about gathering branches to make a bier.

Hanse rode to the edge of the outcropping of rock on which Tempus piled wood and said: "Well, accursed one, are you and your god replete? Stepson told me all about it."

The man straightened up, eyes like flames, and put his hand to the small of his back: "What do you want, Shadowspawn? A man who is respectful does not sling insults over the ears of the dead. If you are here for him, then welcome. If you are here for me, I assure you, your timing is ill."

"I *am* here for him, *friend*. What think you, that I would come here to console you in your grief when it was his love for you that he died of? He asked me," Hanse continued, not dismounting, "to get these. He was going to give them to you." He reached for the diamond rods, wrapped in hide, he had stolen.

"Stay your hand, and your feelings. Both are misplaced. Do not judge what you do not understand. As for the rods, Abarsis was mistaken as to what I wanted done with them. If you are finishing your first mercenary's commission, then give them to One-Thumb. Tell him they are for his benefactor. Then it is done. Someone of the Sacred Band will seek you out and pay you. Do not worry about that. Now, if you would honor Abarsis, dismount." The struggle obvious in Tempus's face for control was chilling, where nothing unintentional was ever seen. "Otherwise, please leave now, friend, *while* we are yet friends. I am in no mood for living boys today."

So Hanse slid from the horse and stalked over
to the corpse stage-whispering, "Mouth me no
swill, Doomface. If this is how your friends fare,
I'd as soon be relieved of the honor," and flipped
back the shroud. "His eyes are open." Shadowspawn reached out to close them.

"Don't. Let him see where he goes."

They glared a time at each other above the
staring corpse while a red-tailed hawk circled
overhead, its shadow caressing the pale, dead
face.

Then Hanse knelt stiffly, took a coin from his
belt, slid it between Stepson's slightly parted
lips, and murmured something low. Rising, he
turned and strode to his stolen horse and scrambled clumsily astride, reining it round and away
without a single backward glance.

When Tempus had the bier all made, and
Abarsis arranged on it to the last glossy hair, and
a spark nursed to consuming flame, he stood
with clenched fists and watering eyes in the billows of smoke. And through his tears, he saw the
boy's father, fighting oblivious from his car, his
charioteer fallen between his legs, that time
Tempus had hacked off an enemy's arm to save
him from the ax it swung; he saw the witchbitch
of a sorceress the king had wed in the black hills
to make alliance with what could not be had by
force; he saw the aftermath of that, when the wild
woman's spawn was out of her and every loyal
general took a hand in her murder before she laid
their commander out in state. He saw the boy,
wizard-haired and wise, running to Tempus's
chariot for a ride, grasping his neck, laughing,
kissing like the northern boys had no shame to

do; all this before the Great King discharged his
armies and retired home to peace, and Tempus
rode south to Ranke, an empire hardly whelped
and shaky on its prodigious feet. And Tempus
saw the field he had taken against a monarch,
once his liege: Masters change. He had not been
there when they had got the Great King, dragged
him down from his car and begun the Unending
Deaths that proved the Rankans barbarians second to none. It was said by those who were there
that he stood it well enough until his son was
castrated before his eyes, given off to a slaver
with ready collar . . . When he had heard, Tempus had gone searching among the sacked towns
of the north, where Ranke wrought infamy into
example, legends better than sharp javelins at
discouraging resistance. And he saw Abarsis in
the slaver's kennel, the boy's look of horror that a
man of the armies would see what had been done
to him. No glimmer of joy invaded the gaunt
child's face turned up to him. No eager hands
outflung to their redeemer; a small, spent hero
shuffled across soiled straw to meet him, slave's
eyes gauging without fear just what he might
expect from this man, who had once been among
his father's most valued, but was now only one
more Rankan enemy. Tempus remembered picking the child up in his arms, hating how little he
weighed, how sharp his bones were; and that
moment when Abarsis at last believed he was
safe. About a boy's tears, Abarsis had sworn
Tempus to secrecy. About the rest, the less said,
the better. He had found him foster parents, in
the rocky west by the sea temples where Tempus
himself was born, and where the gods still made

miracles upon occasion. He had hoped somehow the gods would heal what love could not. Now, they had done it.

He nodded, having passed recollection like poison, watching the fire burn down. Then, for the sake of the soul of Stepson, called Abarsis, and under the aegis of his flesh, Tempus humbled himself before Vashanka and came again into the service of his god.

10

Hanse, hidden below on a shelf, listening and partaking of the funeral of his own fashion, upon realizing what he was overhearing, spurred the horse out of there as if the very god whose thunderous voice he had heard were after him.

He did not stop until he reached the Vulgar Unicorn. There he shot off the horse in a dismount which was a fall disguised as a vault, slapped the beast smartly away, telling it hissingly to go home, and slipped inside with such relief as his favorite knife must feel when he sheathed it.

"One-Thumb," Hanse called out, making for the bar, "What is going on out there?" There had been soldierly commotion at the Common Gate.

"You haven't heard?" scoffed the night-turned-day barman. "Some prisoners escaped from the palace dungeon, certain articles were thieved from the Hall of Judgment, and none of the regular security officers were around to get their scoldings."

Looking at the mirror behind the bar, Hanse
saw the ugly man grin without humor. Gaze
locked to mirror-gaze, Hanse drew the hide-
wrapped bundle from his tunic. "These are for
you. You are supposed to give them to your
benefactor." He shrugged to the mirror.

One-Thumb turned and wiped the dishrag
along the shining bar and when the rag was
gone, the small bundle was gone, also. "Now,
what do you want to get involved in something
like this for? You think you're moving up?
You're not. Next time, when it's this sort of thing,
come round the back. Or, better, don't come at
all. I thought you had more sense."

Hanse's hand smacked flat and loud upon the
bar. "I have taken enough offal for one day, cup-
bearer. Now I tell you what you do, Wide-Belly:
You take what I brought you and your sage counsel, and you wrap it all together, and then you
squat on it!" And stiff-kneed as a roused cat,
Shadowspawn stalked away, toward the door,
saying over his shoulder: "As for sense, I thought
you had more."

"I have my business to think of," called out
One-Thumb, too boldly for a whine.

"Ah, yes! So have I, so have I."

11

Lavender and lemon dawn light bedizened the
white-washed barracks' walls and colored the
palace parade grounds.

Tempus had been working all night, out at

Jubal's estate where he was quartering his mercenaries away from town and Hell-Hounds and
Ilsig garrison personnel. He had fifty there, but
twenty of them were paired members of three
different Sacred Bands: Stepson's legacy to him.
The twenty had convinced the thirty nonallied
operatives that "Stepsons" would be a good
name for their squadron, and for the cohort it
would eventually command should things go as
everyone hoped.

He would keep the Sacred Band teams and
spread the rest throughout the regular army, and
throughout the prince's domain. They would
find what clay they chose, and mold a division
from it of which the spirit of Abarsis, if it were
not too busy fighting theomachy's battles in
heaven, could look upon with pride.

The men had done Tempus proud, already,
that night at Jubal's, and thereafter; and this
evening when he had turned the corner round
the slave barracks the men were refitting for
livestock, there it had been, a love-note written
in lamb's blood two cubits high on the encircling
protective wall: "War is all and king of all, and
all things come into being out of strife."

Albeit they had not gotten it exactly right, he
had smiled, for though the world and the boy-
hood from out of which he had said such auda-
cious things was gone to time, Stepson, called
Abarsis, and his legacy of example and followers
made Tempus think that perhaps (oh just
perhaps) he, Tempus, had not been so young, or
so foolish, as he had lately come to think that he
had been. And if thus the man, then his epoch,
too, was freed of memory's hindsightful taint.

And the god and he were reconciled: This pushed away his curse and the shadow of distress it cast ever before him. His troubles with the prince had subsided. Zalbar had come through his test of fire and returned to stand his duty, thinking deeply, walking quietly. His courage would mend. Tempus knew his sort.

Jubal's disposition he had left to Kadakithis. He had wanted to take the famous ex-gladiator's measure in single combat, but there was no fitness in it now, since the man would never be quick on his feet, should he live to regain the use of them.

Not that the world was as ridiculously beautiful as was the arrogant summer morning which did not understand that it was a Sanctuary morning and therefore should at least be gory, garish, or full of flies buzzing about his head. No, one could find a few thorns in one's path, still. There was Shadowspawn, called Hanse, exhibiting unseemly and proprietary grief over Abarsis whenever it served him, yet not taking a billet among the Stepsons that Tempus had offered. Privately, Tempus thought he might yet come to it, that he was trying to step twice into the same river. When his feet chilled enough, he would step out onto the banks of manhood. If he could sit a horse better, perhaps his pride would let him join in where now, because of that, he could only sneer.

Hanse, too, must find his own path. He was not Tempus's problem, though Tempus would gladly take on that burden should Shadowspawn ever indicate a desire to have help toting it.

His sister, Cime, however, *was* his problem, his alone, and the enormity of that conundrum had him casting about for any possible solution, taking pat answers up and putting them down like gods move seeds from field to field. He could kill her, rape her, deport her; he could not ignore her, forget her, or suffer along without confronting her.

That she and One-Thumb had become enamored of one another was something he had not counted on. Such a thing had never occurred to him.

Tempus felt the god rustling around in him, the deep cavernous sensing in his most private skull that told him the deity was going to speak. *Silently!* he warned the god. They were uneasy with each other, yet, like two lovers after a trial separation.

We can take her, mildly, and then she will leave. You cannot tolerate her presence. Drive her off. I will help thee, spake Vashanka.

"Must you be so predictable, Pillager?" Tempus mumbled under his breath, so that Abarsis's Trôs horse swiveled its ears back to eavesdrop. He slapped its neck, and told it to continue on straight and smartly. They were headed toward Lastel's modest eastside estate.

Constancy is one of My attributes, jibed the god in Tempus's head meaningfully.

"You are not getting her, O Ravening One. You who are never satisfied, in this one thing, will not triumph. What would we have between us to keep it clear who is whom? I cannot allow it."

You will, said Vashanka so loud in his head that he winced in his saddle and the Trôs horse

broke stride, looking reproachfully about at him
to see what that shift of weight could possibly be
construed to mean.

Tempus stopped the horse in the middle of the
cool shadowed way on that beautiful morning
and sat stiffly a long while, conducting an inter-
nal battle which had no resolution.

After a time, he swung the horse back in its
tracks, kicked it into a lope toward the barracks
from which he had just come. Let her stay with
One-Thumb, if she would. She had come between him and his god before. He was not ready
to give her to the god, and he was not ready to
give himself back into the hands of his curse, rip
asunder what had been so laboriously patched
together and at such great cost. He thought of
Abarsis, and Kadakithis, and the refractory upcountry peoples, and he promised Vashanka any
other woman the god should care to choose before sundown. Cime would keep, no doubt, right
where she was. He would see to it that Lastel saw
to her.

Abarsis's Trôs horse snorted softly, as if in
agreement, single-footing through Sanctuary's
better streets toward the barracks. But the Trôs
horse could not have known that by this simple
decision its rider had attained to a greater victory
than in all the wars of all the empires he had ever
labored to increase. No the Trôs horse whose
belly quivered between Tempus's knees as it is-
sued a blaring trumpet to the dusty air did so not
because of its rider's triumph over self and god,
but out of pure high spirits, as horses always will
praise a fine day dawned.

THINGS THE EDITOR
NEVER TOLD ME

Lynn Abbey

I had just administered the coup de grace
to my latest THIEVES' WORLD offering—my
third—when Bob asked if I'd like to have the last
word in SHADOWS OF SANCTUARY. It was an
offer I couldn't refuse, though I'd no idea how I
would put into words the experiences of working on all three THIEVES' WORLD volumes.
After many unsuccessful attempts at getting this
essay down on paper, I began to suspect that
maybe Bob hadn't known the right words either.
He was smiling when he made the offer, and he
doesn't usually give up a by-line that easily.
Sigh. Another example of Things the Editor
Never Told Me.

Actually, a lot of things the editor didn't tell us were things he didn't know himself. We were all naive about the mechanics of a franchised universe back at Boskone of 1978 when the THIEVES' WORLD project was created. It sounded wondrously uncomplicated: we would exchange character sketches and refer to a common street map; Bob would write us a history; Andy Offutt would create our gods. We only had to go to ground and write our five— to—ten thousand words. Fat Chance. Unexpected discovery number one: Sanctuary isn't an imaginary anything; it's a state of mind recognized by the American Psychiatric Association.

We thought we'd gone to ground—it turned out that we'd gone overboard. Bob hadn't told us the things we'd really need to know, and none of us wanted to dictate to the guy who'd created this fun-house, so each of us made great use of the little vicissitudes of life that would add "grit" and "realism" to our stories. My not-gypsy read not-Tarot cards, dealt with necromancers, stole a corpse and witnessed the usual street violence.

It didn't seem too bad until I found the entire book oozing out of my mailbox and read the volume in its entirety. We had Crom-many drugs, magicians, vices, brothels, dives, haunts, curses and feuds. Sanctuary wasn't a provincial backwater; it wasn't even the Imperial armpit; it was the Black-Hole of not-Calcutta. Things could only get worse . . . .

And they did. Bob told us the second volume would be called TALES FROM THE VULGAR UNICORN—the very name incites depravity.

And we rose to the occasion—or perhaps we fell. I explored the unpleasant pieces of my S'danzo's past, gave her a berserker for a half-brother and created Buboe, the night bartender down at the Vulgar Unicorn. Well, Bob said we were supposed to have a scene down at the ol' V.U—but One-Thumb was hors de combat in the bowels of · Sanctuary and no one knew who was running the joint. (I recall one of my confreres created someone called Two-Thumbs—I think that was from spite.) Buboe—a buboe isn't a *person*, a buboe is the rather large glandular eruption that accompanies the terminal stages of the Black Plague; opening it insures death for the opener and the openee.

TALES didn't ooze out of the mailbox; it ate right through the metal. I haven't seen all the stories for volume three yet, but I'm confident the downward spiral has continued. Each set of stories brings new oddments of human behavior, new quirks of character that the authors wouldn't dare put in a universe for which he or she was solely responsible. In Sanctuary, though, where guilt is shared along with the glory, one volume's innuendo becomes the next volume's complete story.

And frankly, nastiness is interesting. If I tell you that the smell of rotting blood can linger for years you might not notice what I don't tell you. Consider for a moment some of the things none of the authors know for sure: the weather in Sanctuary—daily and seasonal. It must be strange. If the Downwinders are downwind of the town then the prevailing wind is off the land—try convincing any coast-dweller of *that*.

As far as the city itself is concerned, I've always imagined it as a sort of late medieval town, out-growing its walls. The Maze is built like the Shambles in York, England, where each storey gets built out over the lower one so everybody can drop their slops directly into the street instead of on their neighbor. There are those who seem to think Sanctuary's like Rome. (Nonsense, Ranke is Rome—or is it that Rome is rank?) They imagine that the town has the rudiments of sewer systems, that the villas are attractive, open buildings and that at least some of the streets are paved. There also seems to be a Baghdad-by-the-sea approach, with turban'd tribesmen and silk-clad ladies, as well as a few indications that we might be dealing with a Babylonian building-style. Since so many of our stories are set in the dark, I suppose it doesn't matter that we don't really agree on what the city looks like.

Of course, nobody, including the Empire, knows how big Sanctuary really is. Anytime one of us needs a secret meeting place we just create one—Sanctuary is either very large or very cramped. You can live your whole life in the Maze or the Bazaar, and yet it only takes fifteen minutes to walk from one end of town to the other—or does it? I'm not sure.

Take the Bazaar, for example. I've spent a fair amount of time in that bazaar and I don't know exactly how it's put together. Part of it is a farmer's market (though I haven't the faintest idea where the farmers are when they aren't at the Bazaar). Other parts are like the cloth-fairs of medieval France, where merchants sell their wares wholesale. Still other parts resemble the permanent bazaars of the Middle-East. Rather than trouble myself with philosophical questions, like how many angels can dance on the head of a pin, someday I've got to figure out how many S'danzo can live full-time in the bazaar.

Moving from angels to gods for a moment—it seems probable that anyone living in Sanctuary would have a personal relationship to the gods—nothing like worship or faith, mind you. The people seem homeric in their religion: the last thing an ordinary citizen wants is dealing with the gods; worship is designed to keep the deities at bay. We have at least two major pantheons represented in the temples and the gods know how many priesthoods trying to control them. They tell me there's a fellow out in California who has made a coherent mythology for the religions of Sanctuary. He's putting his theology into Chaosium's *THIEVES' WORLD* game, but nobody's saying where they're putting the intrepid mythmaster.

Then there's currency—or why we call it THIEVES' WORLD. Since no one knows how the currency works, the townsfolk have no choice but to steal from each other. We sort of agree that there are copper coins, silver coins and gold coins—but we don't know their names or their conversions rates. We say: a few copper coins; or we get very specific and say: nine Rankin soldats—just in case someone else is writing about soldats that weren't minted in Ranke. But how many soldats make a shaboozh—or does it work the other way around? It probably does.

Someday I'll create a money-lender for the town; making change in Sanctuary has got to be an art form. It won't do any good, though. Citizens and authors alike will find reasons not to visit my money-lender. They'll set up their own rates of exchange. The Prince will debase the currency. Vashanka will start spitting Indian-head nickels in his temple. I won't let that stop me. If the editor won't tell me how these things are to be done, I'll just have to start telling *him*.

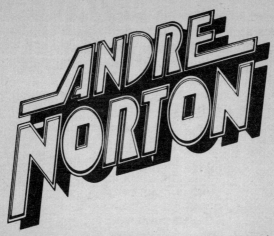

ANDRE NORTON

CONAN

☐ 11577-2	**CONAN, #1**	$2.50
☐ 11595-0	**CONAN OF CIMMERIA, #2**	$2.50
☐ 11614-0	**CONAN THE FREEBOOTER, #3**	$2.50
☐ 11596-9	**CONAN THE WANDERER, #4**	$2.50
☐ 11598-5	**CONAN THE ADVENTURER, #5**	$2.50
☐ 11599-3	**CONAN THE BUCCANEER, #6**	$2.50
☐ 11616-7	**CONAN THE WARRIOR, #7**	$2.50
☐ 11602-7	**CONAN THE USURPER, #8**	$2.50
☐ 11603-5	**CONAN THE CONQUEROR, #9**	$2.50
☐ 11608-6	**CONAN THE AVENGER, #10**	$2.50
☐ 11612-4	**CONAN OF AQUILONIA, #11**	$2.50
☐ 11613-2	**CONAN OF THE ISLES, #12**	$2.50
☐ 11667-1	**CONAN AND THE SORCERER**	$2.50
☐ 11666-3	**CONAN: THE FLAME KNIFE**	$2.50
☐ 11701-5	**THE BLADE OF CONAN**	$2.50
☐ 82245-2	**THE TREASURE OF TRANICOS**	$2.50
☐ 11659-0	**CONAN THE MERCENARY**	$2.50

Available at your local bookstore or return this form to:

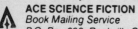

ACE SCIENCE FICTION
Book Mailing Service
P.O. Box 690, Rockville Centre, NY 11571

Please send me the titles checked above. I enclose _____.
Include $1.00 for postage and handling if one book is ordered; 50¢ per book for
two or more. California, Illinois, New York and Tennessee residents please add
sales tax.

NAME _____

ADDRESS _____

CITY _____ STATE/ZIP _____

(allow six weeks for delivery)   A-04

FRITZ LEIBER

FAFHRD AND THE GRAY MOUSER SAGA

COLLECTIONS OF FANTASY AND SCIENCE FICTION